# Summer
## *of the*
# Loon

Deanna Lynn Sletten

**Summer of the Loon**

Copyright 2014 by Deanna Lynn Sletten

ISBN – 10: 1941212107
ISBN - 13: 978-1-941212-10-3

Editor: Sara Wielenberg
Cover Designer: Deborah Bradseth of Tugboat Design

Excerpt from Destination Wedding
Copyright 2014 Deanna Lynn Sletten

# Summer
*of the*
# Loon

# Chapter One

Alison Jenson tucked a stray strand of dark brown hair behind her ear as she wriggled again to try to get comfortable in the narrow airplane seat. She was happy she had a window seat. The airplane from Minneapolis, MN to Duluth was small—only fifty seats in all—with a very narrow aisle, meaning she'd have had a person on either side of her. Sitting by the window meant she could pretend to be busy looking down at the landscape below and not have to make small talk with the older gentleman sitting next to her.

Ali rubbed her sweaty palms over her jean-clad legs as she stared out the window. All she saw below were trees and lakes. Very few towns popped up between Minneapolis and Duluth once they'd left the Metro area. Until about fifteen minutes ago, she was able to distract herself from her destination by texting her best friend, Megan, back in California. But then her phone service was cut off suddenly and she lost contact with her last tie to her old life. Ali already missed Megan and her other friends in California, she already missed her high school in Torrance, and she missed the warm sun and sandy beaches. Most of all, she missed her mom.

The small airplane banked, and Ali saw that they were already making their descent into Duluth. She'd never been to this part of the country before and had no idea what to expect. When her plane had landed in Minneapolis, she'd been delighted to see how large the airport was. During her two-hour delay, she'd wandered the shops and enjoyed a caramel cappuccino and a cookie in a Starbucks. Her phone had informed her that it was fifty-seven degrees outside, which she thought was cold, but apparently it was normal for the middle of May in Minneapolis. Ali had no idea how cold it would be farther north and hoped she'd dressed warm enough in her jeans, UGG boots, and zippered hoodie over a T-shirt.

The plane landed smoothly on the tarmac, and Ali reached down under the seat in front of her to retrieve her laptop backpack. Looking out the window once more, she was surprised to see how small the airport was. She wondered if he was in the terminal, waiting for her. She wondered what he looked like, and how she'd recognize him. She wondered if he was as nervous as she was.

Ali stood, slung her backpack over her shoulder, and followed the other passengers out of the plane and up the ramp into the terminal. This was it. At only sixteen years old, her former life was behind her, and she was walking toward her new life, meeting her estranged grandfather for the very first time.

\* \* \*

Benjamin Jenson stood in the airport terminal behind the crowd of people waiting for the passengers from Minneapolis to disembark. His tall frame allowed him to see easily over the crowd, so he stood in the very back so he could spot his granddaughter before she saw him. He knew he had an advantage. Even though he hadn't seen a photograph of his granddaughter since she was five years old, he knew there'd be no mistaking his Jennifer's child. She'd have Jen's vibrant blue eyes and creamy skin, she'd be tall and slender, and she'd probably have that same stubborn set to her jaw that he remembered so well from his little Jen.

Ben straightened the collar of his blue, plaid, flannel shirt and ran his hand through his salt and pepper hair. At sixty years old, he was in good shape and looked much younger than his age. Years of physical labor working outside had helped to keep his body lean and strong, although being exposed to the elements had etched creases in his face, especially in the corners of his dark blue eyes when he smiled, which he rarely did. He hadn't had much to smile about over the past seventeen years, and most of the people who knew him understood without being told that he was a man of few words. He was a hardworking man, and an honest one, which was all that really mattered in the tough country of the north woods.

Ben wasn't happy at the prospect of having a teenage girl he didn't even know moving in with him. The news of his daughter's untimely death had jolted him severely and brought back a range of emotions that he thought he'd buried deep down inside long ago. Pain, heartbreak, anger, resentment, and guilt had all filtered through the crevices of the locked door to his heart, feelings he thought he'd never have to deal with again. But then, the realization that he was his granddaughter's only living relative and he was responsible for her helped to push those feelings aside, all of them except resentment. *Why should he be responsible for this girl he didn't know?* Ben had grumbled this to himself several times over the past few weeks since he'd found out about Jennifer's death. The last thing he needed was some spoiled city girl from California to come and muck up his life, the life he'd so carefully put back together since the death of his wife, Lizzie.

Because Lizzie would want me to, was the answer he'd hear in his head every time he grumbled.

Ben was snapped out of his thoughts when he heard a woman in front of him squeal with delight at the sight of one of the first passengers filing into the waiting area. Soon, more people followed, and Ben studied each face before moving on to the next. Ben's expression turned into a scowl. *Damn. What if she'd missed her flight from Minneapolis?* The next flight wasn't due until this evening, and they still had a two-and-a-half hour drive back to the cabin. He wouldn't put it past the girl to have missed it. He crossed his arms and continued to wait, all the while convincing himself that it was going to be a long day of waiting.

\* \* \*

Ali saw her grandfather immediately as she passed through the doorway into the waiting area. He was easy to recognize, standing there at the back of the crowd, scowling. He was taller than she'd imagined, and looked younger, too, but there was no mistaking that this man was her relative. The dark hair and intense blue eyes, so much like her own, gave him away, but the strong set to his square jaw was a dead giveaway. It reminded her of her mother when she was stubborn. As she stared at him, Ali saw her grandfather's eyes settle upon her, and recognition filled his gaze. She felt his eyes as intensely as if he'd actually touched her. It was a strange feeling, seeing him for the first time, yet feeling his presence as if she knew him. Straightening her back, Ali lifted her backpack up higher on her shoulder and strode purposefully through the crowd of people toward her grandfather's stern eyes.

Ali stopped only inches from him and stared up at him with questioning eyes. She didn't smile, and neither did he.

"Alison?" he asked, staring down at her.

Ali nodded. She didn't know what else to do. As everyone else around them hugged each other in greeting, they just stood there and stared at each other. Finally, feeling as if she should do something, Ali raised her hand and extended it to him. "It's nice to finally meet you, Grandfather."

Ben frowned down at her and stared at her offered hand as if contemplating whether or not to shake it. Finally, he grasped it in his own large, rough hand, gave it a squeeze, and quickly let it go.

"Well, I see you made your flight," Ben said, his face still stern. "We have a long drive ahead of us. I assume you have more bags." He nodded toward the bag on her shoulder.

Ali merely stared at him. She hadn't expected him to be thrilled that she was here, but she'd hoped he'd show some warmth toward his only grandchild. Her mother had been so affectionate and loving. How in the world had she come from this cold, hard person in front of her?

"I have one other bag," Ali finally answered.

"Only one?" Ben raised his brows.

"Only one."

"Hmmm." Ben turned on his heel and waved for Ali to follow. She did. They made their way to the baggage claim area behind the line of other passengers who had come off her flight.

Ali saw her large, black bag on the carousal and immediately headed over to lift it off. Seeing her struggle with the heavy bag, Ben came up beside her and lifted it easily out of her hands and onto the floor in one smooth motion.

Ali cut her eyes to him. "Thanks," she said through pursed lips as she took ahold of the handle and pulled it away from him.

"Let me carry that for you," Ben offered.

"I can take care of it myself," Ali said.

Ben stared at her for only a second. "Fine. The truck is this way." He turned and walked away with Ali on his heels.

Her grandfather led her outside to a parking lot filled with oversized pickup trucks and SUVs. It was a sunny day, although the air was cool. Ali was glad she'd worn her sweatshirt. When she'd left California, it was eighty-three degrees. Here, it was more like fifty degrees.

They stopped at an extended cab, navy blue, Dodge Ram truck that looked fairly new. Ben took Ali's large bag from her and easily hoisted it up into the back seat of the truck, then walked around to the driver's side and stepped up behind the wheel. The truck was so high off the ground, Ali found she had to literally pull herself up into the cab.

Not a word passed between the two in the pickup as Ben maneuvered his way out of Duluth and headed northwest. Ali had no idea where he lived. She knew he lived on a lake and had owned and operated a resort named Willow Lake Lodge, but that was about all her mother had told her over the years. Ali watched as the road turned from four lanes to two and the landscape turned from homes and businesses to trees. There was nothing for miles and miles except trees.

After riding for a while without her grandfather saying a word to her, Ali pulled her phone out of her pocket and checked for a signal. She had two bars. She quickly texted Megan to tell her she had arrived safely and was with her grandfather.

"That thing won't do you much good once we get closer to home," Ben said into the silent cab.

Ben's sudden words startled Ali, and she looked up at him with wide eyes. His voice was deep and gruff, which didn't make him sound any friendlier.

"There's spotty cell service in Auburn, the town near where we live, but none out at the cabin. It won't be worth the money you pay to have it there," Ben said.

Ali looked down at her phone. It was at one bar now. "I was just texting my friend back home to let her know I made it here," she said. "Her mother wanted to make sure I was safe."

Ben nodded as he continued staring straight ahead at the road. "Is your friend's mother the woman I spoke to? The one you were staying with these past few weeks?"

"Yes," Ali said. "That was Megan's mom, Amy."

"Nice woman," Ben said, the gruffness in his voice softening a little. "It was kind of her to take you in like that."

Ali's heart quickened at his words and she bit the inside of her cheek to stop herself from hurling a nasty retort. Ali had known Megan and her family since the school had moved Ali ahead a year into second grade, and Megan became her best friend. Megan's mother was like a second mother to Ali. Of course they took her in after her mother died. Amy had even offered to allow her to live with them over the next year so Ali could spend her senior year of high school in the same school and not have to transfer. But then Ali's grandfather had agreed to take her in, and there was nothing she or Amy could do about it since he was her only living relative.

Ali felt her grandfather's eyes on her and turned to see him staring at her. She felt compelled to say something. "I've known Megan's family for a long time. They were happy to help."

Ben's eyes narrowed slightly and he nodded toward Ali's phone. "Well, don't expect me to pay for you to have that thing while you're living here. It's too expensive to pay for something that can't be used most of the time."

Ali pocketed her phone and turned her head to look out the side window. She didn't expect the old man to pay for anything for her. She could take care of herself.

The miles dragged on as the silence in the truck grew thicker. Ali wanted to attach her headphones on her phone and block out the silence with music, except her battery was low and her charger was packed in her big bag. So, she sat there as they passed tree after tree, broken up by an occasional body of water or a field of cows or horses. Ali had never seen so much unoccupied land in her life, let alone so many pine trees. Where did all the people live? Occasionally, they'd drive through a small town, or at least a place that had a sign stating there was a town, but all Ali saw was a rundown gas station and maybe a church and a couple of houses. It felt like they were driving to the last place on earth.

Ben pulled over at a small gas station and restaurant in a tiny town about an hour and a half out of Duluth. The parking lot was filled with trucks pulling boats on trailers. It seemed full for such a small town.

"Hungry?" he asked.

Ali shrugged. The little restaurant looked fairly clean, but it was nothing like what she was used to.

"Well, we either eat supper here or else go hungry. We're going to miss supper at the lodge, so we may as well get a bite here," Ben said.

Ali followed him inside and was surprised at how many people were there. Ali and Ben sat at a table by the front window, and after looking at the meager menu, both ordered cheeseburgers and fries.

Ali looked around her. The place was filled mostly with men, and they were all dressed much like her grandfather was, in jeans, T-shirts, and flannel shirts or sweatshirts, and work boots. Many had caps on their heads. She wondered what they were all doing up here in the middle of nowhere.

"Fishing opener was last weekend," Ben said, as if to answer Ali's thoughts.

Ali looked up, startled. "What?"

"The fishing opener. It's practically a holiday up here. All these men are staying at local resorts and fishing."

Ali frowned, trying to understand. "What do you mean by fishing opener? Don't you fish all year around here?"

Ben shook his head. "The season goes roughly from May to February, depending upon the type of fish you're looking to catch. Opening is a big deal. The ice has gone out on the lakes and everyone is raring to get their boats out on the water. It's basically the beginning of the summer season, and it's a good moneymaker for resorts."

Ali nodded even though she really didn't understand much about fishing. Her grandfather seemed happy to be talking about something he enjoyed though, so she listened as they ate their meal and he talked about fish like walleye, northern pike, and crappies. He said he knew every good fishing hole on Willow Lake where his house and the resort was, and he was a fishing guide to tourists who came up to the lodge.

"They never leave empty-handed," he said proudly. Ali knew about malls, crowded parks and beaches, and sunny days all year round, but she didn't know one thing about northern Minnesota, trees, or fishing.

Ali and Ben hopped back into the truck and rambled on down the road as the sun traveled low in the west. Ben seemed a little less stern after telling Ali what he knew about fishing, and there seemed to be less tension in the air between them. Ali checked her phone, and just as her grandfather had said, there was no tower service. She sighed and returned the phone to her pocket.

"If you need to make a call, we can stop in town a moment before heading out to the cabin," Ben offered.

Ali turned and looked at him, surprised by his kind offer. "No, that's okay. I'm sure they got my message."

Ben nodded and kept driving. He broke the silence again. "I'm sorry about your mother," he said, his tone gentle.

Ali had been strong all this time. From the moment she'd been told by the lawyer she was going to live with her grandfather, throughout packing up the small apartment she shared with her mother, and even through the goodbyes to her friends in California and the long flight here. She'd expected a grouchy old man, just as her mother had described him over the years, and he hadn't disappointed her. But hearing him say this, in a soft, caring voice, was the final tipping point that unnerved her to her core. She narrowed her eyes at him. "Not sorry enough to make it to the funeral, though." The harsh words came out of Ali's mouth so quickly, even she was stunned by them.

Ben sat quiet a moment, definitely not the reaction Ali expected. Finally, he said, "I didn't really think I'd be welcome there. Figured it was best to stay away."

Ali turned away as her eyes filled and two tears trailed down her cheeks. *Welcome to Minnesota,* she thought as those incessant trees continued to pass by and the sun sank into darkness.

# Chapter Two

They arrived at the house in darkness with only the half moon and the headlights illuminating their way. Ali had never in her life seen so dark a night sky. Without the illumination of streetlights, building lights, and car lights, it was pitch black in all directions. To top it off, the house had no lights on to welcome them.

"Wait here a minute," Ben said, then stepped out of the pickup with a flashlight and headed into the garage. After a few minutes, Ali heard an engine begin to hum and the garage lights came to life. Her grandfather came back to the truck. "Had to start up the generator," he told her.

Ali had no idea what a generator was.

Ben came around to Ali's side, opened up the back door, and pulled out her suitcase. He lifted the heavy bag easily and walked into the two-stall garage that was attached to the house. Ali wasn't sure what to do, so she picked up her backpack and followed him.

Ben opened a door in the garage that led into the dark kitchen. He set Ali's bag down and clicked on the light, then proceeded farther into the house and turned on another light in the living room.

Ali stood in the small kitchen and looked around her. The walls were split, smooth, honey-colored logs. The kitchen was small but efficient, with an oven and broiler built into the wall ahead of her and the gas burners embedded in the counter on her left. The refrigerator stood by the door behind her, where they'd entered. All the appliances were stainless steel, which surprised Ali because they seemed to be quite new. There was a double sink to her left with a small window over it and counters on either side. The cupboards were also stained a soft honey color and gleamed to a polished perfection in the light. Ali noticed there was no dishwasher or microwave in the kitchen. Over the burners was a pass-through window with a ledge, and she saw that her grandfather was watching her through the opening.

Ali walked into the next room, which held a large, oak dining table and eight chairs. The open room continued straight on to a living room where a large sofa and two reclining rockers sat with a coffee table separating them. All along the wall to her left were windows. Ali walked on the polished hardwood floors to one of the large windows and looked out. With so little moon above, and no outdoor lights, she couldn't see a thing. To her right, down below, there was a light on in the window of a building.

"That's the lodge down there," Ben said. "Straight ahead of you, down the hill, is the lake. That's why it looks so dark. Wait until the full moon, then you'll be able to see it at night."

Ali nodded. She suddenly felt very tired, as if it had been years since she left California instead of hours.

Her grandfather lifted his arm and pointed to a smaller room off the living room. "Through there is the door to the bathroom. It's the only one we have. My room is through the door by the kitchen where we entered."

"Is there somewhere I can plug in my phone? And my laptop?" Ali asked, looking around. She noticed there was no television in the living room. *What did he do for fun around here?*

"You can plug them in upstairs in your room, but it won't do you much good tonight. I turn the generator off at nine every night. I get up early, so I go to bed early. There's an oil lamp in your room if you need light after nine."

Ali just stared at him. She wasn't used to having the electricity turned off each night. "Don't you have power out here?"

"They ran power down to the lodge a few years ago, but I didn't bother to have it hooked up here. Don't need it. I have the generator for all my needs. I don't have television or internet connected here, either. If you want to watch T.V. or use a computer, you'll have to go down to the lodge. And like I said, your cell phone is useless out here. There's a phone down at the lodge, though, if you need to make a call."

Ali blinked and stared at the old man as she absorbed his words. No television, no internet, and no phone, and only a generator for power. She hadn't realized people in the United States still lived like this. Like it was the 1800s or something. And the worst part was that her grandfather looked smug about the fact that he didn't have any conveniences. Like he was showing her a thing or two. Ali sighed.

"I'll show you where your room is," Ben said. "Follow me."

Ben walked back toward the kitchen and Ali frowned. She hadn't seen a staircase anywhere in the kitchen when she came in.

"You coming?" Ben asked gruffly.

Ali sighed again and followed him to the kitchen.

"My room is here." Ben pointed to a door by the refrigerator that Ali hadn't noticed when she walked in. Then he lifted her suitcase and headed back out into the garage. He took a left and flicked on another overhead light. That was when she saw the staircase. It was on the side wall of the garage. Her mouth dropped open as she watched him start up the wooden stairs. *The entrance to her room was in the garage? Could it get any worse?*

Ali reluctantly followed her grandfather up the stairs and

through the lightweight door that had a small window on the top half covered with a curtain. What greeted her was a long, open room the size of the full length of the house. The roof peaked, and slanted down. They were in the attic.

"I hope this is okay," Ben said as he clicked on the overhead light and set the suitcase down on the arms of a big, plaid upholstered chair.

Ali looked around. There was a window on one end of the room, over the bed, and two dormers with large windows to her left at the front of the house. The bed was queen size with a white, wooden headboard and footboard and had a patchwork quilt covering it. A white chest sat at the foot of the bed with a red pillow on top of it so it could be used as a bench. There was a nightstand beside the bed with a small electric lamp and an old-fashioned oil lamp sitting on it, and a white, six-drawer dresser with a mirror on top to the left of the bed. Sitting in one dormer nook was an oak desk and chair. Cherry red curtains were over all of the windows and matched the red patches in the quilt. To the right of the bed was a long bar hanging from the ceiling holding empty hangers on it. Ali supposed this was to be her closet. As she looked around, she thought it wasn't too bad of a room after all.

Her grandfather cleared his throat. "There are power sockets by the desk and dresser, if you want to charge your things. You'll have to wait until morning though, since it's almost bedtime. You should go use the bathroom downstairs, too, before I turn the generator off. You'll want to be sure to keep this door shut tight at night so you don't let any critters in."

Ali's eyes grew wide. "Critters? What type of critters?"

Ben looked at her seriously. "Well, there's chipmunks and squirrels. Then there's skunks and raccoons, they really like to dig around in people's things. I'd advise you not to have food up here at night, either. Bears can smell food from far away."

"Bears?" Ali squealed. "Bears can get up those stairs and in this room?"

"Bears are climbers; of course they can get up a flight of stairs. Of course, I wouldn't worry too much about them. I almost always close the garage door at night so critters don't get into the garbage. I'm sure you won't have a problem, just keep your door shut tight and stay up here at night."

*Oh, great. Not only do I not have lights at night, but now I might get a visit from a bear. I've officially landed in hell.* As Ali contemplated the fact that animals might end up in her bed, she noticed a tug at the corner of her grandfather's mouth and a twinkle in his eyes. Ali narrowed her eyes. *He's enjoying this. He wants to scare me, just for the fun of it.*

"We eat breakfast early, especially now that there are guests staying at the resort. I'll wake you in time to go down to the lodge with me. Jo and her son are nice people, you'll like them."

"Jo?" Ali asked.

"Yeah. Short for Josephine. She and her husband bought the resort from me a few years ago and now I help out around there. Her husband died awhile back. She's a good person." Ben looked around the room a moment, his eyes landing on the red curtains. "Jo helped me get this room ready for you. She made the curtains. The quilt used to be your mother's. My Lizzie, your grandmother, made it."

Ali noticed her grandfather's voice softened when he said "my Lizzie". Maybe he wasn't such a mean old man after all. She reached down and touched the corner of the quilt, rubbing the material between her thumb and forefinger. The fabric was soft from years of washing.

"It's a nice quilt," she told him.

Ben raised his gaze to look into Ali's blue eyes. He nodded curtly, and turned to leave. "Come and use the bathroom before lights out," he reminded her, then let the door bang behind him as he left the room.

Later, after Ali had unpacked a few things she needed, and used the bathroom, she pulled back the old timeworn quilt on her bed and slipped between the soft sheets. The sheets were new, as were the pillows and the blanket under the quilt, but the quilt was from another time. A time when her mother had been young and carefree, before her life changed course. Ali ran her hand over the soft fabric, and thought about her mother and how she'd slept under this quilt that her own mother had lovingly made for her. The quilt was made from yellow cotton, denim blues, red calico, pink corduroy, and white cotton that had turned creamy with age. Ali wondered if it had been made from clothes her mother had worn as a child and outgrown. She wondered if her mother had been happy as a child, lying under this quilt. Suddenly, the light beside her bed went out, and the hum of the generator grew silent. Ali sighed. Nine o'clock. She lay back and listened to the nighttime sounds of the woods in the distance as tears streamed down her cheeks.

* * *

Long after he'd turned the generator off, Ben sat in his chair in the living room with only the golden light of the oil lamp. Usually, he was sound asleep only minutes after the lights were out, but not tonight. After his granddaughter headed back up to her bedroom, and he closed the garage door and locked it, and after he turned off the generator, he found he wasn't sleepy.

Ben rocked back and forth in his chair, watching the shadows on the walls around him as the flame flickered in the lamp. Outside, the frogs croaked in a nearby swamp, and an old hoot owl called out into the night. Usually, these sounds of the night lulled him to sleep, but not tonight. Tonight, he was worried he'd made a mistake, having his granddaughter move out here and live with him. As much a mistake for him as for her.

Ali was used to living in the city with access to television, cell phones, and that blasted internet everyone seemed to need these days. What the hell would she do out here, in the middle of the woods?

Ben couldn't help but smirk when he thought about how frightened she'd looked when he'd told her to watch out for critters coming up to her room, especially bears. He'd only been kidding. Of course he'd make sure she was safe up there. But she didn't understand his sense of humor yet, and how serious he could look when he was pulling a person's leg. Then again, how would she know if he was kidding? She didn't know him from Adam.

The moment he'd seen her at the airport, he was surprised to find that she didn't have her mother's square jaw, although she sure could tighten it stubbornly when she wanted to, just like his little Jen had. No, her face was a soft oval, like his Lizzie's. And those eyes. They were the same vibrant blue as her mother's, the same blue as his. She was a striking girl, with her long, dark hair and light skin, standing tall and lean. All he could think was that he'd have his hands full keeping the boys away from her.

Ben ran his hands through his thick hair and stood, staring out the window into the dark night. Ali's comment earlier in the truck reverberated in his head. He'd been trying to be nice, saying he was sorry for her mother's passing. And he was. After all, she'd been his daughter. But when Ali had said, 'Not sorry enough to make it to the funeral,' it had shook Ben to his core. He had wanted to go to the funeral. He'd wanted to fly out immediately after hearing his daughter had died and hold Ali in his arms and grieve with her. But deep down, he knew he wouldn't have been welcome there. Nor should he have been.

Below, down at the lodge, the light in the kitchen still burned. Jo would still be up, baking fresh bread for the morning and doing about a hundred other chores necessary for running a resort. She ran it just as smoothly as he and his Lizzie had years before, always baking and cooking delicious meals for the guests and providing the perfect north woods experience for each and every person who came to stay. Ben helped as much as he could, cutting firewood, cleaning the outdoor areas, keeping the boats in working order, and so many other small chores in addition to taking guests out on fishing and hunting trips. Chase, her son, helped out, too. He was a hardworking boy, and Ben had enjoyed watching him grow up. But raising a boy was so much different than a girl. Ben knew this from experience. Having Ali here was going to be a handful, for sure.

Ben finally went to bed and lay there for some time before sleep eventually fell over him. His last thoughts were of his Lizzie, as they always were each night, and how much he missed her gentle guidance, even if he hadn't always listened to her.

# Chapter Three

Ali awoke with a start in the dark room. Slivers of sunlight seeped in through the red curtains, leaving an orange tint across her bed. Lying on her stomach, arms above her head, Ali lifted her head a little and squinted at the small battery powered alarm clock she'd placed on her nightstand. Five forty-five a.m. She closed her eyes and dropped her head back on the pillow.

"Ali, wake up. It's time for breakfast."

Ali's eyes shot open and she quickly rolled over in bed to see where the gruff voice had come from. Standing over her was a dark shadow. It took her a moment to come to her senses and realize it was her grandfather.

Ali fell back again on the bed, holding her hand over her pumping heart. "Geez, you scared me half to death," she told the looming shadow.

"You sleep like the dead," he said. "Been trying to wake you for over five minutes. It's time to get up for breakfast. If you aren't downstairs in ten minutes, I'm going without you." Ben turned and stomped out of the room. Ali heard his heavy boots retreat down the stairs.

Ali groaned. *Who in the world eats at dawn? I'm not even awake, let alone hungry.* She shook her head to try to wake up and finally rolled over enough to pull herself up and out of the bed. Standing there in the semi-dark room, she remembered that there was internet down at the lodge, and her tired face brightened a little. She pulled the string on the light hanging from the ceiling, and the room filled with light. Excited that the generator was running, Ali plugged in her phone and hoped he wouldn't turn it off when they headed down to the lodge for breakfast. Then she dressed hurriedly, ran the brush through her long, straight hair, grabbed her laptop bag, and headed down the stairs. She caught up to her grandfather, who was standing on the cement slab outside the garage, waiting for her.

"Well, it's about time. Almost left without you. Let's go."

Ali turned to follow her grandfather down the hill when suddenly she stopped. Her eyes touched the scenery, and she involuntarily drew in a breath. The scene spread out before her was breathtaking, like a painting or photograph of the most serene place on earth. Dew glistened on the grass all around her, and the crisp, morning air gently caressed her cheeks. Down the hill lay the lake, peaceful and still. It looked like a small cove, with land protecting it on both sides, but then opening up to many more coves over miles of acres. Directly across the lake from the house stood a tall, rocky cliff, where pine trees and moss jutted out of the rock. Down the gravel road, to the right, sat the resort on a point of land that spread out like a peninsula into the crystal blue water. A forest of trees, blue sky, and deep blue water surrounded Ali, and she couldn't help but be amazed at the spectacular beauty of it.

"It's so beautiful," she said, her voice a reverent whisper.

Ben stopped and glanced at her in surprise. He looked in the direction of the lake where Ali was staring, and finally nodded. "Yes, it is," he agreed.

Suddenly, a tremulous wail sounded from high above as a shadow swooped across Ali, making her duck involuntarily. The shadow continued on, finally landing on the still water with a splash and then gracefully swimming forward, leaving a trail in its wake. It called again, a long wail that echoed off the water and the cliff.

"What was that?" Ali exclaimed, still ducking and looking up into the sky for more wailing creatures.

Ben chuckled, which made Ali draw up to stand tall again, embarrassed.

"It's a loon, silly," Ben said. "Haven't you ever heard a loon before?"

On the water, the loon called out again, a long, laughing wail as if making fun of Ali too.

"No," Ali said, crossly. "I lived near the coast. I'm used to seagulls and pigeons, not crazy birds that laugh at you."

Ben sobered at Ali's tone and spoke in a kinder voice. "He's calling to his mate to let her know where he is. We have a couple of pairs of loons nesting around the lakeshore, in separate coves. One parent goes off to feed while the other guards the nest. You can practically set your watch to their feeding times. Around six every morning, one or another will fly over the house and then the next one will fly over about nine. Then about nine at night, they head back to their nests. You'll hear them almost every time they fly over the house."

"If they live on the lake, why do they fly over the house?" Ali asked, interested now in these strange birds.

"They feed on different lakes in the area, and there are loons nesting on each of the lakes. About a mile behind the house, there's a smaller lake, more like a pond, I'd say. There are loons nesting there. And about two miles north of here, there's another larger lake. This lake has eight coves and covers miles of area, so the loons fly from cove to cove."

"Oh." Ali tried to absorb everything her grandfather told her.

"Come on. We're late for breakfast," Ben said, leading the way down the gravel road to the resort.

Ali followed him, but kept her eyes on the sky in search of loons so they wouldn't scare her a second time.

Ben led Ali down to the rustic, log lodge and through a

squeaky screen door that led into a screened-in porch facing the lake. Through there, he opened a heavier door that led them into the kitchen. They were greeted by the aroma of freshly flipped flapjacks, scrambled eggs, bacon, blueberry muffins, and rich, black coffee. Ali's stomach, which just moments before didn't feel hungry, was suddenly growling, reacting to the delicious smells.

Standing at the oversized stove, flipping bacon and flapjacks, was a short woman with long, strawberry blonde hair pulled back into a ponytail. She wore jeans and a plain T-shirt under her white apron, and sensible sneakers. As Ali and Ben entered the kitchen, the woman turned from her work and smiled wide.

"Ali. You're finally here!" the woman exclaimed, running over and pulling Ali into a warm embrace. Ali froze a moment, not knowing quite what to do. But the woman held her so tight that Ali couldn't help but give in and return her hug.

Pulling away, the woman smiled up at Ali, her pale, blue eyes twinkling. "My, aren't you the prettiest girl I've ever seen. And look how tall you are. I've been waiting for this moment the minute your grandfather told me you were coming. Finally. Another female in the house. I won't be outnumbered by men anymore."

Ali watched as Ben shook his head and walked over to the stove to take the flapjacks off and check on the bacon. The woman winked at Ali, then clapped her hands over her mouth.

"Oh, my goodness, " she exclaimed. "How silly of me. I'm gushing all over you and you don't even know who I am. I'm Jo, short for Josephine, but everyone just calls me Jo. I own this old lodge, which means I'm the chief cook and bottle washer." Jo smiled again, and it was such a warm, sweet smile that Ali couldn't help but smile back.

"It's nice to meet you," Ali said. Jo had freshly scrubbed, pale skin with a dash of freckles that ran across her cheeks and nose. She looked no more than fifteen years old, although Ali knew she had to be older. Jo's friendliness was so contagious, Ali couldn't help but be drawn in by Jo's fresh-faced looks and genuine smile.

A door swung open behind Jo and in walked a young man carrying an empty platter. "We need more flapjacks," he said in a deep voice. "Those men are eating faster than I can bring them food."

Ali looked up into deep blue eyes that immediately reminded her of the lake outside.

"Honey, come meet Ben's granddaughter, Ali," Jo said, waving the young man over. "Ali, this is my son, Chase. He's graduating high school this year, so you two are really close in age. I hope you both will be good friends."

"Hello," Chase said, smiling down at Ali.

Ali smiled back, but didn't say a word. Chase's long, lean body was several inches taller than hers, and he had sun-bleached blonde hair that curled at the nape of his neck. He had a golden tan and his smile was as infectious as Jo's.

"Are you all just going to stand there gawking at each other or are you going to help me with breakfast?" Ben said, pulling the platter out of Chase's hands. Ben turned back to the stove, grunting in disgust, and began filling the platter with flapjacks.

Ali blushed a deep red.

"Don't get your flannel shirt tied in a knot," Jo said to Ben, winking once more at Ali before heading back over to the stove.

Chase quickly picked up a basket of muffins and headed back out the swinging door.

"Ali, go ahead and grab a plate and fill it with whatever you want to eat. There's cold milk in the fridge, or juice if you want it. Just make yourself at home," Jo said. She picked up the fresh platter of bacon and scrambled eggs and headed out to the dining room.

Ali stood there, uncomfortable about not helping out when everyone else was working.

Ben walked over, grabbed an empty plate, and began filling it from the platter of eggs, flapjacks, and bacon that had been left on the table in the kitchen. "If you don't help yourself around here, you'll starve," he said.

Ali sighed, picked up a plate, and began placing food on it.

As Ali ate her breakfast in silence alongside her grandfather, she looked around the kitchen. It was a large, square room, big enough to contain commercial grade appliances, generous counter space, and a large oak table with two long bench seats that could easily seat eight people. There was nothing fancy about this room. Everything was plain and utilitarian, yet the honey colored log interior, red and white checked table cloth, gleaming pans hanging over the butcher block island, and cheery red and white curtains in the window over the sink made it feel very cozy. But it was Jo's friendly smile as she ran to and from the kitchen to serve the guests that filled the room with warmth.

Ali wasn't used to eating such a big breakfast, so she was finished by the time Jo and Chase came in and sat down to eat. As the two latecomers filled their plates with food, Ali took her dishes to the sink and rinsed them, then stacked them into the dishwasher tray that sat on the stainless steel counter beside the commercial grade dishwasher.

"Now Ali, you don't have to work your first day here," Jo said from her seat at the table. "Come over and sit and tell me all about yourself."

Ali reluctantly returned to the table and sat on the bench across from Jo and her grandfather, who was finishing up his mug of coffee. Chase sat just a foot away from Ali, seemingly concentrating on his food.

"How was your flight here?" Jo asked, giving her full

attention to Ali.

Ali answered all her questions about her flight, the friends she'd left behind, whether or not she enjoyed school, and if she'd left a boyfriend behind. Jo asked the last question with a wink, and Ali saw her grandfather roll his eyes when he heard it.

"No boyfriend," Ali answered, embarrassed. "I was too busy with school and other things."

"Good," Ben said, getting up and walking over to the sink to rinse his mug. "I don't need some lovesick boy coming out to visit you."

Ali stared at him but didn't say a word.

"Don't listen to him. He's just an old grouch," Jo said.

Ali saw a small smile appear on Chase's face.

"Humph. I'm taking a few of the guests out fishing," Ben said. "You coming along, Chase?"

Chase shook his head. "I have to run to town for Mom later."

Ben nodded, then pointed his finger at Ali. "Stay out of trouble while I'm gone," he said, then he was out the door.

Ali's eyes followed him as he left the room. She sighed. Ali hated that he treated her like she was three years old. She stood and headed over to the sink and began rinsing and stacking the dishes that Chase and Jo were bringing in from the outer room. Before Jo came back into the kitchen a second time, Ali had already started a load in the dishwasher and was stacking a tray for a second load.

"You know how to use that dishwasher?" Jo asked, surprised. It wasn't a regular dishwasher, but the heavy-duty type found in restaurant kitchens. It washed dishes quickly so several loads were done in a matter of minutes.

Ali shrugged. "I've used a similar one before," she said, as she continued rinsing and stacking dishes.

Jo cocked her head and quietly watched the young girl

with interest.

Once the dishes were washed and the kitchen was in order again, Ali picked up her laptop bag. "My grandfather said you have Internet here in the lodge," she said, hopefully. "Would it be okay if I signed onto it?"

"Oh, I'm sorry honey," Jo said. "We do have Internet, but it's dial-up and very slow. It's hooked up to that dinosaur of a computer we have out in the main room. You're welcome to use it, but if you're anything like Chase, it'll frustrate you."

Ali's face dropped. "Oh."

"Chase always goes to the coffeehouse in town to use their Internet when he has homework to do. They have wireless. All the kids go there."

"There's a coffeehouse in town?" Ali asked, surprised. She hadn't seen much of Auburn, the nearest town, when they drove through last night. She'd assumed there wouldn't be much there except for a gas station.

Jo smiled. "Yep. Chase is going to town to run a few errands for me in a bit. Why don't you go with him? He can drop you off so you can use your computer. I bet you want to talk to your friends."

Ali nodded. "Are you sure it'll be okay with my grandfather if I go into town?"

Jo waved her hand through the air. "Don't worry about Ben. If I say you can go, then you can go."

Ali decided she really liked Jo.

Jo drew closer to Ali, her expression serious. "I hope I don't upset you by saying this, dear, but I am so sorry about you losing your mother. Jen was a nice girl, and beautiful, too."

Ali looked up with interest. "You knew my mother?"

Jo nodded. "Oh, yes. Of course, I was years older than she was. I've been working at this lodge since I was sixteen, and I worked for Ben's parents first, then Ben and Lizzie until my husband and I bought it. Jen was as cute as a button from the day she was born, and you never saw parents who doted on their daughter as much as Ben and Lizzie did. Why, Jen used to shadow her father everywhere he went. She had no desire to learn about cooking or cleaning, she wanted to fish and hunt with her father. And he let her. Every morning, come rain or shine, you'd see those two out in the boat at five a.m. with their lines in the water. They were quite a pair."

Ali frowned as she tried to picture her grandfather doting on her mother. She had trouble imagining it.

"Oh, dear. I'm so sorry if I made you feel sad. I didn't mean to go on and on," Jo said.

"No, it's okay. I like hearing about my mother. I really don't know too much about her life when she lived here."

Jo walked over and gave Ali a big hug. "Well, you just come talk to me anytime about anything you want to know. I'll be happy to tell you about your mother, your grandmother, and anyone else you're curious about. Okay?"

Ali nodded. It felt good to have an ally here in this place that seemed so foreign to her.

# Chapter Four

As Ali waited for Chase, she wandered through the main part of the lodge. Beyond the kitchen's swinging door was a huge, open area that held four big tables like the one in the kitchen. Each was covered with the same red and white checked tablecloth as the kitchen table. Beyond the tables was a great room with a massive stone fireplace, huge leather sofas, and overstuffed chairs. A flat screen television was hung over the fireplace mantel. The ceiling was peaked and log beams were exposed. High on the walls were mounted animal heads— two deer, a moose, and a black bear that looked like it was jumping out of the wall. Ali shivered. The thought of killing all those animals made her sick. Other than the dead animals, though, the room was warm, cozy, and very North Country.

"They give you the creeps, don't they?"

Ali jumped at the voice behind her. She turned to see Chase standing only inches away.

"Kind of," she said honestly. "Did you kill them?"

Chase shook his head. "These have been here for years. I think Ben and his dad killed them and had them stuffed. I hunt, just like everyone else does around here, but I don't feel the need to hang animal heads like trophies."

"That's good, I guess," Ali said, uncertain. She wasn't used to the idea of hunting and killing animals, even if it was legal. But she guessed if she was going to live here, she'd have to get used to it.

Chase smiled. "Ready to go to town?"

Ali nodded and followed Chase through the kitchen where she retrieved her backpack. After a quick wave to Jo, who was busy baking a chocolate cake, they went outside and headed over to a faded red pickup truck.

"Is this your truck?" Ali asked after they were seated inside the cab and Chase had started the engine.

"Yep. I know it's not much, but it gets me to town and back. I'm hoping when I go to college in the fall that I'll be able to buy something newer to drive."

"Where are you going to college?" Ali asked.

"Duluth," Chase said. "I know it's not far, but I want to be close enough to home in case my mom needs me. Of course, she always has Ben to help her, and now you," he said with a grin. "But I still feel like I shouldn't be too far away."

"Have you already graduated high school?" Ali asked. It was only the middle of May and she thought it was too early for school to be let out. In California, she would have been going until mid-June.

"No. We're done at the end of May. Ben said he fixed it with the school so you wouldn't have to start school here until the fall. He didn't think you'd want to go for only a couple of weeks."

"How thoughtful of him," Ali said sarcastically, turning to stare out the window. In truth, she was relieved she didn't have to start school here yet. It was bad enough she had to go to a strange school for her senior year, but at least she had the summer to get used to the idea.

The two sat silent for a few minutes as Ali watched the endless procession of trees stream by as the truck bumped along on the gravel road.

"He's not all that bad, you know," Chase said softly.

Ali looked at him, startled. "What?"

Chase smiled at her. He had perfectly straight, white teeth. Between his good looks and easy-going nature, Ali had yet to find anything wrong with him, except for the fact that he killed animals for sport.

"Ben. He's not really all that bad," Chase said. "I've known him all my life, and even though he puts on that grumpy act, he's really not a bad guy. Once you get to know him, you'll know what I mean."

Ali shrugged and turned back to stare out the window.

\* \* \*

Chase dropped Ali off at the coffeehouse and said he'd be back as soon as he finished his errands. Ali stood on the sidewalk and watched him drive down the street toward the gas station-slash-hardware store. Auburn was bigger than she'd expected, but still tiny compared to a real town. The sign at the outskirts of town announced that Auburn had a population of 862 people. Ali wondered if they changed the sign every time a new baby was born or someone died.

Looking down the street, Ali saw a grocery store near the gas station, three different bars, and a small movie theater. She wasn't surprised to see that the movie showing this weekend had come out over a year ago in California.

Sighing, Ali hoisted her backpack up on her shoulder and entered North Country Coffeehouse. "Everything around here is named North Country," Ali grumbled. But the minute she walked into the cabin-like setting, the aroma of sweet coffee and fresh baked goods lightened her attitude and made her smile.

A middle-aged woman wearing jeans, a black polo, and a white apron greeted Ali with a friendly smile. "What can I get you?" she asked.

Ali ordered a caramel cappuccino and couldn't resist

ordering one of the fresh, frosted brownies in the display case. There were so many delicious treats to choose from including cookies, extra-large muffins, scones, and lemon bars. The list went on and on. But the brownies looked heavenly.

As Ali stood at the counter and waited for her order, she noticed a large chalkboard displaying the lunch and supper food selections. North Country Coffeehouse offered sandwiches of all varieties as well as homemade soups. Ali hoped she'd get a chance to spend a lot of time here and try their food.

Once her order was ready, Ali carried her tray toward the back of the building and sat down at a table in a corner by an unlit fireplace. The interior was exactly what she'd expect from the name with its tall ceilings with exposed beams and ductwork, slatted pine walls, blue calico curtains hanging in the windows, and large, thick rugs over the polished hardwood floors. Small tables sat around the room and in the back corner, two tan cushy sofas faced each other with a coffee table between them. Music played softly throughout the building, most likely an area radio station that played songs from the 60s through the 90s. Ali heard an old Beach Boys tune playing and was immediately homesick for California.

Ali was the only customer in the place, which seemed strange to her. She'd never sat at a Starbucks or café at home that wasn't crowded with people no matter what time of day it was. She supposed this was such a small town that most people came in early for their coffee, then filtered in again as lunch time grew near.

Ali pulled her laptop out of her bag and turned it on. She drank her cappuccino and ate her brownie while she waited for her computer to load. She'd been right. The brownie was heavenly, and she ate every last bite.

Ali sighed as she waited for her computer to turn on. She'd bought it second-hand two years ago from a girl at school who was just going to throw it out. Ali took it to a computer geek friend to clean it out, and so far it had worked pretty well. But it was getting slower and slower to load, and if it died, she didn't know what she'd do. She didn't have enough money saved to buy a new computer. She hoped it would run for at least one more year, until she could finish high school and start working full-time.

When her computer finally came on, Ali thanked the computer gods and logged onto the Internet, using the code the woman at the counter had given her. She opened up her chat program and hoped her friend, Megan, would be online.

"Ali? Is that you?" Megan's smiling face appeared on the screen.

Ali's heart jumped. It had been only twenty-four hours since she saw her best friend, but it seemed like a lifetime.

"Hi, Megan. I'm so happy I caught up with you."

"Oh, my God, Ali. It seems like forever since we talked. What happened yesterday? We were talking when you were on the plane and then, nothing. I tried calling you several times last night and you didn't answer. I thought you'd fallen off the planet."

Ali smiled. It was so good seeing Megan again, even if it was on a computer screen. Megan's sun-bleached, blonde hair was pulled back in a smooth ponytail and her green eyes sparkled with excitement. Ali wished she could reach through her laptop and give her a big hug.

"The connection was cut-off on the plane. And there isn't any cell connection or Internet at my grandfather's house," Ali told her. "It's going to be hard to stay connected. I have to come to town just to use my phone or my computer."

"Are you kidding me?" Megan asked, a look of astonishment on her face. "No cell phone or Internet? Where are you now?"

"I'm in a small town about fifteen miles from my

grandfather's house. He lives way out in the boonies. You wouldn't believe it. And my bedroom is in the attic. I mean, it's large and it's nice and all, but it's still an attic. I feel like I've completely left civilization," Ali said, relieved to finally have someone to talk to. Someone who knew her through and through and could sympathize with her.

"That's awful," Megan said. Then, in a quieter tone, she asked. "What's your grandfather like? Is he nice?"

Ali sighed. She'd only spent a few hours with him so far. She really didn't know what he was like yet. "He's okay, I guess. He's kind of grouchy and bossy. But he's used to living alone, so I guess he's not really sure what to think of me yet."

"Are there any other people around where he lives?" Megan asked.

"Oh, sure. There's the lodge just down the hill from his cabin. We ate breakfast there this morning and I met the owner, Jo, and her son, Chase. They seem nice, so far."

"That's good," Megan said. "So, what's this Chase guy like? How old is he? Is he cute?"

Ali frowned. "I don't know. I mean, he's eighteen, and he's graduating high school this year. He's cute, I guess. But what does that matter? I'm not looking for a boyfriend. I just want to get this next year over with and go back to California to be with my real friends."

"Oh, that reminds me," Megan said. "I'm meeting up with the other girls to go to the mall in a few minutes. I guess I should get going."

Ali's heart sank. She wished she was going to the mall with Megan and the girls. "Okay. Say hi to everyone for me. And to your mom, too. Did she get my message yesterday?"

Megan nodded. "She says hi, too. I really miss you, Ali. I can't wait until I can see you again. So, I can't call you or email you or anything while you're at the house?"

"You can email me, I'll just have to wait until I come to

town to read it, though. And no, my phone doesn't work out there. I'm not even sure what I'm going to do about it. I need a job if I want to pay for phone service, and I'm not sure where I'll get a job around here."

Megan shook her head. "Sounds too bleak to me. I gotta go. Love you. Take care, and I'll email lots of photos and stuff, okay?"

Ali tried to smile, but failed miserably. "Okay. Love you, too. Bye." The screen went dead. Ali felt like crying.

"Hi. Can I get you anything else?"

Ali jumped at the voice that came up beside her. She looked up to see a girl standing over her. The girl had on the same black polo and white apron as the woman who'd served Ali earlier, but she was much younger. She was slightly plump and had pale blonde hair, creamy white skin with freckles, and hazel eyes. She was staring down at Ali and her eyes seemed to be dancing.

"Uh, no thanks. I'm fine," Ali answered.

The girl still stood there, as if trying to decide something. Ali noticed her name tag said Kat on it.

"Are you Chase's girlfriend?" The "Kat" girl finally asked.

Ali frowned and stared at her. *What kind of a question was that?*

"No," Ali answered.

"Sorry," the girl said, grimacing. "I shouldn't have asked you that. I do that sometimes. I just blurt out what I'm thinking. It's just that I saw Chase drop you off, and I don't recognize you, so I thought maybe you were someone new he met."

"Oh," Ali said. *Don't recognize me? Are strangers in town so rare that people around here freak out when they don't recognize people?*

The girl stuck out her hand. "I'm Katrina. My friends call me Kat. My parents own the coffeehouse, and I work here, too. Are you new in town or just staying at a resort around here?"

Ali shook Kat's hand. "I'm Alison Jenson. Ali. I'm new around here. I just moved here to live with my grandfather."

Kat's hands flew to her mouth and her eyes grew wide. "You're old man Jenson's granddaughter? Oh, my goodness. I should've known. That's why Chase drove you in here, huh? You're living out by the resort."

Ali nodded. *Old man Jenson?* "Is that what people call my grandfather around here? Old man Jenson?"

Kat covered her mouth again with her hands. "Oh, crap. I did it again. See, I just run off at the mouth. My mother is always telling me to think before I speak, but I just can't seem to do it." Kat took a breath, then continued. "Some people call him that, especially the kids in town, but we'd never call him that to his face. He's just so grouchy all the time that he scares the crap out of everyone. Sorry, I know he's your relative and all, but don't you find him intimidating?"

Ali smirked. Kat really did say whatever she was thinking, and Ali found it amusing. Over the last twenty-four hours, Ali had been careful with every word she said around her grandfather, so it was refreshing to hear someone just tell it like it is.

"Yes. He does seem kind of intimidating," Ali agreed. "But I don't really know him well yet, so I can't really say what I think of him."

Kat smiled, then pulled out the chair opposite of Ali's and sat down. "He's probably fine. He just seems scary since he never talks to anyone or smiles," Kat said. "At least you get to live near Jo and Chase. Jo's a sweetheart, and Chase…" Kat's eyes grew dreamy. "Well, he's just the cutest thing in the world. Don't you think? Every girl in high school wants to date Chase but he doesn't ask anyone out." Kat sighed.

Ali thought it was funny how Kat swooned over Chase. "He's been really nice," Ali said. "And Jo seems very nice, too. I've only been here for a day, so I don't know anyone well yet."

"Are you still in high school or did you graduate already?" Kat asked.

"I'll be a senior in the fall," Ali told her.

Kat clapped her hands with delight. "So will I! We can be friends and hang out together. I'll introduce you to all the kids, even though the girls will be jealous of you since you're so pretty. But it will be fun to have someone new in town for a change."

Ali's brows rose. *The girls will be jealous? I doubt it.*

"I guess I should get back to work. It's getting close to lunch time and it gets busy in here then. Will you be coming into town often? I hope to see a lot more of you."

"I'm hoping I can come to town a lot. It's the only way I can talk to my friends back in California," Ali said.

Kat stood. "Wow. California. I bet you miss it there. You'll really miss it when winter comes. It's way too cold around here."

"I do miss it. But mostly, I miss the people I know out there."

Kat cocked her head and looked at Ali, her eyes dancing again. "You know, we always hire someone to help around here in the summer. It gets busy when the tourists start coming to the resorts and crave specialty coffees. My mom hasn't hired anyone yet. Would you be interested? I can tell her about you."

Ali's face brightened. "Maybe," she said. "I do need a job to keep my phone service going. I'm not sure if my grandfather will let me use his truck to come into town to work, but I could ask him. Can I get back to you?"

"Sure," Kat said, smiling wide. "Okay. I'll leave you alone so you can finish what you're doing. I'm so happy you came to town, though. We're going to have so much fun together." Kat turned and headed up to the front of the shop. Ali couldn't help but smile. Kat was so friendly and energetic that it made Ali feel welcomed in this small community.

Ali sat for a while checking her email and responding to a couple of friends who'd written to her already. Then she texted Megan on her phone to see how shopping was going. The girls sent her a picture of them in front of an escalator at the mall. Instead of making Ali feel happy, it just made her feel sad she wasn't with them.

After a while, Ali heard the bell on the front door to the coffeehouse tinkle and then Chase's deep voice say hello to Kat. She heard Kat talking, but couldn't make out what she was saying. Then she saw Chase heading back to where she sat, a cup in his hand.

"Did you talk to your friends?" Chase asked, taking the seat that Kat had abandoned.

Ali nodded. "I talked to Megan and answered a few emails. Megan and some other friends texted me a photo of them at the mall." Ali handed Chase her phone and he looked at the photo and nodded.

"Cute," he said, then handed it back to her.

"Did you finish your errands?" Ali asked.

"Yep."

The two sat there a moment in silence before Ali busied herself with turning off her computer and sliding it back into its padded case. Chase picked up her backpack and held it open so she could slip it in. It was a simple gesture, but Ali thought it was really nice of him. Kat was right. Chase was a nice guy. As she thought about what Kat had said earlier, she couldn't help but grin.

"What's that silly smile for?" Chase asked, taking a sip of his coffee.

"I hear that you're a big, dreamy catch around here. All the girls want to date you," Ali said.

Chase grimaced. "You've been talking to Kat. She's nice, but don't believe everything she says. Sometimes she gets carried away."

Ali grinned wider. "Sounds more to me like the girls in this town are all in love with you. So, why don't you have a girlfriend, since you're so popular?"

Chase sighed. "I'm not popular. It's a small town and everyone knows everyone. And I've known most of the girls in high school since Kindergarten. I'm not interested in dating girls who I've known all my life."

Ali shot him a surprised look. "You mean you don't date at all? Ever? Didn't you go to your prom? Take a girl to a movie here in town? Anything?"

"I didn't say I never dated," Chase said. "I just don't date girls I go to school with. Yes, I went to my prom, but I invited a girl I met from another school. And I have dated, a little. I just don't meet that many girls around here. Besides," Chase added, growing serious. "I'm not letting anything distract me from going to college in the fall. Especially a local girl."

"I didn't mean to make you mad," Ali said, feeling sorry she'd teased him, especially since she didn't know him too well. "I was only teasing."

"I know you were. You didn't make me mad. But sometimes it's hard living in a small town. Everyone talks about everyone else, and it gets annoying." Chase looked at his watch. It was nearly noon. "We'd better head back to the lodge. I'm sure Ben is already back with the fishing group, and if they've caught fish, he'll want help cleaning them."

Ali nodded. She reached for her backpack, but Chase picked it up before she could, stood, and slung it over his shoulder. He smiled at her then, that adorable perfect smile, and Ali suddenly understood why all the girls in town had a crush on him.

# Chapter Five

Ali spent the rest of the afternoon unpacking her bag and settling into her new room. After she'd hung her clothes on the pole that served as a closet, and placed smaller items in the dresser drawers, she put her laptop computer on the desk in the window alcove and some pens and a pad of paper in the desk's drawers. Reverently, she set a framed photo of her mother and her on the top of the dresser. It was over a year old, but it was the most recent one she had. She stared at the photo for a long time, remembering how happy they'd been that day, hanging out with Megan and her mom, Amy. Ali's mom had looked pretty that day, her eyes clear and her smile easy to entice. It had been a rare day, and one that Ali had treasured for a long time afterward, when times became tougher.

Ali turned away from the photo and sat at the small desk a while, staring out the window at the scenery below. The lake sparkled in the afternoon sun. With no wind today, it looked like a sheet of glass, smooth and shiny. But then a duck would land in the water, or a boat from the lodge would drive by and the water broke into a cascade of shimmering ripples. The lake was nothing like the ocean that Ali was used to. The ocean was always moving, rushing onto shore, wave after wave. The lake, however, moved in slower motion, making it peaceful and calming.

As the day warmed up, so did the attic room, so Ali went downstairs in search of something to drink. There wasn't much in the refrigerator. In fact, there wasn't anything to drink at all. She found a glass in one of the cupboards and turned the cold tap on, but nothing came out of the faucet. "No water?" Ali asked, confused. Then she realized that the generator probably had to be on in order for the water to turn on. That seemed strange to a girl who was used to city water running all the time. Ali sighed. She'd have to wait until she went back down to the lodge to have something to drink. Jo's refrigerator was stocked full with drinks and food. Maybe Ali could ask her grandfather if they could buy a few groceries to keep at the cabin, just in case she was hungry or thirsty.

Ali wandered out of the kitchen and around the cabin. There was a smaller room off of the larger living room that held a small sofa and an antique oak desk. Ali walked over to the desk and noticed a small, framed photo there. She lifted it up and looked into the kind face of an older woman. "My grandmother," she said softly. "His Lizzie." She studied her grandmother's photo, a woman she'd never met or even seen a picture of before. Her grandmother looked to be about the same height as Ali's mom and had a slender build. Her hair was dark and straight, framing her face, just long enough to curl under her jaw, and her eyes were a deep brown. Ali looked up into the antique gilt-framed mirror that hung over the desk and studied her face. She lifted her hand and traced her jawline down to her chin. "I have my grandmother's oval face," Ali said, smiling. That was where she'd inherited it from. Her mother's face had been square and strong, like her grandfather's. But her grandmother's face was softer. Ali gently traced her finger over the photo of her grandmother, happy to have made a connection with her. Then she carefully set the photo down and left the cabin, heading back down to the lodge.

\* \* \*

"Where's the girl?" Ben asked Jo as he dropped a bucket of freshly cleaned fish onto the counter by the sink and started the tap to wash the fillets.

"You mean Ali? Your granddaughter?" Jo asked from across the kitchen where she was cutting up potatoes and placing them in a large pan of water.

Ben looked over his shoulder at Jo, frowning, but then turned back to his fish cleaning. "Yeah. Where's Ali?"

"She's setting the tables for supper out in the dining room. She's been a big help all afternoon."

"Humph," Ben grunted.

"I'm thinking of asking her if she'd like to work here this summer," Jo continued, ignoring Ben's grunt. "I always hire extra help in the summer and she'd be perfect. What do you think?"

Ben turned from the sink again and looked at Jo as if she'd lost her mind. "What in the world would a spoiled city girl know about working at a resort?" he asked. "Do you really expect her to help with cleaning, cooking, and making up cabins?"

Jo stopped cutting potatoes and looked directly at Ben. "She seems very capable to me. She helps out without even being asked, and she seems to know her way around a kitchen."

"Humph," Ben grunted again, returning to the fish. "If you ask me, she should be helping without being paid anyway since she'll be eating here for free."

Jo set down her knife, wiped her hands on her apron, and walked over to where Ben stood. She reached over and turned off the tap, making Ben turn his attention to her.

"What?" Ben insisted.

"Ben, I don't think you're giving Ali enough credit. She doesn't seem to be a spoiled city kid to me. She's a nice girl, and seems to be a hard worker. So, do you mind my asking her to work here, or not?"

Ben stared at Jo for one long moment, then shrugged. "Fine. It's your money." He turned back to the sink and turned on the cold tap again to clean his fish fillets.

Jo smiled and patted his arm gently, then walked back to where she was cutting up potatoes.

"Women," Ben muttered, shaking his head. "They're always trying to talk you into things."

Jo just ignored him and continued preparing supper.

* * *

Ali smelled the fish frying from the outer room long before she entered the kitchen. After she'd set the tables, Jo had told her to relax a while before supper because once the men came in to eat, there'd be plenty to do. Chase was helping her grandfather outside, cleaning out the boats and putting away fishing gear, so Ali had just wandered around inside the lodge and then walked around outside a while until she finally came inside again.

As Ali entered the kitchen, the fish smell grew stronger. She wrinkled her nose. Ali didn't like fish, but it looked like the catch of the day was on the menu for supper tonight.

"Sweetie, can you grab a stack of plates from the cupboard? And get down a platter for the fish, please?" Jo asked as she carefully tended the fish fillets in the large, black, cast iron pan on the stove. Next to it, two huge pans were boiling.

Ali did as she was asked, counting out enough plates for the settings she'd placed earlier and four more for her, her grandfather, Chase, and Jo. Then she pulled down the platter from the open shelf beside the cabinets. Seeing a few pans and dishes in the sink, Ali began running hot water to wash them.

Jo came over to get some paper towels to line the fish

platter with and patted Ali on the shoulder. "You're a lifesaver," she said, smiling.

Ali and Jo worked side-by-side in the kitchen. Ali pulled condiments and butter out of the refrigerator and took them to the tables in the outer room. As one platter of fish became full, Ali pulled down another platter and lined it with paper towels as Jo had done, then handed it to Jo. Cornbread muffins were baking in the oven, and when the timer buzzed, Ali pulled them out and placed them into cloth-lined baskets that Jo had already prepared. The muffins smelled heavenly, and Ali couldn't wait to taste one. All the while Jo stood at the stove, frying fish, turning each fillet over carefully so it would brown just right. When the potatoes were done boiling, Ali carried the heavy pot over to the sink and poured them into a strainer, then put the steaming, quartered potatoes into serving bowls and covered them with aluminum foil to keep them warm. She did the same with the cut carrots that had been boiling in the other pot.

Just as the clock struck six, Ali heard the men coming into the room beyond and Ben and Chase walked through the back door into the kitchen. The four began serving supper to the men in the outer room. Freshly brewed coffee was poured, water glasses were filled, and the food was brought out to the tables. Ali pitched right in alongside Jo, Chase, and her grandfather, making sure the guests had everything they needed before the four finally returned to the kitchen and served up their own supper.

"Ah, nothing like fresh fish," Ben said as he filled his plate with fish, potatoes, cooked carrots, and a warm corn muffin.

Jo and Chase dug right in too, but Ali hesitated when the platter of fish came her way.

"What's the matter? Don't you like fish?" Ben asked.

Ali looked at the three faces that stared back at her. "I've never really liked fish," she said, feeling bad after having watched Jo work so hard to prepare it.

Ben frowned at her. "Well, that's because you've never had fresh water fish before. This is Walleye, the best fish you'll ever taste." He forked up a fillet and placed it on her plate. "Go ahead, try it. You won't know if you like it unless you do."

Ali looked down at the fish, then up at Jo.

Jo smiled encouragingly. "Just try a bite, dear. It really isn't fishy at all. If you don't like it, you certainly don't have to eat it."

Ben grunted and started eating his own food.

Ali scooped a few potatoes onto her plate and mashed them with her fork like she'd seen everyone else at the table do. She buttered them, then took a warm cornbread muffin and buttered it also. When she could no longer put off trying the fish, she broke off a small piece with her fork, took a deep breath, and placed it in her mouth, chewing it quickly.

Chase had been watching her the entire time with a small grin on his face. Finally, he asked, "Well? Do you like it?"

Ali swallowed. She was surprised there was no fishy taste, and the texture wasn't gooey, either. It actually tasted good. "Yeah. Actually, I do," she said.

Jo smiled wide and continued eating and Chase winked at Ali. Ben, however, grunted again. "Of course you like it," he said. "It's the best fish there is."

Ali sighed. She ignored her grandfather's comment and dug right into her supper, even eating a second piece of fish. Ali especially enjoyed the cornbread muffins. Slathered in butter, they were heavenly.

Later, after everyone had finished supper and had enjoyed a piece of the chocolate cake Jo had made earlier, Ali helped Jo clean up the kitchen. Chase and Ben had gone off again to work outside, although Ali had no idea what they were doing. As the two women finished up the last of the dishes and wiped down the counters and stove, Jo casually asked Ali how she'd learned so much about working in a kitchen.

"I worked at a small restaurant for the last two years," Ali told her.

Jo stopped and looked at the young teen. "Really? As a cook or a waitress?"

"I started as a dishwasher, cleaning off tables, setting them, and running the dishwasher," Ali said. "After I turned sixteen, the owner let me wait tables so I could earn tips. I made a lot more money that way."

"So, you've been working since you were fourteen?" Jo asked.

Ali shrugged. "Longer than that, if you count babysitting for neighbors. I started babysitting nights and weekends when I was twelve. It wasn't a lot of money, but at least it was something."

"Well, you certainly are a hard worker," Jo said, smiling at Ali. "What about here? Are you thinking of finding a summer job?"

"I'd like to," Ali said. "I need money if I want to keep my phone working. Kat at the coffeehouse asked me if I'd like to work there this summer, but I'm not sure if my grandfather would let me drive his truck back and forth to town. Plus, I still have to get my Minnesota driver's license before I can drive by myself."

"Maybe I can help," Jo said. "I was wondering if you'd like to work here, at the lodge. You could help me with meals and cleaning out the cabins and rooms. I usually hire someone for the summer, and I thought you'd be perfect since you're such a good worker and you live right here."

Ali's eyes grew wide and she smiled broadly. "Really? That would be great. I'd love working here with you."

"Good. I can only pay you minimum wage. I hope that's okay."

"That's fine. When do you want me to start?"

Jo laughed. "It seems as if you've already started, what with all the work you've done already."

"Oh, I don't mind. I like helping you."

"How about tomorrow morning?" Jo asked. "The guests will be here until the afternoon but then we can get started on cleaning up the cabins and getting them ready for next weekend. For now, we'll only be busy on weekends, but as soon as June hits, we'll have guests here pretty much all the time."

"This is so great. It will be perfect. Thanks, Jo." Ali was so excited about having a job for the summer that she reached out and gave Jo a big hug without even thinking about it.

Jo hugged her back tightly. "I'm happy, too. This will be a great summer."

* * *

Evening settled in early as the sun slowly slipped below the cliff across the lake. Ali sat on the old wooden dock that jutted out into the water, her legs dangling over the edge, her bare feet skimming the cold water. The spring chill made Ali shiver, making her happy she'd worn a heavy sweatshirt. Everything was peaceful. The water barely rippled, the breeze blew lightly, and the leaves on the trees swayed slowly.

A loon swooped high above Ali and landed smoothly on the lake, laughing as it touched the water. It swam very close, allowing Ali to study it. She marveled at its black and white checkerboard back and its long, graceful neck and head that looked like black velvet. Then, when she least expected it, the loon dived straight down into the water. Ali waited and watched for what seemed like an eternity before it finally appeared again, a little farther away from her, shaking the water droplets from its head.

"You're beautiful," Ali said aloud.

"Who? Me, or the loon?" Chase asked as he came up behind her on the dock.

Ali turned, surprised she hadn't heard or felt him walk up behind her. She'd been so engrossed in watching the loon, she'd forgotten she wasn't alone here.

"The loon, silly," she answered. "I've never seen one close up before. He's so beautiful."

Chase slipped off his sneakers and sat down beside Ali on the edge of the dock. "Yep. They're pretty amazing. There are a couple of nests here on the lake. Maybe sometime I can take you out in the canoe and show you."

Ali turned and looked at one of the old wooden canoes lying upside down on the shore. It didn't look all that safe to her. "Why not a boat?" she asked.

"A boat would make waves which might swamp the nest. Loons nest close to the edge of the water because they can't maneuver very well on land. Their legs are too far back on their bodies to walk very far. With a canoe, we could skim up closer to the nest to see it without causing waves."

Ali tipped her head and looked at Chase. He was sitting so near, the sleeve of his sweatshirt was skimming her sleeve. His blonde hair was tousled, and his face was lightly tanned. He'd been cleaning fish all afternoon with her grandfather, yet he didn't smell fishy. He smelled like lemons.

Chase turned to look at her. "What?"

Ali quickly looked away. "I smell lemons," she said.

Chase raised his hands and smiled. "Lemon hand cleaner. It takes the fish smell away."

"Oh," was all Ali could manage.

They sat in silence a while as the night sky grew darker. Ali heard chattering in the trees above and croaking on the ground close by.

"Is the croaking a toad?" she asked.

"Yep. Frogs, too."

"What's that chattering? A bird?"

"A chipmunk," Chase said. "Probably yelling at a blue jay to get away from its nest."

"I guess I have a lot of animal sounds to learn," Ali said. "So, does a bear make a sound before it attacks?"

Chase laughed. "Was Ben teasing you about bears coming up to your room?"

Ali frowned. "He said if I have food up there, one might come up."

"He's just pulling your leg. I mean, a bear could get up there if he really wanted to, but it's unlikely, especially since Ben closes the garage door at night. Don't take everything Ben says seriously. He likes to tease."

"Hmmm." Ali didn't find her grandfather's sense of humor funny.

The loon was across the lake by now and began swimming faster, finally lifting its powerful wings and taking flight up and over Ali and Chase. It called out as it flew away, its tremulous call loud and musical.

"He's going back to his own lake. His own home," Chase said, watching it fly away.

Home, Ali thought. She no longer knew where home was.

* * *

Ben and Jo sat on the swing in the screened-in porch facing the lake. The sun was almost down, the work was all done for the day, and now they could relax in the few minutes they had left before night fell.

"What do you think they're talking about?" Ben asked, nodding his head in the direction of the dock where Ali and Chase sat.

"The mysteries of life, I suppose," Jo replied with a grin. When Ben slid a disgusted look her way, she continued. "More likely they're talking about living up here, the lake, maybe even that loon swimming out there."

"They're sitting awfully close together," Ben said, grumbling.

"So. You're sitting awfully close, too," Jo said, referring to him being only inches away from her, his right arm draped casually behind her over the back of the swing.

"That's different. I'm old. I can do whatever I want," Ben said. He slid over even closer to Jo, making her laugh. This brought a smile to his lips.

"I offered Ali the job. She was excited about it," Jo said.

"Humph. Well, don't come complaining to me when she doesn't give you an honest day's work."

"I don't think that'll be a problem," Jo said. "She's a hard worker. She's been working in one form or another since she was twelve."

Ben's brows rose as he turned and looked at Jo. "Twelve? Whatever for?"

Jo shrugged. "She didn't say. She babysat for neighbors for two years and then she started working in a restaurant when she was fourteen."

Ben's gaze turned back to where Ali and Chase sat on the dock. "Hmmm."

"You should ask Ali to go fishing with you in the morning. Remember how much Jen used to enjoy it? Maybe Ali will, too. It would give you two time together to talk," Jo told him.

Ben frowned. "What? Are you kidding? I could barely get her out of bed for breakfast. You think she's going to want to get up before five to go sit in a boat for an hour?"

"Wouldn't hurt to ask, would it?"

"What in the world would we talk about?" Ben asked.

Jo sighed. "Just stuff. Her mother, maybe. How her mother died. How she feels about it. Ali's been through a lot this last month, maybe even longer. It wouldn't hurt for you to connect with her and let her know that you care."

Twilight was upon them. The frogs and toads were busy with their nightly chanting and the loon flew off the lake, heading home, his laughter echoing in the evening sky. Ben looked over at Jo. She looked like a young girl, even though there were only nine years between their ages. Her porcelain complexion was soft and smooth, and a smattering of freckles ran across her cheeks and nose. Her lips were full and still held a rich, rose color, and when she smiled, the tiny lines around her pale blue eyes only made her lovelier. Jo was the only woman, besides his Lizzie, who'd ever gotten away with bossing him around. But he never gave up without a fight, or at least without having his say first. In the end though, Jo usually won.

"The girl's been here less than forty-eight hours and you've already given her a job, and now you want me to take her fishing and talk to her about her feelings. Don't you think we should give her a few days to adjust to this new life?" Ben asked softly.

Jo smiled up at him. "She's not going to adjust until she's comfortable around you and feels like she belongs here. No better time than the present to start making her feel at home."

Ben shook his head, but didn't respond. He reached up and tugged playfully at Jo's ponytail, which only made her laugh, then stood, stretched, and headed out the screen door.

"Let's head up," Ben called out to Ali.

\* \* \*

Ali sighed and said goodnight to Chase before slipping on her sneakers and following Ben up the gravel road to the cabin. His flashlight beam led the way, and once they were there, Ali waited inside the garage while he started up the generator.

"Do you mind if I take a quick shower?" she asked. It was almost nine o'clock and she was afraid if she didn't shower tonight, she'd have to go another day without one.

Ben waved her on. "Go ahead. Make it quick."

Ali rushed up the stairs to her room and grabbed her night clothes and bathroom items, along with her blow dryer, then headed back down and into the bathroom. She showered quickly, afraid her grandfather might turn the lights off, and the water with it, in the middle of her shower. She combed out her hair and dried it, dressed in her night clothes—a T-shirt and boxer shorts—then hesitated a moment, wondering if she should leave her bathroom items in there. She finally decided if she was going to be living here, she needed her things in the bathroom, so she left her shampoo and conditioner on the rim of the tub, her blow dryer under the cabinet near the clean towels, and made a space in the medicine cabinet over the sink for her toothbrush and paste. She stepped out of the bathroom with her wet towel and washcloth in hand and stopped when she saw her grandfather sitting in one of the rocking recliner chairs in the living room.

"I left some of my things in the bathroom. Is that okay?" Ali asked.

Ben shrugged. "Don't see why you shouldn't. You live here now."

Ali bit her bottom lip. He always sounded angry. "Where should I put my wet towel?"

Ben stood and walked over to her. "Hang the towel over the shower curtain rod to dry so you can use it again. No sense wasting water washing a towel that's practically clean. There's a basket on the washing machine out in the garage where you can put your wet washcloth."

"Washing machine?" Ali asked. She didn't remember seeing one.

"Yeah. It's under the staircase in the garage. You must

have missed it."

Ali nodded, then ran back into the bathroom and hung up her towel. She wrinkled her nose at the thought of reusing the same towel, but she'd just have to get used to his ways. When she walked out of the bathroom again, her grandfather was no longer in the living room. She found him in the kitchen, drinking a glass of water.

"I noticed there wasn't anything in the fridge when I was in here this afternoon," Ali said, hesitantly, as her grandfather stared at her with those stern eyes. "Could we buy some pop or juice or something to have here? Maybe some fruit to snack on, the next time we go into town?"

Her grandfather seemed to be mulling this over. "I usually eat and drink everything down at the lodge," he said. "But I guess it wouldn't hurt to get a few things for up here."

Ali smiled at him. A small, slow smile, but one nonetheless. Instead of making her grandfather happy though, it seemed to unnerve him.

"Well," he said gruffly. "It's time I turn out the lights. We get up early around here."

Ali nodded and turned to go, but then stopped when her grandfather spoke again.

"Say. Jo was thinking you might like to go out fishing with me in the morning. I go out early, by five o'clock, so you'd have to be up and ready on time. Is that something you'd like to do?"

Ali stood, dumbfounded. She wasn't sure if she should say yes or no. It sounded like it was Jo's idea, not his, and maybe he really didn't want her to go with him. "Um, sure. I'd like to go. But I'm starting work tomorrow with Jo at the lodge. Will we be back in time?"

Ben nodded. "I'm always on time for breakfast. We'll only go out for an hour. Do you have an alarm clock?"

Ali nodded.

"Good. Dress warm. Be ready to go by five to five. If you're not down at the dock by then, I'm going without you," Ben told her.

Ali nodded, then headed out the door to the garage. She placed her washcloth in the basket on the washing machine, headed up to her room, and closed the door tightly. She wasn't sure she even wanted to go fishing with her grandfather, but she didn't know how to tell him no. Besides, if it was Jo's suggestion, then she'd give it a try.

She lit the oil lamp just moments before the generator shut off and the light went out. Then she set the alarm clock early enough so she could dress and get down to the dock on time. Tonight, after she'd blown out the oil lamp and slipped underneath the timeworn quilt, no tears came as she lay there listening to the nightly music from the woods. She fell into a deep sleep quickly, exhausted from her long first day of her new life.

# Chapter Six

Ali was startled awake by a high-pitched beeping and it took her a few moments to remember that she'd set her alarm. It was pitch black in her room so she had to feel around on the nightstand for the flashlight she kept by her bed, hoping she didn't knock the oil lamp over. Finally, she found the flashlight and turned it on, then turned off the offending alarm. Four twenty-five a.m. Her days were getting longer and her nights were getting shorter.

Ali sighed and reached for the matches to light the oil lamp, but stopped when she realized she heard the hum of the generator. She reached over and clicked on the bedside lamp. *Yes! Lights.* Her grandfather was already up and actually using electricity.

Ali shivered. The room was chilly, which reminded her that her grandfather had told her to dress warmly. Hurriedly, she headed over to where her clothes hung and picked out something to wear. She figured layers for the day would be best, so she put on a T-shirt, a thick, hooded sweatshirt, jeans, heavy socks, and her sneakers.

Ali stood in front of the mirror that was connected to the dresser and quickly tied her hair up into a ponytail. Then she grabbed her flashlight, in case the lights went out again, and ran down the stairs to use the bathroom. The large garage door was already open. *Great, I could have run into a bear.* Instead, she ran into her grandfather in the kitchen where he was standing by the sink, drinking a mug of coffee.

"I'm heading down to the boat. Hurry on down. I'll be turning off the generator in a minute," he told her.

Ali literally ran to the bathroom to brush her teeth before the water pump turned off. She didn't want to go all day without clean teeth. The lights snapped off just as she was finishing. It grossed her out that she wasn't able to flush the toilet, but there was nothing she could do about it. Not having electricity on all the time sucked.

Ali stepped outside, her flashlight held tightly in her hand. She couldn't see a thing in the dark. The air was chilly and nipped at her face and hands. She hoped she'd be warm enough out on the water. *Who in their right mind goes fishing before sunrise?* Ali picked her way carefully down the gravel road to her grandfather's dock, her flashlight beam leading the way.

"Hop in. Let's get going," Ben said when Ali stepped onto the dock.

Ali ran her flashlight over the boat. This was the first time she'd seen it close up. It was fairly large, maybe sixteen or seventeen feet long, had a full-length windshield, and four seats in back and one seat up in front of the windshield. From what she could see, it was black on the outside and gray on the inside, but in the dark, it was hard to tell. The motor on the back looked huge to Ali. She had no experience with boats, but it looked big enough to speed across the lake without ever touching the water. One thing was certain—her grandfather wasn't cheap when it came to his boat.

Ali gingerly stepped down onto the side bench in the boat and then onto the floor. The boat rocked back and forth from her weight.

"Can you swim?" Ben asked.

Ali's brows rose. "Uh, yes. Why?"

"If we swamp the boat, it's good to know you can swim."

"Are we going to swamp the boat?" Ali asked, not sure if

he was teasing or serious.

"Not if I can help it," Ben said. "Here." He handed her a life jacket. "It will save you if you fall in. It'll help keep you warm, too."

Ali slipped on the bulky life jacket and snapped it tight. Her grandfather stood from his seat at the wheel and helped her adjust the vest tabs so it fit properly. This was the closest he'd ever stood next to her. Ali could smell his spicy aftershave. *He smells like a grandfather.* She smiled up at him, but he didn't smile back.

"Don't want it sliding off if you fall in," he said gruffly. "Now, sit down and let's go."

No sooner had Ali sat in the seat across from her grandfather then he turned the key and the boat motor came to life. He stood, untied the front and back of the boat, then backed out from the dock. Soon, they were buzzing across the lake at a rapid speed that scared the life out of Ali.

After a few minutes, the boat slowed to a crawl.

"Here we are," Ben said. "I want to try this spot and see how it is before I bring any of the fishing groups out here."

Ali stared over at him. It was still dark out, but her eyes had adjusted enough to see him clearly. "How did you know where you were going in the dark?" she asked, her heart still pounding from the fast ride across the lake.

"I've been driving on this lake since I was a kid. Know it like the back of my hand," Ben said.

"Even when you can't see the back of your hand in the dark?" Ali asked.

Ben shook his head. "Let's just get to fishing. Do you know how to bait a hook?"

Ali frowned at him. "I've never been fishing. Ever."

Ben just shook his head again and got to work. He pulled out two fishing rods from a side compartment then reached into a bucket on the floor and pulled out a minnow to bait Ali's hook. "Pay attention to how I do this," he told her. "I'm not baiting your hook every time you lose a minnow."

Ali watched as he pushed the hook through the middle of the small, silver minnow. The thing wiggled and squirmed, and she thought she was going to be sick.

"You want me to kill one of those little fish like that? Gross."

Ben rolled his eyes. "It's bait. It's a minnow. That's what they're for. How the heck do you expect to catch a fish without something on your hook?" He handed her the fishing rod, making sure it was pointed out over the side. "Now, this is how you use the reel. This little lever moves over and releases the line. When you've let out enough line, you move it back and it'll stop. Don't let it go too slack, though. It'll tangle up the line. This little handle is how you reel in the line. Got it?"

Ali nodded. "Aren't I supposed to toss the line far out into the water? That's what they do on all those fishing shows."

"Not today," Ben said. "We'll work on casting another day. Just let the line out until you feel it hit the bottom, then stop it and reel it up a roll or two. You don't want your bait lying on the bottom, you want it floating where the fish are."

Ali did as he said. She dropped the line until she felt it stop and start to go slack, then reeled it up a little. "How do you know that there are fish here?"

Ben had already baited his hook and cast his line out into the water. "Because I know all the good spots on this lake," he said, sounding superior. Then, to Ali's surprise, he chuckled. "Plus, my fish locater here tells me there are fish right under us." He pointed to a small screen that was bolted to the dashboard of the boat. On the TV-like screen, Ali saw little cartoon fish of all sizes swimming by.

Ali smirked. "So, you do like technology."

"When it's useful, like for catching fish, I do."

They sat in silence for a while with Ben casting out his line every now and again. The motor chugged quietly as they moved slowly across the water.

Ali sat, her fishing pole held firmly in her hand. She had no idea what she was doing. "How will I know when a fish tries to eat my bait?"

"You'll feel a little tug on the line, just the tiniest nibble. When you feel that, just hold still until it nibbles again. Walleyes like to inspect their food before they open wide and suck it in. That's why you feel the nibble. The fish will barely touch the minnow, then it will strike. So, when you feel the second tug, that's when you want to pull up fast with your rod and hook it." Ben showed what he meant by jerking his rod up high in one swift motion.

Ali sat quietly for some time, concentrating on feeling a tiny nibble. She had trouble believing that a fish in this wide-open lake would actually choose her minnow to latch onto. It seemed to her like finding a needle in a haystack.

The sun was slowly rising, casting a golden gleam over the water. Ali was finally able to see around her, and was surprised when she couldn't see the house or the lodge. Her grandfather had said there were several coves on the lake, so she assumed they were off in one of them. The water was still, the sky peaceful. She began to understand why her grandfather enjoyed his early mornings out on the lake. It was the perfect place to sit, relax, and reflect.

"Jo said you've been working since you were twelve," Ben said, interrupting her thoughts as he cast out his line again.

Ali shrugged. "Yeah."

"Was there a reason for that?"

Ali looked up at him, wondering what he was getting at. "Just wanted my own money, that's all."

Ben nodded. "Well, that's a good thing. So, what is it that my Jen did out there? What kind of work, I mean."

Ali stared at the end of her fishing rod as if she was more

interested in fishing than the conversation. "She worked as a secretary sometimes. Sometimes she worked at a store. Jobs weren't always easy to get and keep."

Ben looked over at Ali and frowned. "Jen was always a hard worker. She did well in school and always helped out at the lodge. I'm surprised she didn't find more permanent work."

"She did the best she could," Ali said defensively.

"I'm sure she did," Ben said. "Yep. My Jen was a hard worker, always was. And she sure liked to fish and hunt, too. Why, she'd beg to not have to cook and clean at the lodge so she could go out on the fishing tours with me instead. My Lizzie just said to let her go along. It was better than forcing her to work at something she didn't enjoy. Did your mom ever mention how she and I went out fishing every morning?"

Ali shook her head. She was relieved the conversation had turned from what her mother did in California to when she was younger. "No. She hardly ever said anything about her childhood or this place."

Ben wrinkled his brow. "Hmmm. That surprises me. My Jen loved the mornings on the lake. She'd always come back with a stringer of fish. We'd have a competition on who'd catch the most walleye, and she almost always won."

Ali sat a moment, trying to picture her mom as a young girl or teen who hung out with her father and fished. They probably laughed and teased each other, like fathers and daughters do. It made Ali sad, because she'd never had the chance to have a relationship like that with her own father. Ali didn't even know who her father was.

"I like that you call my mom and grandmother what you do. My Jen and my Lizzie. I bet it made them feel good to have someone feel that way about them," Ali said, wondering how it would feel to have someone claim her as lovingly as that.

Ben sat silent and didn't respond.

Ali turned and looked at her grandfather. He was staring out at the lake.

"Did I say something wrong?" Ali asked.

Ben slowly shook his head. "No. I was just thinking how that term didn't always go over well. When she got older, your mom told me that it made her feel as if I owned her by calling her my Jen. I didn't mean it that way, but I guess now I can understand how she felt."

Ali didn't know what to say. Her grandfather seemed upset, and she didn't want to make things worse. She sat, concentrating on her line. Suddenly, she felt a tiny tug on the end of the pole. Ali held her breath. Was a fish actually nibbling on her bait? She waited, holding her rod very still. The tug came again, and this time Ali pulled up hard on the line, just like her grandfather had told her to do. The line went taut, and suddenly something was pulling at the rod in her hand.

"I got one!" Ali yelled.

Ben turned. He lay down his own rod and came over beside her. "Reel it in slowly. Let it give you some fight, but not too much. I'll get the net."

Ben opened up the center of the windshield and reached through to pick up the large fishing net. He came up beside Ali again and got the net ready by the side of the boat to grab the fish.

"Oh, my God! It's really fighting. I can't reel it up," Ali shrieked.

"Just reel it in slowly. Hang on tight to the rod. Get it up here and I'll grab it with the net," Ben said, excitement rising in his voice.

Ali reeled and reeled, but it seemed to take forever to bring the fish up. Finally, she could see it just below the surface of the water.

"Yep. You have a keeper. It's a walleye. Pull up on the rod so I can get the net under it," Ben told her.

Ali pulled, but she had trouble getting the fish to go where she wanted.

"Come on, girl. Pull it up before we lose it," Ben hollered.

"I'm trying. You don't have to yell at me," Ali shouted back angrily.

For a second, Ben stared at her with his eyes narrowed, but then his face softened a bit and he said in a kinder tone. "Sorry. I know you're trying. Let's get this fish in."

Ali concentrated on the fish again and this time when she tugged, it lifted up high enough so Ben could get the net under it. She reeled in carefully so the line wouldn't tangle while he lifted the fish up into the boat.

"Now, that's a fine fish you caught," Ben said, smiling. He grabbed a pair of long nosed pliers and a rag and wrapped his hand around the middle of the fish. Carefully, he pulled the hook out of the fish's mouth with the pliers. "Good thing I filled the live well with water. This one's going home with us." Ben opened a trap door in the front of the boat and dropped the fish inside. Immediately, the fish began splashing in the shallow water.

Ali's eyes shone bright. "That was fun. Do they always fight like that?"

Ben chuckled. "Sometimes. Wait till you catch a northern pike, then you'll have a fight on your hands."

"I can't wait," Ali said.

Ben picked up her hook and put a fresh minnow on it. "Okay, go at it. With you in the boat, we're going to fill out our limit in no time."

Ali smiled wide.

\* \* \*

By the time Ben and Ali made it to the lodge for breakfast, Ali had caught two more fish and Ben had caught one. They were joking and laughing on their way into the kitchen.

"Look at what Ali caught this morning," Ben said, holding up the stringer of fish. "I'd say we have a natural fisherwoman here."

Jo ran over to see the fish while Chase smiled at them from the stove where he was stirring the scrambled eggs and flipping bacon. "Oh, my goodness. Those are nice looking fish. Ali, you caught your own supper. Isn't that amazing?"

Ali smiled in response, then quickly washed her hands and started helping Jo with breakfast.

Ben couldn't have been prouder if he'd caught all the fish himself. Not only had Ali done a good job on her first day of fishing, but she seemed to have enjoyed being out there, too. He was in high spirits. Maybe having his granddaughter living with him wasn't going to be so bad after all.

"After breakfast, you need to have Jo issue you a fishing permit," Ben told Ali. "I don't want to be caught on the lake with you fishing illegally, now that we know you're so good at it."

Ali looked over at her grandfather and nodded.

Ben left the kitchen to place the fish in the sink in the fish cleaning house, washed his hands thoroughly, then returned to the kitchen. Jo, Chase, and Ali had already served the men in the other room and were just getting ready to sit down and eat their own breakfast. Ali brought over the pot of coffee as Ben sat down and poured some into his mug.

"Thanks, Ali," Ben said cheerfully.

Jo, Chase, and Ali looked at the usually grumpy old man with surprise registered on their faces, but didn't say a word.

The foursome ate their hearty breakfast amidst tales of Ali's first fishing day, mostly told by Ben.

"You should have seen her out there," Ben boasted. "She was all squeamish about baiting her hook, but after her second catch, she baited that hook all by herself and caught the third one. Yep. I think she's moved over to the dark side. She's becoming a true northern Minnesota girl."

Ali grinned, looking embarrassed at all the attention.

"Sounds like you two had a fun time," Jo said. "See, Ben. Having someone along was actually fun for a change. Wasn't it?" Jo winked at Ben, but he pretended to ignore her.

"Ali can come out with me anytime she wants," Ben said, looking over at his granddaughter. "She's good luck."

Ali beamed, pleased at the praise Ben was showering on her.

They joked and laughed a while longer, then Chase got up to bring more food out to the men in the dining room and Ali followed with the coffee pot to refill their mugs. Soon, all four of them were busy in the kitchen, bringing in dirty plates and platters, rinsing dishes and pans, and stacking the dishwasher trays. Jo started packing a lunch for Ben and the men he was taking out fishing. Working at the sink by the steamy dishwasher, Ali grew warm, so she pulled off the heavy sweatshirt she'd worn fishing and hung it on the coat hooks by the door. Underneath, she'd worn a basic, scoop necked T-shirt that fit her figure perfectly without being too tight. She walked back over to the sink, not noticing the three pairs of eyes following her. In the two days Ali had been here, she'd worn a sweatshirt, and this was the first time Chase and Jo had seen how slender and shapely she was. Chase stopped scraping the plate over the garbage and stared at her.

Jo saw the expression on her teenage son's face and looked like she was going to break out into laughter. She turned back to packing up the lunch.

"Oh, boy," Ben grumbled.

Ali turned from the sink at her grandfather's words. "What's wrong?" she asked, looking confused.

"Put your eyes back in your sockets, boy," Ben said gruffly. "Haven't you ever seen a girl before?"

Ali blushed and turned back toward the sink. Chase turned crimson and went back to scraping the plate, but only managed to drop it into the garbage can and had to retrieve it from the gooey, sticky mess.

Ben looked over at his granddaughter then back at Chase and rolled his eyes. It all came back to him why he hadn't wanted to deal with a teenage girl living here. Girls who looked like Ali could get into trouble real fast. He'd lived it once already. He didn't want to live through it again. With a disgusted sigh, Ben left the room.

# Chapter Seven

Ali and Jo spent the morning and afternoon going over details about the work Ali would be doing. Ben had left with four of the men to go out on one more fishing trip before they checked out and departed. Chase had disappeared into the fish cleaning house to clean the fish Ali and Ben had caught that morning. Ali didn't see him the rest of the morning or afternoon, and wondered if he was avoiding her because of what her grandfather had said to him. She'd been surprised at the fuss taking off her sweatshirt had caused. After all, she was wearing a decent T-shirt that wasn't offensive or skin tight like the ones her friends in California usually wore. Although, she had to admit that the look on Chase's face this morning had been both comical and flattering. He was a cute guy who was also friendly and sweet, so the fact that he thought she looked pretty enough to stare at was a compliment. But she knew immediately that her grandfather hadn't been amused. When he'd left, he'd had that same grumpy, disgusted look on his face that he generally wore. She had thought they'd made some headway this morning in their relationship, but now she felt they were back at square one, all because she took off her sweatshirt.

Forgetting her grandfather, Ali concentrated on everything Jo told her. Ali wanted to do a good job for Jo because she really liked her and didn't want to disappoint her.

"When the men get back from fishing, they'll pack up

their gear and then we can get to work on their cabins. If they've caught any fish, Ben and Chase will clean them and pack them up in dry ice for the men to take home. That's when we're the busiest, when the guests check out and we have to get the cabins ready for the next guests."

Jo showed Ali where the laundry room was. It was just off from the kitchen and held a commercial size washer and dryer. A large linen closet was also in the room where the bedding, blankets, and towels were stored when not in use. There was also a closet stacked full of toilet tissue, Kleenex boxes, packaged soaps, and other necessities for the rooms.

"This washer and dryer work fast and hold big loads," Jo said. "I can usually get the sheets and towels done quickly. If you ever want to do your laundry here, that's fine, too. I do most of Ben's for him."

Ali looked at Jo, surprised. "You do? Why? There's a washer and dryer up at the cabin."

Jo waved her hand through the air. "Oh, I don't mind. I just mix his shirts and jeans in when I do Chase's laundry." Jo chuckled. "Ben washes his own underclothes and towels up at the house. Guess he doesn't want me touching his unmentionables. But I know that he's chincy about running his generator, so don't be afraid to do your laundry down here."

Ali nodded, but she couldn't help but wonder why Jo would do her grandfather's laundry. It seemed strange to her. Ali figured she'd do her own laundry at the cabin. She didn't want anyone, especially Chase, to see her unmentionables, as Jo so delicately put it, either.

Jo showed Ali around the grounds to where each of the eight cabins was nestled around the point. "All of our cabins are named for the wildlife around here, except one," Jo told her. "Since so many men come up here for fishing and hunting, the cabins have always had masculine-type names. We have the Bear, Moose, Deer, Wolf, Elk, Mallard, and Loon cabins. But I set aside the cutest one for a family or honeymoon cabin and named it the Lady Slipper cabin. That's our state flower. There had to be one girly cabin in this place."

Ali chuckled. Jo, wearing jeans, a T-shirt, and a flannel shirt as a jacket didn't exactly represent a girly girl. It was funny that she wanted a feminine cabin among all the masculine ones.

"Are there usually just men staying here?" Ali asked.

"Oh, heaven's no. As soon as school lets out, we have a lot of families staying here. That's why we have that little play area over near the lodge with the tire swing, slide, and monkey bars. Ben and Chase will put out the swimming dock in a couple of weeks, too. The kids love diving and jumping off of it into the lake. And there are trails close by where families can go biking or hiking, although they have to bring their own bikes. There's a wonderful old Indian trail across the lake up behind the cliff. You can walk it all the way up to the top of the cliff or way back into the woods. A lot of guests enjoy doing that."

Ali nodded, trying to take it all in.

Jo took Ali into one of the cabins that wasn't being used. It had a front living room area with a small kitchen and table and chairs. There were two separate bedrooms, one with twin beds and the other with a full size bed, and a small bathroom with a stall shower. Everything looked cozy and very clean. The beds had soft, puffy quilts on them and the windows had cute red-striped curtains hanging across them. Woven scatter rugs kept the polished wood floors from being cool underfoot. Jo pointed out that each cabin had a small woodstove in it too, for heat. "It gets cold around hunting season and we also get a lot of men up here for ice fishing in the winter. Ben chops a lot of wood in the fall to keep these cabins heated."

Ali stared at Jo. "Ice fishing?"

Jo laughed. "Sorry. I forget this is all foreign to you. We put out small fishing houses on the lake in the winter and the men cut out holes in the ice and fish right through it. Some of the men bring up their fancy fish houses that are like small cabins on wheels and stay in them. Ben helps the men find good spots on the lake."

Ali wasn't too sure about walking out on a frozen lake, let alone driving a heavy vehicle out on it. She thought that people in Minnesota did strange things.

Each cabin was nestled in its own grove of trees which made them feel private, and four of them had lovely lake views from their spot around the point. Ali fell in love with the Lady Slipper Cabin. Jo had done it up in soft pink and coral hues, making it seem more like a fairytale cottage than a cabin. It stood on short stilts right in front of the point and had a large, screened-in porch facing the lake. The point was rocky, and there were huge boulders jutting out into the lake that the water splashed softly against. It was a dreamy, peaceful setting. A wonderful place to sit back and get lost in.

The men soon came back and packed up, and just as Jo had said, Ben and Chase packed up their fresh fish for them to take home. Ali and Jo soon became immersed in changing bed linens and sweeping and vacuuming out the cabins. Ali learned how to run the washer and dryer and had washed several loads of sheets and towels and folded them, storing them in the linen closet. The hours went by quickly, and before Ali realized it, it was supper time.

Since there was only the four of them, Jo made up a quick supper of fried fish, cornbread, baked potatoes, and raw veggies. There wasn't much conversation between them that night, mostly because they were all tired from the busy weekend, but there also didn't seem to be any tension in the air, which was a relief to Ali.

When Ali rose to help Jo with the dishes, Jo waved her away. "You've worked enough for today," she told Ali. "Why don't you go outside and enjoy what's left of the day? Ben will help me with this."

Ali saw Ben frown over at Jo in response, but he kept silent. Ali reluctantly took her sweatshirt off the hook by the door and stepped outside.

There was a chill to the evening air as Ali wandered out onto the dock. So far, the weather had been mostly cool, and she wondered if it ever grew hot this far north. She walked to the end of the dock and stood there, arms crossed, gazing out over the lake. There was no breeze, not even a hint of one, and the lake was smooth as glass. The rocky cliff across the lake reflected in the water like a mirror image. Ali watched a loon out in the distance as it dived for food, then came up, continually poking its head into the water before diving again. She laughed at it, thinking how funny it was that the loon kept peeking down into the water. She supposed it was looking for food, but it looked silly to her anyway.

Footsteps tread lightly on the dock behind her, and Ali turned to see Chase walking toward her.

"It's nice and smooth out on the lake tonight. Want to go for that canoe ride to see the loons' nest?" Chase asked, grinning.

"Sure," Ali replied. She followed him back up the dock to where the canoes were lying upside down on the shore. Chase had on a pair of tall, rubber boots, which Ali thought looked funny, but she didn't say so. She helped him turn the canoe over, then glide it halfway into the lake on the sandy shore. That was when she realized why he was wearing the funny boots.

"Go ahead and get in," he said. "I'll push you out farther, then get in myself."

"Shouldn't we wear life jackets?" Ali asked.

Chase shook his head. "We'll stay along the edge of the shore where it's shallow. You couldn't drown even if you wanted to," he teased.

Ali hesitantly stepped in, careful not to get her shoes wet.

She moved up to the front of the canoe and sat on the narrow bench, facing Chase. Chase pushed the canoe farther out into the water, then carefully stepped in and sat at the back. He picked up one of the paddles that lay on the floor and started gliding the canoe in the water with strong, smooth motions.

"Should I paddle?" Ali asked, feeling useless just sitting there while he did all the work.

"It's okay, just relax," Chase told her. "I can manage fine."

Ali sat, her hands holding the sides of the canoe, and watched Chase as he effortlessly maneuvered the canoe. He used long, smooth strokes, first paddling on one side, then lifting the paddle to run it through the water on the other side. They glided through the water, only leaving a small trail in their wake, hardly disturbing the crystal water. Even though Chase made it look easy, Ali suspected it took muscle to keep paddling so evenly. Chase was tall and slender, but Ali thought he must have muscles hidden under his sweatshirt from all his outdoor labor around the lodge, muscles that now were able to guide them so easily around the lake.

"Do I look funny?" Chase asked.

Ali snapped out of her reverie and her eyes grew wide. She'd been caught staring, and her face warmed in embarrassment. "No," she said, finally. "You just do that like it's so easy."

"It is, if you've been doing it most of your life," he said, that adorable grin of his on his face.

Ali noticed how blue his eyes looked here on the water, as if they'd turned an even deeper blue to match the lake. Quickly, she turned away so she wouldn't be caught staring at him again.

Chase paddled the canoe along the edge of the lake shore, careful not to get too close in case they came upon a nest by the water. He headed around to the edge of the cove closest to the cliff. As they neared the shore, he stopped paddling and pointed to a spot by the shore. "Over there," he said quietly.

Ali looked in the direction he was pointing. There sat a loon in a nest of grass and reeds, its body puffed up for warmth. Not far from the nest swam another loon, casually eating, ignoring Ali and Chase.

"She must have finally laid her eggs," Chase said quietly. "Last week they were just building the nest. That's her mate in the water. She wouldn't let any other loon besides him near her nest."

Ali watched, mesmerized by the serenity of the lake and the beautiful creatures that called it home. They were a family, and soon they'd have babies that would follow them out onto the lake and learn to survive, just like their parents. It was a heartwarming sight to see.

"They're so beautiful," Ali whispered to Chase. "So different from any other bird I've ever seen." She looked over at Chase, who seemed just as captivated by the mother bird on the nest as she was. Ali knew he'd probably seen them a million times, yet he still enjoyed watching them, and that warmed her heart. Chase was more than just a nice guy; he was truly a good person.

"There's another nest in the other cove behind the cliff," Chase said softly so as not to disturb the loons. "Maybe we can go see that another day when we have more time."

Ali nodded. "Jo said there's an Indian trail over by the cliff. Do you think we could hike it someday?"

Chase smiled and nodded. "Sure. It's a date."

Ali watched as he picked up the paddle and started turning the canoe back toward the lodge. The sun was falling slowly behind the cliff, and soon night would be upon them. She concentrated on watching the loons as their canoe slipped away, but in her mind, all she could hear was Chase telling her, 'It's a date'.

\* \* \*

Ben stood at the open kitchen door, a dishtowel in his hand, drying a pan but watching Ali and Chase in the canoe out on the lake. "Now, what do you suppose they're up to?" he asked Jo gruffly.

Jo stood by the sink, rinsing the few dishes from supper and stacking them into a dishwasher tray. "Don't worry about those two. Chase said he was taking Ali to see the loons' nest, that's all."

"Humph. They're not even wearing life jackets. They'll fall in and drown. Do you know how cold that lake water is this time of year?"

"They're not going to drown in four feet of water, silly. He's staying by the shore. And yes, I do know how cold the water is this time of year. Been skinny dipping in it a few times in the spring, remember?" Jo threw Ben a wink, but he only scowled at her.

"Better not be any skinny dipping going on in this lake this summer," Ben said as he marched over to the rack of pans and set the one he'd been drying down. "A girl as pretty as that granddaughter of mine can end up in an awful lot of trouble, that's all I know."

Jo sighed as she shut off the water and turned to face Ben, placing a hand on his arm. "Ben. She's a good girl. Will you just give her a chance? You're already accusing her of causing trouble when she hasn't done one wrong thing. She's a good worker, and a sweet girl. Be nice, will you?"

Ben looked at Jo and realized she was telling him exactly what his Lizzie would have told him if she were still here. Jo was a lot like his Lizzie had been, smart, confident, compassionate, and intuitive. He knew he should just give in and do as Jo said, but he didn't like letting his guard down. He'd lived through losing his daughter because of a mistake she'd made long ago. Could he live through that again?

Ben reached up his hand and covered Jo's, which still lay

on his arm. "I'm trying," he finally said. "It's difficult. I wasn't prepared for her coming here. Heck, I wasn't prepared to ever meet her, period."

Jo stepped closer to Ben. "She never expected to be here either. Remember that. This is harder on her than on you."

Ben nodded and wrapped his arms around Jo's small body. Her face reached his chest, and she turned and snuggled into his warmth, fitting perfectly. "You know, I didn't mean skinny dipping was off limits for everyone," he said, chuckling. "Just for Ali."

Jo laughed, then turned from his embrace to finish up her work.

\* \* \*

Later that evening, Ali stood in front of her dresser mirror brushing out her damp hair. She'd come up to the cabin just before sunset with her grandfather so she could shower before the lights went out. Tonight, she wore an oversized T-shirt and snuggly soft pajama pants for bed since it grew so cold at night. As she brushed her hair, she examined her reflection in the mirror. People at home had always told her she looked just like her mother, except for her dark hair. Now, she knew she looked like people other than her mom. Her face was shaped like her grandma Lizzie's and her dark hair and brows came from her grandfather. It felt strange, not knowing these people all her life but being made up of different parts of them. Ali wondered if her mother had lived, would she have ever met her grandfather or known what her grandma Lizzie looked like?

Her grandfather had been quiet on the walk back up to the cabin and Ali hadn't said anything to him other than goodnight when she passed him in the living room on her way up to her room. There he sat again, in the rocking recliner whose identical mate sat empty beside him. Ali wondered if her grandma Lizzie had always sat in the other rocker in the evening, and if he sat there now, wishing she was still there.

Ali and her grandfather had something in common. They'd both lost people they loved.

Ali pulled back the comforter and sheets and sat down on the bed. She lit the oil lamp, in case the generator was turned off suddenly. Reverently, she ran her hand over the soft quilt, thinking about how her mother had once slept under this same quilt, maybe even when she was the same age as Ali. Less than a month ago, Ali had been living in their small apartment, working at the restaurant, and going to school with her friends. Each night, she'd come home from her waitressing shift to find her mother passed out on the sofa, an empty bottle tipped over on the coffee table. It could have been wine, vodka, or whiskey, it didn't matter. Her mother always found a way to bring a bottle into the apartment and drain it before Ali came home from work. Each night, Ali helped her mother up gently and walked her to bed, tucking her in like she was the child and not the parent. That had been their routine over the past several months, and at the time, Ali didn't know what they'd do when they were eventually evicted from the apartment for late rent and would have to leave.

Ali had lived that scenario several times throughout the years. Her mother would fall into a depression and start drinking for months, then get help, clean up, and find a job for a while, then plummet back down into drinking. It didn't help that the doctors gave her prescription medications like pain pills and sleeping aids, thinking these would help her cope better. The drugs only helped to send her mother off on a drinking binge again, and Ali was always left to care for her.

Then the night came when Ali came home and couldn't wake her mother up. The booze and the sleeping pill bottles sat on the coffee table, both empty.

Tears ran down Ali's cheeks as she crawled under the

covers and pulled them up tight around her. No one knew for sure if her mother had accidently overdosed or taken her own life. Ali didn't know for sure. But the fact that her mother didn't care enough about her to try to stay sober hurt Ali deeply. Ali had loved her mother despite everything, but it hadn't been enough.

As Ali lay in her bed, the lights went out, and after a time her eyes adjusted to the darkness with the aid of the oil lamp's flame flickering, leaving shadows on the walls. In a split second, her old life was gone, and now here she was, trying hard to adjust to a new one. She didn't know if her grandfather loved her, or if she'd ever find it in her heart to love him, either. She liked Jo, and Chase had been very nice and welcoming to her. All she knew for sure was that she would try her hardest not to disappoint the people in her new life as she must have disappointed her mother, who had chosen to check out from their life rather than love her.

# Chapter Eight

The next morning, Ali met her grandfather down at the boat as she had the morning before with her brand new fishing license in her pocket. Ben didn't say a word, acting as if her coming fishing was as normal as the sunrise, and soon they were off across the lake to a new spot he wanted to try.

After baiting her own hook and dropping her line in the water, Ali was startled by her grandfather's gruff voice.

"I made a thermos of hot cocoa instead of coffee today. It's just the powdered type, nothing fancy, but you can have some if you like."

Ali nodded and Ben poured some of the steaming liquid into a travel coffee cup with a lid and handed it to her. She took a sip, savoring the rich, creamy drink. "Thanks," she said. Ali knew he preferred coffee, and that he'd made the cocoa just for her, but she didn't mention it. He'd only deny it anyway.

They sat in silence and fished. Ben cast his line every so often and Ali dropped in her line, slowly reeled it up, then dropped it back in several times in the hope of catching a walleye's attention. Soon, the sun peeked over the horizon and rested its golden rays across the lake. Just as the sun touched the lake, a loon flew over Ben and Ali, loudly announcing its presence with echoing laughter.

"On time, as usual," Ben said as the loon skimmed the water and came to rest, leaving a V-shaped trail in its wake.

Ali watched as the loon dipped its head down in the water,

then dove and disappeared. "Do they look down into the water first to spot their prey?" Ali asked.

"Yep," Ben replied.

"They look funny when they do it," Ali said. "I've noticed they can stay underwater for a long time."

"That's right. A loon can stay down there for up to a minute. They grab their food and sometimes even have it eaten before they come up. They also eat small pebbles from the lake floor. It helps their digestive system grind food up since they eat the fish bones and all."

Ali listened intently to her grandfather. She was intrigued by the loons and wanted to learn everything about them.

"That's why I'm so careful not to let a line break when I catch a fish," Ben continued. "When that happens, hooks, sinkers, and sometimes pieces of tackle end up on the bottom of the lake and the loons pick them up and swallow them by mistake. The lead is poisonous to them. Not to mention any loose line that they can tangle up in. I once saw a duck with fishing line tangled tightly around its neck. Poor thing was going to slowly choke to death just because some fisherman wasn't careful."

Ali frowned. She hated thinking about any living creature suffering. "What happened to it?"

"I shot it. Put it out of its misery."

Ali's mouth dropped open. "You what? You killed it? Why didn't you just try to help it?"

Ben looked over at Ali, a crease appearing between his brows. "It was a duck. The damn thing would never have let me cut fishing line off its neck. Besides, it was hunting season, so shooting him was legal. And he tasted good, too."

Ali just stared at her grandfather, not sure if he was kidding or not. She decided he wasn't. "Well, I hope you never shoot one of the loons," she said crossly.

"The loon is the state bird. It's illegal to kill them. Besides, even if a person did, they aren't worth eating. Too much bone and too little soft flesh. If I can't eat it, I'm certainly not going to kill it," Ben said matter-of-factly.

"Well, that's good to hear," Ali said, rolling her eyes.

After sitting in silence a while longer, Ben spoke up again. "I saw you and Chase out in the canoe last night. Did he show you the loons' nest?"

Ali's eyes lit up. "Yes. It was so cool. He said he'd take me to see another one, and maybe we can even go hiking on the old Indian Trail by the cliff sometime."

"Well, that's nice. Chase, he's a good kid. And smart, too. You know, he plans on going to college this fall," Ben said.

Ali glanced guardedly at her grandfather. "Yes, I know. He said he's looking forward to it. He doesn't want anything to get in the way of his going."

"That's right. I wouldn't get too attached to the boy if I were you. You wouldn't want to do anything to muck up his plans."

Ali took a deep breath to calm the anger rising inside her. She knew exactly what her grandfather was getting at. He didn't want her getting in Chase's way of going to school. As if she'd want to trap him in a relationship or worse yet, get pregnant like her mother.

"You don't have to worry about me," Ali said, turning away from him. "I don't plan on hanging around forever, either."

Ben didn't reply. Ali hoped he got the message.

* * *

Ali spent the rest of the morning helping Jo finish cleaning the cabins and washing linens. Chase had school for the next two weeks, so he was gone all day. Shortly after noon, Jo and Ali stopped for a bite to eat and then Jo told Ali to go relax for a while. "The cabins are clean and ready for this weekend. Why don't you go outside and enjoy the beautiful weather?"

Reluctantly, Ali slipped on her sweatshirt and headed outdoors. It was still chilly outside compared to the weather she was used to in California, but it felt good. She thought she might go up to the cabin and dig out her Kindle so she could sit out by the lake and read. She hadn't packed any of her favorite books because they would have been too heavy. Megan's mom, Amy, had given her an inexpensive Kindle e-reader for Christmas last year, and thanks to all the freebies on Amazon, Ali had filled it up with books she wanted to read.

As Ali passed by the resort's dock, she noticed her grandfather was in one of the smaller motorboats working on the motor and grumbling to himself. She was still upset with him over what he'd said that morning in the boat, so she decided to steer clear of him. It seemed every time they started getting along fine, he said or did something to mess it up. It was almost as if he didn't even want to try having a good relationship with her.

"Hey, Ali. Come here a moment, will you?" Ben hollered out to her from the dock.

Ali sighed, but turned and walked down the dock to where he was.

"Will you hand me the wrench?" he asked, not even looking at her. "I have this dang thing apart and can't let go of it or it'll fall to pieces."

Ali knelt down and looked into the metal toolbox. She pulled out the smaller wrench, since what he was working on looked small, leaned over, and handed it to her grandfather.

"So, you know what a wrench is," Ben said, taking the tool.

"I've used one a time or two," Ali said. There'd been many times Ali had to fix a leaking faucet or pipe under a sink in one of the many old apartments they'd lived in through the years.

The building managers were never around, there was never extra money to hire a plumber, and her mom didn't take it upon herself to fix things, so Ali learned how. But she wasn't about to share that information with her grandfather.

"These damn old motors, they're useless," Ben said as he pulled the starter cord and nothing happened. "Should just dump them all and buy new ones."

Ali stood there, not quite sure if she should leave, or stay and listen to him complain. Just as she thought she'd leave, her grandfather looked up at her.

"Are you all done with your work?" he asked.

"Yeah. Jo said we're all done."

"Good. Why don't you make yourself useful?" Ben reached into his pants pocket, pulled out a ring of keys, and tossed them to Ali. Ali reached out and caught them before they fell into the lake, a startled look on her face.

"I need some more spark plugs and a roll of screen so I can fix a few window screens in the cabins. Do you know where Chet's Hardware Store is in town?"

Ali nodded.

"Do you remember how to get to town?"

Ali nodded again.

"Good. I'll have Jo call Chet so he'll have everything ready when you get there," Ben said.

"You want me to drive into town alone?" Ali asked, surprised.

Ben frowned, the crease in the middle of his eyebrows growing deep. "You're sixteen, aren't you?"

"Well, yes, but I only have my driver's permit. I don't have a license yet," Ali told him.

Ben frowned deeper. "How long have you been sixteen?"

"Since January," Ali told him.

"Well, why the heck didn't you get your license yet?"

"I took all the classes and driver's training," Ali said. "But between going to school and working after school, I never got a chance to take the driving test." Ali had actually spent every bit of her money to pay for driver's training classes, which were expensive, and simply couldn't afford to go and pay for her license. But if she told him that, he'd have too many questions about why her mother hadn't paid for it.

Ben let out a long sigh. "Well, we can't have you living up here and not driving. How the heck are you going to get to school every day if you can't drive yourself?"

Ali shrugged. "I guess I thought there'd be a school bus."

"Dang school bus doesn't come all the way out here. You have to go two miles down the road to be picked up. If you're going that far, you might as well drive all the way yourself."

Ali didn't know how to respond. He was making her feel bad for not having a driver's license, but it wasn't her fault.

"Well, now we're going to have to go to the county offices and get you a dang driver's license," Ben said, sounding disgusted. "That means we have to make a trip into Grand Rapids. I'll call over there to see if we can do it all in one day, otherwise it will mean two wasted days."

Ali's first reaction was to apologize, but then she decided she shouldn't have to. It wasn't her fault she didn't have a driver's license. Besides, she would have had to get a new one here anyway.

Ben picked up a rag and wiped his hands. "Guess I'll be making a trip into town. Can't finish working on this motor without spark plugs." He stepped out of the boat and walked past Ali, heading down the dock. A few steps away, he turned and looked at Ali, who still had the truck keys in her hand. "You coming?" he asked, then turned and walked away without waiting for her to reply.

Ali suddenly realized that going into town meant she might be able to text or chat with Megan. She started walking fast to catch up to her grandfather. "I'll just grab my phone," she told him as he headed into the fish cleaning house to wash his hands. Ali had left her phone in the kitchen where she could recharge it. She ran in and grabbed it. Jo was standing at the butcher block island, mixing up some batter.

"We're going into town," Ali told her. "Do you need anything?"

"Why, isn't that sweet of you to ask, dear. That old Ben wouldn't have thought to ask me. But no, I don't need anything today. You go ahead. I'm just going to finish making these chocolate chip cookies."

Ali's eyes lit up. She loved chocolate chip cookies. "See you in a bit," she said and turned to run out the door, almost slamming into her grandfather.

"I would have asked you if you wanted anything," he grumbled to Jo. Jo grinned at him but didn't reply. "Well, come on, girl. Let's get going."

Ali followed her grandfather up the hill to the cabin where his truck was parked. She reached out to hand him the keys, but he brushed them away.

"You drive. I want to make sure you know how."

Ali stopped and stared at the big pickup truck. She'd never driven anything so large before. She walked around to the driver's side, pulled herself up into the seat, put the key into the ignition, and started it up. The truck hummed. Ali studied the dashboard and steering wheel to make sure she knew where the turn signal and lights were, adjusted the seat so she could reach the pedals, then adjusted the mirrors. She was happy to see the truck was automatic and not stick shift.

"Let's get going," Ben said. He was already belted into the passenger's seat.

Ali bit her lower lip, pulled the seatbelt around her, sat up a little straighter, put her foot on the brake, and snapped the gearshift into drive. Hesitantly, she pulled the big truck out of the driveway and turned left onto the gravel road.

Ali drove slowly down the gravel road, not quite knowing how fast she should go. There were no speed limit signs, and the road was narrow and curvy, so staying on the far right was difficult. She was afraid if she took a turn too fast, she'd hit a car if it was coming from the other side. She was just starting to feel comfortable behind the big truck's wheel when her grandfather spoke up.

"You drive like an old lady. You can go faster, otherwise we'll never get to town."

Ali reddened, more from embarrassment than anger. "I'm just trying to get used to driving this thing," she blurted out. "I've never driven anything this big before."

"What kind of car did you drive?" Ben asked.

"We had a Cavalier. It was really small compared to this." Ali thought back to the old, beat-up car. Her mom had bought it used and they'd been driving it for over five years. The body was rusting out, the tires were bald, and the engine leaked oil. There was never any money to put into it, and sometimes it just didn't run at all. Ali got used to taking the city bus or getting a ride from friends most of the time.

Ben cocked his head, looking interested. "What happened to the car? Did you sell it?"

Ali shrugged. "It really wasn't much of a car. Amy, Megan's mom, said she'd see what she could do about it and send me any money she could get."

"What about your furniture and other household items? What happened to all of that?" Ben asked.

Ali kept her eyes on the road. She was uncomfortable with her grandfather's questions, especially since he hadn't bothered to come out for the funeral or to help her move out of their apartment. She wanted to ask him why he cared all of a sudden when he hadn't cared before, but she didn't dare start a fight with him while she was driving.

"Amy helped me store some of it, and she was going to

sell the rest for me. We didn't own all that much that was worth any money, so it doesn't really matter what happened to it."

"Hmmm," Ben said thoughtfully. "Well, I know this might feel like driving a tank to you, but you can go a little faster."

Ali pushed down a little more on the gas pedal and sped up, happy that the conversation had turned away from her life in California and back to driving.

As they entered Auburn, Ben interrupted the silence. "Why don't you drive on down to the coffeehouse and you can stay there while I go get my supplies. You can have one of your fancy coffees and play with your phone. Nothing but a bunch of nosy old men in the hardware store anyway. No sense in you standing there being stared at."

Ali turned right and drove down to North Country Coffee. She pulled into one of the slanted parking spaces and put the truck in park, but left it idling. As she opened the door to hop out, her grandfather nudged her arm.

"Here," he said, offering her a ten dollar bill. "Might as well get a snack, too."

Ali looked at the money but hesitated in taking it. She wasn't used to anyone giving her money.

"It's okay. Take it," her grandfather urged her as he slid over behind the wheel. His tone had softened and his face wasn't creased in its usual frown. "I'll come get you in a bit."

Ali reached over and took the money. "Thanks." She hopped out and headed inside the coffeehouse without looking back.

Ali's nerves calmed the moment she entered North Country Coffee. The smell of the sweet coffees and the baked goods was soothing. Entering the coffeehouse reminded her of going to Starbucks with her friends back in California, and all the tension from the morning drifted away.

The place was practically empty again, except for two

older women sitting in the back corner with bowls of steaming soup. As Ali walked up to the counter, the woman who'd waited on her the first time, Kat's mom, came up behind the counter with a welcoming smile.

"Hi," she said. "It's Ali, right?"

"Yes," Ali replied.

"I'm Karen," the woman said. She wiped her hand on her apron and reached over the counter to shake Ali's hand. "It's so nice to meet you. The first time you came in, I didn't know you were Ben's granddaughter, until Kat told me. I was sorry to hear about your mother's death. She was a sweet person, and pretty, too. Now that I look at you, I can see a lot of your mother in you."

Ali stood there uneasily. It felt odd that everyone knew who she was and had known her mother. "How did you know my mother?" she asked.

"I went to school with her here, although she was two years ahead of me. Everyone knows everyone in a small school. Your mother was very smart and always nice to everyone. Anyway, I just wanted you to know that I was sorry, and if there's anything I can do for you, let me know."

Ali nodded. She thought it was nice of this stranger to be so kind to her.

"Speaking of which, Kat said she asked you if you'd like to work here this summer. I think that's a great idea. Are you still interested?"

In the excitement of getting the job at the lodge, Ali had forgotten about the job offer at the coffeehouse. "Thanks, but Jo offered me a job at the lodge so I accepted that. I figured it would be easier to work right near where I lived so I wouldn't have to drive into town."

Karen smiled at Ali. "That's wonderful. Jo's a sweetheart, you'll love working for her. Kat will be disappointed, though, but I can see how it will be easier for you to work there at the lodge. So, what can I get you? The same as you had before? A caramel cappuccino?"

Ali looked at Karen in surprise. How did she remember what she'd ordered last time? "Yes, please," Ali said. She considered getting a brownie, too, but decided against it. There were always plenty of homemade baked goods at the lodge to eat.

Karen made up Ali's drink, then poured it into a large cup and popped a lid on it. After Ali paid, Karen picked up one of their customer appreciation cards and punched three holes in it, then handed it to Ali.

"Once you have ten punches in this card, you get a free coffee. I gave you credit for the two you already bought, and a punch just for being new to our little town. I hope to see you in here often," Karen said with a warm smile.

Ali thanked her, then looked around for a place to sit. The two women in the back of the coffeehouse were looking at her and smiling, so Ali smiled back. *Do they know who I am, too? Does everyone in this town know who I am and about my mother?* Ali decided to sit outside instead and left the building. She sat down on the wooden glider bench just outside the coffeehouse.

The town was fairly quiet, but there were a few people milling around. The bar across the street, The Loon's Nest Bar & Grill, was open, and every now and then someone would walk in or out of it. Ali supposed people were eating lunch there. Just down the street was another bar, The Beaver's Den, and it looked to be open, also. Farther down the street were a post office and a small bank, which surprised Ali. *A bank in this tiny town? Amazing.*

Ali sipped her coffee, and then turned her attention to her phone. It was almost two o'clock, so it was noon in California. She hoped Megan would be out of class heading to lunch and would be able to text or chat with her. Ali sent a message to Megan and waited for a response. The video chat screen popped up almost immediately and there was Megan's smiling face, staring at her.

"Wow, it's about time I heard from you," Megan said excitedly. "I'm still not used to the fact that I can't text you or talk to you anytime of the day or night."

Ali smiled wide. It felt so good to be talking to her best friend from home. "I know. It seems like forever since we last talked. So, what are you up to?"

Megan said she was just sitting down to lunch with their friends at school and she passed her phone around the table so everyone could say hi to Ali. Seeing all her school friends made Ali feel homesick.

Once the phone was back in Megan's hand, she asked, "What have you been doing? You're so lucky you don't have to go to school. It's too bad, though, that you won't be going to school with us next year. So, what's going on?"

Ali told Megan about her job at the lodge. "Now I'll be able to pay for my phone service so I can keep talking to you," Ali said.

Megan wrinkled her nose. "What kind of work are you doing there?"

"I help cook the meals, serve meals to the guests, clean the cabins, and do laundry. Stuff like that," Ali said.

"Oh."

Ali tried to ignore Megan's halfhearted response. Ali knew that Megan thought it sounded terrible because Megan used to think that Ali's job at the restaurant was awful, too. But Ali made much more money at the restaurant with tips added to her pay than Megan made working part-time at the clothing store in the mall, and Ali had needed all the money she could earn.

"I know it doesn't sound like much," Ali said. "But it's a job, and I need to make my own money."

"Yeah, I guess so," Megan said. Then her face brightened.

"At least you get to be around that cutie, Chase."

Ali grinned and rolled her eyes. "We're just friends," she said. "He's leaving for college this fall, and I don't plan on getting involved with anyone here."

"Are you kidding?" Megan asked. "He sounds like he's definitely worth getting involved with." Some of the girls around the table were asking, "Who, who?" and Ali heard Megan telling them about Chase. "See, it's unanimous. Everyone here thinks you definitely need to hook up with Chase."

Ali laughed. She missed her friends so much. "Not going to happen," she said.

"Well, I'd better go. I have to finish eating and lunchtime is almost over," Megan said. "Miss you. Call again real soon, okay?"

Ali's heart sank. She didn't want to say goodbye already. "Okay, I'll try. Miss you, too."

Megan showed the phone to everyone again and they all waved and said goodbye, then the screen popped off. Ali was left alone, sitting on the bench with her coffee, feeling like she lived on another planet, far away from her friends, instead of in another state.

Sighing, Ali started looking through her emails to see if any of her other friends had contacted her. Megan had left her three emails, which made Ali feel better, and another friend had sent her one. As she sipped her coffee and read her emails, a shadow crossed over her and Ali looked up into the face of a man. He was tall and had thick, wavy dark hair, a tan face, and piercing blue eyes. He was dressed in slacks, a button down shirt, and a sports jacket. He didn't look menacing, but the way he stared at her caused a shiver to go up Ali's spine.

The man nodded, then walked across the street and entered The Loon's Nest.

Ali didn't know why the man had stared at her, or why it

bothered her. *Probably just another local wondering who I am.*

A while later, Ben pulled up in his pickup and parked in front of where Ali sat. He walked past Ali and into the coffeehouse, shouting out a greeting to Karen. "Got any real coffee back there?" Ali heard him asking. She sighed. She couldn't tell if he was teasing or being grouchy. A few minutes later, he came out with a cup of coffee and a bag in his hand. He sat down beside Ali and scooted the bag over next to her.

"Have one," he said.

Ali looked up at him. "What's in there?"

"Scones. Karen makes the best ones around, but don't tell Jo I said that. She might get jealous."

Ali pulled out a scone and took a bite. It was delicious.

Ben took the other one and started eating it as they sat there side by side on the glider.

"So, did you get a chance to talk to your friends?" Ben asked between bites.

"Yeah. But it feels like I'm a million miles away from them," Ali said.

Ben turned and looked at her. "Hmmm. I guess their lives are a lot different from yours here," he said. "Guess that's to be expected."

"I suppose so," Ali said, but she wasn't happy about it.

"Would you rather be there?" Ben asked bluntly.

*Damn right I would.* Ali thought it but she didn't say it out loud. "I just miss everyone, that's all," she said instead.

Ben nodded.

Across the street, the man who had stopped and stared at Ali walked out of the bar and nodded at Ben. Ali watched as Ben's expression turned into a sneer.

"Who is that man?" Ali asked. "He was staring at me earlier."

The sneer on Ben's face deepened. "He's nobody important. He only thinks he is. Stay away from him. As far as

I'm concerned, he's trash."

Ali's eyes widened at her grandfather's words. She'd heard him be grouchy, sarcastic, and even condescending, but she'd never heard hatred in his voice before. Apparently, he really disliked this man.

"Come on, let's get back," Ben said, rising from the bench. "I have work to do, and you have a driver's test to study for."

This time, Ali sat in the passenger's seat and her grandfather drove. As they drove down the street, Ali caught a glimpse of the tall, dark haired man again. She wondered who he was, and why her grandfather hated him so much.

# Chapter Nine

Back at the lodge, Ali asked Jo if she had a driver's manual she could study.

"I'm sure Chase still has one in his room. Let me go dig it out for you," Jo told Ali. Sure enough, there was one in Chase's desk drawer and Jo handed it over to Ali. "Did you have a nice time in town?" Jo asked. "Were you able to talk to your friend?"

Ali nodded. "Yeah. Megan was at lunch with all our friends from school, so I was able to say hi to everyone. It seems weird, though, them being so far away."

Jo gave Ali a hug. "I know this is hard on you, dear. Everything changed so quickly for you. You can talk to me anytime about anything, remember that. I want you to feel at home here."

Ali held back the tears that were threatening to fall. She really liked Jo, and she liked Chase, too. She wasn't sure about her grandfather yet, but she could tell that he tried to be nice to her sometimes. She couldn't go back home, and she didn't feel like this was home either, but she appreciated Jo's kindness and warmth. "Thanks," was all Ali could manage, then she went out to one of the leather sofas in the main room, curled up, and began studying the driver's manual.

Awhile later, Chase came into the main room with a cookie in his hand and dropped his heavy backpack into one of the chairs. "Mom says you're studying for your driver's test," he said.

Ali smiled up at him. It was hard to not smile around him because he almost always had that cute grin on his face and his eyes twinkled. *It would be easy to have a huge crush on him.* The thought came out of nowhere, and it surprised Ali. *He's just a friend, he's just a friend,* she reminded herself.

"Do you want me to test you?" Chase asked, coming over and sitting down on the sofa beside her.

"Uh, sure." Ali handed Chase the booklet and he turned to the back where the practice test was.

"Okay. If you approach an intersection without a stop sign or signal, you: A. Should always stop before driving through the intersection, B. Must yield the right-of-way to all vehicles, or C. Should slow down and be ready to stop, if necessary."

Ali thought a moment. "C?"

"Yep, you're correct," Chase said. "Next question: If you have a tire blowout, you should: A. Brake hard to stop the car immediately, B. Let the car slow to a stop, or C. Continue driving until you reach a garage."

Ali giggled. "Is that a real question?"

Chase nodded seriously. "Yep."

"Hmmm. C. Drive until you get to a garage," Ali said, smiling.

Chase chuckled. "No, seriously, this is a real question."

"It's silly. What does it have to do with actual driving?"

"Tires blow out all the time. You'll be a danger to yourself and the entire state of Minnesota if you don't know the answer to this question," Chase said, trying to look serious but failing miserably.

Ali shook her head. "Fine. B is the correct answer then."

Chase nodded. "Whew. I thought for sure you'd flunk this test."

Ali picked up a small pillow off the sofa and threw it at Chase. He ducked, and it went right over his head. "Missed me."

Ali got up, grabbed another pillow, and smacked him with

it. Chase started laughing and grabbed for the pillow and they both fell down on the sofa, Chase on top of Ali, laughing hysterically. They were laughing so hard, Ali couldn't even fight back when Chase took the pillow away from her and started tickling her.

"Okay, okay," Ali yelled between fits of laughter. "I give. Stop!"

Chase stopped tickling her. He was on his hands and knees on the sofa, leaning over Ali's prone body. Their faces were only inches apart, and they both were breathing heavily, trying to catch their breath. For one brief moment, their eyes met and Ali's heart did a little jump.

"What in the heck is going on in here?"

Ali and Chase both looked up at the gruff sound of Ben's voice. He was standing a few feet away, his arms crossed, frowning at them.

Chase sat back on the sofa as Ali slowly rose up to a sitting position. Both teens were still breathing heavily.

Ali picked up the driver's manual from the floor and showed it to her grandfather. "Chase was just helping me study for my driver's test," she said, trying to look serious but her grin gave her away.

"Humph. So is that what you call tumbling around on the sofa and screeching?" Ben asked. "Studying for a test?"

Both teens nodded.

Ben shook his head, turned, and headed back into the kitchen. Ali and Chase stared at each other a moment, then broke out into another fit of laughter.

* * *

Ben stomped into the kitchen and stopped in front of the butcher block island where Jo was kneading bread dough. "Do you know what those two were doing in there? They're horsing around on the sofa, that's what," Ben said, answering his own question.

Jo didn't even look up. She continued working on the dough. "Are they horsing around with or without clothes on?" she asked.

"Well, of course they had clothes on," Ben said, appalled. "Don't you think I would have said something if they didn't have clothes on?"

Jo looked up and winked at Ben. "Then it's okay. As long as they keep their clothes on, we're good."

Ben let out a long, exaggerated sigh. "Don't you take anything seriously? You know darn well what horsing around leads to."

"Oh, yeah, I remember what it leads to," Jo said, grinning at Ben. "I wouldn't mind a little horsing around myself." She waggled her eyebrows at him.

"Dammit, woman. This is serious. Do you want to become a grandmother before your time?"

Jo sighed. She wiped her hands on her apron and walked around the island to stand directly in front of Ben. "That's not going to happen, Ben, and you know it. They're just having fun. Have a little faith in Ali. She's a good girl. And you've known Chase his whole life. Do you think he's so stupid that he'd ruin his future by doing something reckless?"

Ben tightened his lips into a thin line. "Teenagers do stupid things all the time," he said.

"Don't punish Ali for her mother's mistakes. I think Ali's had it hard enough already. I doubt she's in a hurry to mess up her own life." Jo turned and went back to kneading the bread dough.

Ben stood there a moment, thinking about what Jo had said. *Is that what he was doing? Transferring Jen's mistakes onto Ali?* He walked back over to Jo and looked at her, his expression no longer angry. "I just don't want to live through that again. Is that so wrong?"

Jo shook her head. "No, it's not. But you have to trust her, Ben, or else you'll push her away, too."

Ben walked around behind Jo, gave her a hug, and kissed the top of her head, then walked to the door. "I'm taking Ali on Thursday into Grand Rapids to get her driver's license. If there's anything you need me to get for you, make a list." With that, he stepped outside.

Ben walked over to the dock and looked out at the lake. A loon swam peacefully in the water, along with the ducks that also fed in the cove. Ben thought about Ali's fascination with the loons. He thought about his Jen's love of wildlife and the outdoors. His thoughts turned to his Lizzie, and how she'd been gone almost seven years now. Times changed. Life changed. People came and went. Yet each year, the loons came and nested in the same place they've nested for years. They found their mate and continued the cycle. For them, no change was the key to survival.

Ben thought about Jo's words. 'Don't punish Ali for her mother's mistakes.' His anger all those years ago had pushed his Jen away, and Lizzie had never truly forgiven him for it. Even though he'd tried to set things straight with Jen, she never came home. And Lizzie had lived with the pain of not seeing her only daughter or knowing her only granddaughter. Yet, it was hard. Every time he looked at Ali, he saw his Jen, he saw his Lizzie, and he was reminded over and over again that she was the very reason his Jen had left them forever.

\* \* \*

After supper was eaten and the dishes were cleaned up, Ali and Chase took a walk around the cabins and out to the rocky point. It was breezy out, and the night air had a chill to it. Ali and Chase had both slipped on sweatshirts to ward off the cold. Once they reached the point, they climbed up on two of the large boulders that stood side by side and sat, enjoying the warmth the rocks had absorbed during the day.

"It feels like sitting on a heated chair," Ali said, giggling as Chase nodded agreement.

The water lapped against the rocks as the breeze caressed Ali's cheeks. The sun was low in the sky behind them, causing long shadows from the trees to fall over them. Ali felt like she was nestled at the very tip of the world.

"Do you think Ben was mad at us tonight?" Chase asked, interrupting Ali's thoughts.

Ali shrugged. Her grandfather had been very quiet at supper, only speaking when he had to and to tell her they'd be going to Grand Rapids on Thursday for her driver's test. Apparently, he knew someone in the office there who had arranged for Ali to take both the written and driving test all in one day. Ali was excited to go into a bigger town where she hoped she could make arrangements to update her phone plan and maybe do a little shopping for necessities. But Ben's sour mood had dampened her excitement. After supper, he'd said he was heading up to the house for the night and she should be up there before lights out.

"He's afraid I'm going to muck up your life," Ali said, turning to face Chase. Her expression was half-serious, half-smiling, but Chase only frowned at her words.

"Muck up my life? Were those his words?" Chase asked.

Ali chuckled. "Yep. He said not to get too attached to you and not to muck up your life."

Chase shook his head. "Don't worry too much about Ben. He takes everything so seriously. I'm sure he meant well." Chase picked up a flat pebble and spun it sideways through the air, skimming the water. The pebble jumped three times on the surface of the lake before dropping in.

"Cool," Ali said, watching the pebble. She turned to face

Chase. "Why do you always defend my grandfather, even when he's being a jerk?"

It was Chase's turn to shrug. "I don't know. I guess because I've known him so long, he's practically like a second father to me. After my dad died, Ben took it upon himself to teach me things he knew my dad would have. And he's always been fair to me. It's only been lately that he's been acting weird, and I'm sure it's because he hadn't really planned on you being here."

Ali stared out at the water. "It's not like I planned on coming here, either," she said sadly.

Chase reached over and placed his hand on her arm. "I'm sorry for the reason you had to move here, but I'm glad you came," he said.

Ali looked up into his kind, blue eyes. Moving here hadn't been easy, especially after losing her mother so suddenly. But having Chase here made it much easier.

"Tell me about your father," Ali said. "I mean, if you don't mind talking about him."

Chase removed his hand from Ali's arm and wrapped his arms around his legs. "I don't mind. What do you want to know?"

"How long has he been gone?" Ali asked.

"He died in 2007. I was twelve. It seems like a long time ago, though."

"How did he die?" Ali asked in a hushed whisper.

"My dad used to log in the winter to make extra money. Logging can be dangerous. He was working near a pile of freshly stacked trees when it came loose and rolled. The pile rolled right over top of him and crushed him." Chase said the words quietly.

"I'm sorry," Ali told him. "I bet it was really hard on you and Jo."

Chase nodded. "It was. Ben had been helping out a little

around the lodge before that, but after my dad died, he started helping out more to make things easier for my mom. And he spent a lot of time with me, making sure I had someone to talk to."

Ali looked up at him in surprise. "My grandfather talked about feelings with you?"

Chase chuckled. "No. Not feelings exactly. But he was there when I'd get angry or sad. Mostly, he'd take me out fishing, or we'd go out hiking, looking for good hunting spots. He kept me busy so I wouldn't just sit around being upset all the time. It helped."

"What was your dad like? What did he look like?" Ali asked, interested in Chase's father. She'd never had a father or even a man in her life that acted like a dad, so she was always interested in other kids' fathers.

"He was tall, and he was kind of rugged looking, like you'd expect from someone who worked outside. He had really thick, wavy black hair and his face was always tanned, even in the winter. He was a hard worker, but he also liked to have fun. He'd joke and tease a lot. He was a nice guy."

"Your poor mom. It must have been awful being left alone with a resort to run and a kid to raise," Ali said.

"She had a hard time at first. I remember her being sad a lot. I was afraid she'd want to sell the resort and we'd have to move. But she hung in there. I don't think she could have kept going without Ben. He really did take it upon himself to make her life easier."

Ali thought about her grandfather and how he tried to make things difficult for her, but at the same time, he'd do something nice, like giving her the money today for the coffee and buying her the scone. And it was he who insisted she get her driver's license, but he also grouched about having to go to do it. Ali sighed. She wasn't sure if she liked her grandfather, or if he liked her, but she didn't have much choice in the matter, at least until she finished high school.

Ali and Chase sat there awhile, looking out over the lake. It was peaceful, sitting there in the fading daylight, listening to the water lapping against the rocks.

"I haven't heard you say anything about your mom," Chase said, hesitantly. "I mean, it's okay that you don't, but if you want to, I'm here to listen."

Ali turned sad eyes to Chase. "I haven't said much because I'm afraid I'll say the wrong thing, and I don't want my grandfather judging my mom."

Chase frowned. "How do you mean?"

Ali took a deep breath. "My mom was a good person, but she didn't always do things the right way. She had problems. I don't want my grandfather to know that, though. He'll find something mean to say about her then."

Chase shook his head. "I'm sorry to hear your mom had troubles, but I think you've pegged Ben wrong. He's only ever said nice things about your mom. I think he really loved her. I don't know what happened between them that made her stay away, but I do know it made him sad. I don't think he'd judge your mom harshly."

Ali sighed. "I don't know, Chase. Maybe he's different with you. I guess I'll just have to get to know him better, that's all."

Chase smiled over at Ali, and her heart warmed at the tenderness in his gaze.

"Come on," he said, standing up and balancing on the boulder. "You'd better get up to the cabin before he turns the lights out on you." Chase reached down and offered his hand to Ali, which she accepted, and he pulled her up to her feet. They stood there a moment, hands clasped, looking into each other's eyes. A loon flew overhead, his sing-song voice echoing across the cove. Both teens looked up at the same time, and the moment between them was gone.

"Don't let me muck up your life, okay?" Ali said, half-teasing as they both climbed down from the boulders and picked their way over the rocks and onto the mossy ground.

"I don't really see you mucking up my life," Chase said, looking at her seriously. "If anything, you only make it nicer." He reached for her hand again, and they walked back to the lodge in silence.

# Chapter Ten

The week went by quickly for Ali as she helped Jo prepare the cabins for the weekend guests and studied for her driving test. She looked forward to the evenings after supper when she and Chase could hang out together. They'd sit on the dock, or take a walk in the woods. When they were out of sight of the lodge, Chase reached for her hand and held it as they walked together. Ali liked that. She knew that Chase liked her, but he hadn't tried to kiss her yet, and she wondered why. The thought of him kissing her made her nervous and tingly all at the same time. She'd never been kissed before, so she didn't know how it felt, but she bet that a kiss from Chase would be sweet, warm, and just plain wonderful.

Thursday morning came and Ali and her grandfather were off in the truck to Grand Rapids. It was an hour's drive away and he wanted to leave early, so right after breakfast, they hopped in his truck and left.

The drive was a quiet one with no conversation and no music playing on the stereo. Ali wondered if they even had any radio reception this far out in the country. She hadn't yet asked her grandfather about stopping at the phone store or at a department store where she could buy a few necessities. About half an hour into the drive, she took a deep breath and spoke up.

"Grandpa?" she asked, saying this name for him aloud for the very first time. It felt strange to her. "Do you think, maybe, after the driving tests, we could go to the phone store so I can change my mailing address?"

Her grandfather looked over at her with a surprised look on his face. Ali didn't know if it was from being called "grandpa" or from her question about the phone store. He seemed to recover quickly, though, and replied after a moment's thought.

"I guess we can do that. I don't know where it is, though."

Ali pointed to her phone. "It has GPS. I can find the directions on my phone as soon as I have a signal."

Ben nodded, but didn't reply.

Ali took another deep breath. "And, if it's not too much trouble, can we stop at a discount store so I can buy a few things? I have my own money."

Ben looked over at her again. At least he wasn't frowning. "Well, I guess since we're in town anyway, we can stop somewhere," he said. "I think there's a Walmart in town. Will that do?"

Ali smiled and nodded. At home, she'd shopped at the Walmart and at dollar stores for most of what she needed. At least she knew she'd be able to get the same things here. She thought it was funny that he'd said he thought there was a Walmart in town. Ali cocked her head and looked at her grandfather quizzically.

Ben turned and saw her staring at him. "What?"

"You *think* there's a Walmart in town? Don't you ever go there to buy things you need?" Ali asked.

Ben frowned. "Why the heck would I? I can buy everything I need in Auburn at Chet's Hardware."

"What about personal items like clothes and stuff?" Ali asked.

"Jo usually picks up that stuff for me when she comes into town. I don't need much. A few flannel shirts, some work jeans. I can get boots and coats at the L&M Fleet Supply store when I need them."

"What about stuff like oil, filters, and parts for the truck and boats? Wouldn't that stuff be cheaper at a place like Walmart than at Chet's?"

"Bite your tongue, girl," Ben said. "If Chet heard you say that, he'd have a fit. It may be a little cheaper at one of those big stores, but I believe in supporting the small, family businesses."

Ali shrugged. She found it strange that her grandfather was too cheap to have electricity at his house but he'd overspend on everyday items.

Once they were in town, Ben turned off on a side street which led them to the office where Ali could take her written test and road test. After standing in line for a few minutes, it was their turn at the counter, and Ali saw her grandfather actually smile at the clerk.

"Hi Carol. How's it going?" Ben asked the middle aged lady behind the counter.

Carol smiled back at him. "Busy, but fine. You'd think a small town like this wouldn't have so many drivers." Carol turned to Ali and smiled at her. "So you're Jen's little girl, eh? Nice to meet you, Ali. You sure are a beauty, just like your momma."

Ali stood there, confused, but answered her. "Thank you."

"This is Carol. She's your Grandma Lizzie's niece. She's the reason you were able to take both tests on the same day," Ben said.

"Oh, well, thank you," Ali said, shaking the woman's hand. "It's nice to meet you." Carol was short and round with short, dark hair that was beginning to gray at the sides. She didn't really look much like Ali's grandma Lizzie, but she had a nice smile and seemed friendly.

"Well, it wasn't easy to arrange, dear, but I know what an old grouch Ben can be and it wasn't worth it telling him he had to come back a second time," Carol said with a wink. "I was happy to do it for you."

Carol got to work looking over Ali's paperwork from California. Ali had a driver's permit and a signed certificate that stated she'd completed driver's training. Carol gave Ali new paperwork to fill out, then sent her to sit at a row of tables and chairs with dividers where the electronic driving tests were. Ben went over to sit on a long bench by the wall and started reading a hunting magazine.

After Ali finished the test, she waited in line again and when it was her turn, Carol looked over her test. "Congratulations, Ali. You only missed one answer. That's good, otherwise you'd have to reschedule your driving test."

Ben paid the fees for both tests. Ali hadn't expected him to. "I brought money to pay for this," she told him, but Ben shook his head.

"I'll take care of this," he told her.

Ali thanked him but felt funny about his paying. She was used to paying her own way.

Ali's appointment for her driving test was in a half hour, so she and her grandfather sat out in the truck to wait for the instructor. She had to use the truck for the test, and she was nervous about parallel parking. Chase had set up a practice spot for her at the lodge, so she had practiced parking it a few times, but if she missed just once on the test, she'd have to take it over again.

"Nervous?" Ben asked, looking over at Ali.

"A little. Mostly about parallel parking this big rig."

Ben waved his hand through the air as if it were nothing. "You'll do fine," he said.

Luckily, his prediction was correct and forty-five minutes later, Ali left the building with a piece of paper that stated she had a brand new Minnesota driver's license.

"Where to now?" Ben asked as he got behind the wheel.

Apparently, he wasn't going to ask her to drive around Grand Rapids. Ali looked up the phone store address on her phone, found it, and told him where it was.

They drove there and Ali hurried in and made the necessary arrangements. The phone store clerk tried talking her into a new phone and plan upgrade, but Ali declined. She had always had the least expensive plan available because she couldn't afford to spend too much on her phone service. It meant she had to be careful about the minutes she used, but it was better than having no phone at all. Ali set it up to pay by mail, and gave them her new address. She'd have to open a bank account somewhere and find a way to get money in it so she could write a check or transfer from an account. She hadn't figured out where she'd do that yet. She thought about banking at the little bank in Auburn, that way she could deposit money there easily. Everywhere else was too far away. She decided she'd ask Jo where the best place to bank was.

When Ali hopped back into the truck, Ben headed to the other side of town and pulled into the Walmart parking lot. They walked inside and Ali was surprised to find it was such a big store. She grabbed a hand basket and looked at her grandfather, who looked lost in the mob of people.

"I'll just let you do your shopping and catch up with you in a bit," Ben told her. "Meet me in front of the first checkout. Get what you need, I'll pay for it." With that said, he wandered off in the direction of car supplies.

Ali was glad he'd left her to be on her own because some of the things she needed, like new underwear, a bra, and other personal items, would have probably embarrassed him. She set out for the personal care items first, then headed over to women's clothing. Since she was familiar with the store brands, she knew exactly what would fit her, so it didn't take long to pick out a bra and underwear. She also picked out new socks, and four scooped-necked T-shirts like the ones she already had. They were on sale, so she was able to get more than she'd planned on. Ali skipped the jeans because she'd never had any luck fitting into the brands here. She walked through the shoe department looking for some new sneakers but didn't see anything that she thought would hold up to constant wear. Finally, she was finished, so she headed over to the front counters and waited for her grandfather. She could hardly believe it when she saw him heading toward her with a cart full of items.

"What's all this?" she asked with a grin on her face.

Ben wrinkled up his face. "Don't you go telling Chet about this, you hear? You were right. Oil, filters, spark plugs, and a whole bunch of other stuff I usually buy at his store are so much cheaper here. I guess I have been missing out by not coming here to stock up."

Ali laughed. "Don't worry, your secret is safe with me."

They got in line and Ben paid for their items. There was a teenage girl ringing up their purchases, so Ali took a chance and asked her, "Is there a secondhand clothing shop around here?"

The girl smiled and nodded. "Yep. It's called Rosie's, and it's right downtown on Third Street. You can't miss it."

Ali thanked her. They loaded up their cart and headed out to the truck.

As they settled into the truck's cab, Ali asked her grandfather if they could make one more stop at Rosie's on Third Street. He agreed, and soon they were parked in front of the small shop on a tree lined street in the older part of town.

"Are you sure this is the shop you're looking for?" Ben asked, looking confused.

Ali nodded. "I need some new jeans and maybe a pair of shorts. All of mine are getting pretty worn out. I'll hurry," she said as she opened the truck's door and started to step out.

"Wait a minute." Ben reached into his back pocket and

pulled out his wallet. He took out two one hundred dollar bills. "Here. Will this be enough?"

Ali looked at the money in his outstretched hand and wavered. Once again, she was amazed he was so readily handing her money. "I don't expect you to buy everything for me," she said. "I have some money of my own."

"I said I wouldn't pay for your silly phone that you can barely use, but I will pay for things you need," Ben said gruffly. "Here, take it."

Hesitantly, Ali took the money. "Thanks. I'm sure I won't need this much, so I'll bring back the change." She stepped out of the truck and headed inside the store.

* * *

Ben sat and watched Ali walk inside the store. He stepped out of the truck and leaned against its side, looking at the shop. It was a beautiful day. The temperature was mild with the sun shining overhead. He'd parked the truck under a big oak tree, and stood there, enjoying the shade. As he stared at the store, he frowned. "Gently used clothing" the sign in the window stated.

Ben wondered why Ali thought she had to buy used clothes instead of new ones. Did she think he was that cheap? Or that he didn't have enough money to buy her nice things? The more he thought about it, the angrier he became. Sure, he may seem cheap to her because he didn't have electricity hooked up at the house but that was because he didn't like depending upon a company for something he could supply himself. He didn't have a computer or a phone because he just plain didn't need one. Who in the world would he call or email? Everyone important in his life lived at the lodge. He may not own a lot of fancy things, but he didn't scrimp when it came to the things he did own, like household items, his truck, or his boat. And he'd always been able to afford nice things for his Lizzie and Jen. By the time Ali came out of the store with a big bag under her arm and a smile on her face, Ben was fuming.

They both climbed back into the truck's cab and Ali handed Ben one-hundred and ten dollars.

"Is that all you spent?" he asked. "Your bag is full."

"Yep," she answered, practically beaming with delight. "Rosie's is a nice store. There were so many great clothes in there in practically new condition for good prices. Look," she slipped a pair of jeans out of the bag. "I bought two pairs of Levi's Silver jeans for only twenty dollars each. Do you know what these sell for in the stores? Eighty-five dollars a pair. And I got a sixty dollar American Eagle sweatshirt for only fifteen dollars. Can you believe it? They look just like brand new. I bought two pairs of Levi's shorts and a pair of sneakers, too. I just can't believe that people buy these great clothes then resell them after barely wearing them."

Ben stared at his granddaughter in utter surprise, his earlier anger dissipating. He'd never seen anyone so excited before about buying used clothes. Still, he felt like he wasn't being a good guardian by letting her buy second hand clothes to wear.

"You know, we could have gone to a clothing store and bought you some new clothes. There's a mall around here somewhere. I don't expect you to buy used clothes," Ben told her.

Ali laughed lightly. "Are you kidding? Who'd pay full price for these things when you can get them practically new for so much cheaper." She folded the jeans and slipped them back in the bag.

"I may seem cheap to you, but when it comes to family, I can certainly afford nice things," Ben said, his blue eyes flashing. "No granddaughter of mine needs to wear hand-me-downs when I can afford better."

Ali's smile faded from her lips. "I said I didn't mind."

"Well, maybe I do. It's nice that you want to be careful with money, but when it comes to personal things like clothes, you can have new. My Lizzie and Jen always had nice things. They never wore second hand clothes."

Ali's jaw tightened and her blue eyes matched her grandfather's angry ones. "Second hand clothes are all I've ever worn," she said tightly.

Ben's anger slowly left him as Ali's words sank in. He watched as Ali turned away from him to stare out the window. He knew he should apologize for being angry with her, but he wasn't too good at saying he was sorry. He started the truck and pulled out of the parking space, heading the truck toward home.

\* \* \*

It was late afternoon when Ben and Ali arrived back at the cabin. Ali quietly thanked her grandfather for her purchases then disappeared up to her room. Ben unloaded the items he'd purchased and stored them in the garage. With one long look up the staircase to Ali's room, he sighed and walked down to the lodge.

When Ben walked into the kitchen, Jo's face lit up. She'd been putting away the food supplies that came on the food truck every Thursday, but she stopped what she was doing and walked over to where Ben stood.

"So, how'd it go?" Jo asked. "Did she pass her tests?"

Ben nodded. He walked over to the cookie jar and pulled out one of the chocolate chip cookies Jo had made earlier in the week and started eating it.

Jo frowned. "Didn't you two stop for lunch? I swear, Ben, you can be so forgetful." Jo took some lunchmeat out of the refrigerator and started making a sandwich for Ben. "So tell me, how was the trip to town? Did you two get a chance to talk?"

"Cripes, woman," Ben said. "Why are you all full of questions today?" He accepted the sandwich Jo handed him with a nod.

"Because you don't tell me anything without my asking, that's why," Jo responded. She headed back over to the pile of dry goods she'd received that day and started putting them away in the pantry.

"What kind of mother do you think my Jen was?" Ben asked.

Jo stepped out of the pantry. "What?"

"I asked what kind of mother do you think my Jen was? Do you think she was a good mother to Ali or a bad mother?"

Jo walked over to Ben and sat down on the bench beside him, facing him. "I don't know. What brought this on?"

"Ali's worked for years to have her own money. I just found out she's owned second hand clothes her whole life. And we both know how Jen died. A drug and booze overdose. What kind of life did Ali have? What kind of mother was Jen? And why?" Ben asked, the frustration growing in his voice.

"Maybe there was never enough money for new things," Jo said. "Jen was a single mother. Earning money for rent, clothes, and food can be expensive."

"And booze? And drugs? Those are expensive, too. Did Ali do without because her mother was buying things she shouldn't have bought?" Ben asked.

"Does it matter now?" Jo asked. "Jen is gone and Ali is here now. Ali's a good girl and a hard worker. Jen must have been enough of a good influence for Ali to turn out that way."

Ben shook his head. He looked up at Jo and gave her a half smile. "You always find the good in a situation, don't you?"

Jo winked. "Someone around here has to."

"She never talks about her mother, you know. Why do you think that is?"

"I don't know, but she will when she's ready. Just give her time." Jo stood and went back to her work.

Ben finished his sandwich. His thoughts turned back to the day Jen had told him and Lizzie that she was pregnant. They'd fought. She'd run off. He could have helped her all these years. He could have made sure Ali was okay and had what she needed. He may have even been able to help Jen with her addiction problems, if that was what she'd had. But Jen had never contacted him, never let him know she'd needed help. It had been easier for him to ignore the fact that he had a daughter and granddaughter out there, somewhere, than to come face to face with it. Now, it was coming back to haunt him, and he wasn't handling it very well.

# Chapter Eleven

The days flew by, especially the weekends when guests came to the lodge. Ali had worked hard as a waitress, but keeping up with cabin cleaning, meal preparation, and serving kept her busier than she'd ever been before. She didn't mind, though. She was earning money, and that made it all worthwhile.

Ali had asked Jo what she should do about a checking account, and Jo had suggested she open an account with the bank in Auburn. "As long as you aren't saving hundreds of thousands of dollars, you're safe there," Jo had teased her. Ali didn't have hundreds of thousands of dollars, so she did as Jo suggested.

Ali fell into a routine as the days went by. Each morning she'd get up early and sit in the boat with her grandfather. At first, she'd gone out with him only because he'd asked, but now she went out because she actually enjoyed it. The mornings were usually cool, with a mist rising off the lake as the sun came up. The loons always flew in before the boat headed into shore, and Ali loved watching and listening to the majestic birds. Sometimes her grandfather talked about the wildlife in the area, but mostly they just fished in silence. Ali enjoyed the peace of the lake in the morning, the stillness of the water, and the beauty of the sunrise. They almost always brought back fish, and enjoyed the competition between them, seeing who'd catch the most fish for the day.

In the afternoons, Ali looked forward to Chase returning home from school and spending time with him. On weekends, they were both too busy to do much together, but on weekday afternoons, they found an hour or two to walk to the point and sit, or glide through the water in the canoe. They'd talk, which Ali enjoyed the most, getting to know each other better. They talked about their childhoods, their friends, their dreams for the future. The more Ali learned about Chase, the more it reaffirmed that he was truly a nice guy with a good heart. And each day, they grew closer as friends.

Ali asked her grandfather to teach her how to start up the generator so she could go to the cabin some afternoons and wash clothes. Ben grudgingly agreed to show her, and she'd go there between work at the lodge and toss in a load of clothes or her sheets or towels, whatever needed to be done, and read books on her Kindle while she waited for each load to wash and dry. After finding fresh, clean towels in the bathroom and fresh sheets on the bed on a regular basis, her grandfather stopped grumbling about her using the generator during the day.

On two occasions, Ali borrowed her grandfather's truck to go into town in the afternoon so she could talk to Megan on the phone. She always went to the coffeehouse for a caramel cappuccino and a brownie, visited a few minutes with Kat's mom, Karen, then connected with Megan for a chat. But each time, Ali came away feeling sad instead of happy. With each phone call, she felt the distance between her and her best friend growing wider. Megan was out in California enjoying an entirely different lifestyle from Ali and having fun with friends. Ali was no longer a part of that life. Ali mentioned it to Chase one evening as they sat at the end of the dock, their legs dangling over the edge and their feet in the cool water. He'd asked her why she'd been so quiet all afternoon and at supper.

"I went into town and talked to Megan today," she told him. "Our lives are so different now. I don't feel as connected to her as I once was. I feel like I'm losing my best friend."

Chase wrapped his arm around her waist and she scooted over closer to him. "I can be your new best friend, if you'd like," he said softly.

Ali looked up into his gentle blue eyes. "I'd like that," she told him. "But do you really want to talk to me about clothes and makeup and boys, and all those silly things girls talk about?" she asked with a grin.

Chase smiled. "You can talk to me about anything, and I'll listen to most of it, or pretend to listen if I find it boring. But you can't talk to me about boys. I don't want to hear that you like anyone except me."

Ali laughed. "Deal."

* * *

The month of May came to a close and Chase was finally graduating from high school. On the last Friday afternoon of May, the graduation was held. Ali, Ben, and Jo sat in the bleachers in the gymnasium along with the rest of the town of Auburn and watched as the graduates crossed the stage and accepted their diplomas. Ali had stared at the old school building in amazement. It looked to be built in the early 1900s, was three stories high, had a small gymnasium in the center of the school with a stage and balcony seating above, narrow stairways leading up and down to the different levels, and tiny classrooms. She couldn't believe that people still went to school in a place like this, and she really couldn't believe that she'd be attending school here in the fall.

Right before the ceremony started, Kat had caught sight of Ali and run down the row of bleachers to sit beside her.

"Do you mind if I sit with you?" Kat asked.

Ali shook her head. "Do you have a relative graduating today?"

"No. But I know the whole graduating class. Everyone comes to graduation. It's like a big event here."

Ali nodded. It seemed strange to her, but she still wasn't used to small town living. At her old school, you had to get tickets for family members to attend graduation and it lasted hours. There were only twenty-five kids in Chase's class, so graduation was going to last a matter of minutes.

Ali watched with pride as Chase accepted his diploma. He turned and smiled up at their little group in the bleachers. She figured he was smiling at his mom, but she hoped the smile was for her, too. Afterward, everyone met outside on the lawn for congratulations and family photos.

Kat was running around, congratulating everyone, then came back to stand beside Ali. "Are you and Chase coming to the graduation party tonight?" she asked.

Ali's brows rose. Chase hadn't mentioned a party.

"Chase didn't tell you, did he?" Kat asked, rolling her eyes. "Chase never comes to any of the parties. But he can't miss this one. It's for graduation. It's the biggest party of the year."

"Where is it at?" Ali asked, curious about this party that Chase had forgotten to mention.

"It's out at The Landing," Kat said.

"Where's that?"

"Oh, it's just an old campground no one uses anymore out at the point on Black Lake. Chase knows where it is, he just never comes to any of the parties. Try talking him into coming, okay? I can introduce you to some of the kids in our class and point out all the ones you won't want to be friends with," Kat said, grinning.

Ali smiled. Kat was always so full of energy, Ali wondered if she drank too much coffee at work.

Jo and Ben had to get back to the resort because it was a Friday and Jo had to take care of the arriving guests. Jo had made a cake to celebrate Chase's graduation and they were going to eat it after supper. It was Chase's favorite—carrot cake with cream cheese frosting. The four finally piled into Ben's truck and headed off.

"Kat mentioned a graduation party tonight," Ali said to Chase in the back seat of Ben's truck. "Are you going?"

"I don't know," Chase said. "I never do. It's really not the kind of thing I go to."

"Why?"

Chase nodded toward his mother and Ben in the front seat. Ali realized he didn't want to talk about the party in front of them.

"Oh, go on and tell her, Chase," Ben piped up. "We all know the kids go out in the woods and have a drinking party for graduation. It's not a secret."

Chase shook his head. "Can't get anything past Ben," he said to Ali.

Later, after supper and cake, Chase asked Ali if she'd like to go with him for an hour or so to the party. "I don't usually go to those things, but it is graduation," he said.

Ali wavered. She wasn't too fond of being around a bunch of drunk people, and she didn't know if her grandfather would allow her to go.

"You both should go for a while," Jo piped up. "I know Chase will be responsible and not drink. It's probably the last time you'll be around all your classmates for a long time. Go and enjoy."

Ben frowned, but didn't say anything.

"Grandpa? Is it okay?" Ali asked.

"Well, Jo went ahead and already said yes, so I guess I can't say no now," Ben said gruffly. "But be back by eleven. And no drinking."

"Midnight," Jo said. "And I agree. No drinking."

Ben rolled his eyes as he stood up and started helping Jo clear off the table.

An hour later, Chase and Ali were in his truck heading down a gravel road the size of a cow path. Ali had asked Chase earlier what she should wear. He'd said her T-shirt, jeans, and sneakers were fine, but to be sure to bring a heavy sweatshirt because it would be cold by the lake, even with a bonfire.

"See," he'd said with a wink. "I can talk about clothes when I have to."

Ali had worn a pair of the new jeans she'd bought at Rosie's as well as the American Eagle sweatshirt. She'd left her hair down, just pushing it back behind her ears. The blue sweatshirt made her eyes a brilliant blue, especially with her dark hair framing her face. Chase had smiled wide when he saw her before they headed out in his truck. Ali liked making him smile.

It was after nine when they arrived at the party. Ali couldn't figure out how Chase could see where he was going with the sky so dark and the road so narrow. As they pulled in next to a row of cars parked to the side, she saw a bonfire roaring, and the lake sparkling in the moonlight. Music was blasting from somewhere, and kids were already laughing and making all sorts of noise that echoed off the body of water.

Kat saw them first as they walked up to the crowd around the bonfire. She had a plastic cup in her hand and it spilled a little as she ran up to them.

"You made it," Kat said, a little too loud. "I'm so happy you're here." She linked arms with Ali as if they'd been best friends forever, and led her toward the bonfire. Chase just shook his head and followed them.

"Hey, look everyone. The prom king is here. Long live the king!" a boy with shaggy, brown hair yelled as Ali, Kat, and Chase drew closer to the fire. Soon, another boy joined in on the chant of "long live the king" and they both laughed hysterically, as if it was the funniest thing they'd ever heard.

Ali looked over at Chase with a teasing grin. "You were

prom king?"

Chase rolled his eyes. "Someone had to be," he said. "Okay, guys. Everyone heard you for miles around, so shut up now." Chase turned to Ali. "These two idiots are my friends, Jake and Eric. Don't get too close, though. They're insane."

"Oooooh, lookie," Jake, the shaggy-haired kid said. "The prom king brought a princess." He stepped up closer to Ali, his eyes wide. "And she's really pretty, too. Hi pretty princess."

Chase's eyes narrowed. "This is Ali, you jerk. Stop acting stupid."

Jake bowed low in front of Ali, and Eric did the same. The cups in their hands spilled all over the ground in front of them, but they didn't seem to notice. "So happy to meet you, Princess Ali," Jake said.

"Just ignore them," Kat said to Ali. "They're already drunk. They were drinking right out of the tap a few minutes ago."

A tall girl with long, blonde hair sidled up beside Chase and linked her arm around his. "Chase can't be the prom king without his queen," she said, smiling up at him. Ali saw Chase try to pull away, but the girl held on tightly.

"More like Queen Bitchalot," Jake said in a pretend whisper, then laughed loudly at his own joke. Eric laughed along.

The girl's eyes narrowed at the two boys. "Shut up, you jerks. Chase? Are you going to let them talk to me like that?"

Chase sighed.

Kat whispered in Ali's ear. "That's Emily. She's been after Chase for years. She's the banker's daughter, and she's a spoiled little snot. She hangs out with those two." Kat pointed out two other girls coming up beside Emily. "They're Ashley and Kelsey, and they follow Emily everywhere. They're all going to be seniors this fall, too. Have you seen the movie *Mean Girls*? Well, we all think it was written about these three."

Chase disengaged himself from Emily, told Ali he'd be right back, then grabbed Jake and Eric by their arms and dragged them off toward the fire. Emily stood there a moment, her lips pursed and a crease between her brows, looking like she might scream. But then she turned her sights on Ali, softened her face, and came to stand in front of her with her two friends right behind her.

"So, you're old man Jenson's granddaughter," Emily said, giving Ali the once over.

Ali just stood there and stared at Emily. She'd dealt with many spoiled kids over the years, and some really mean ones, too. She could handle Emily if she had to.

"I hear you're cleaning cabins at the resort this summer," Emily said, smirking. "I'm sure it's the perfect job for you." Emily's two friends snickered behind her.

"What's it to you?" Ali asked, looking straight into Emily's eyes.

Emily's eyes narrowed. She looked Ali up and down again. "Chase is too good for you," she told Ali. "If I were you, I'd just forget about him. He'll drop you as fast as he does all the girls he dates." With that, Emily and her friends laughed, turned, and headed back to the fire.

"Stupid little bitch," Kat said, taking a sip from her cup. "I've had to put up with her my whole life. I should pour water on her and see if she melts."

Ali turned and smiled at Kat. "She's not worth the trouble. I've found it's easier to ignore people like her."

Kat nodded reluctantly. "My mom always says that too, but girls like her make me so mad. Don't worry, though, there are a few nice girls in school." Kat grabbed Ali's arm. "Come on. Let's go get you a beer."

Ali shook her head. "You go ahead. I don't want one right now." She spotted Chase standing by his friends and went to stand with him while Kat went to get a refill. Chase had a cup in his hand which was half full, and Ali frowned at him as she drew near.

"Don't worry. I'll only have this one," he whispered into her ear.

Ali relaxed and listened as the boys talked about basketball games they'd played in at school. Chase introduced Ali to three boys, Brandon, Steve, and Matt, who were going to be seniors with her in the fall. Matt's eyes grew wide when he looked at Ali. "You're so pretty," he said, then turned red when he realized he'd said it aloud. Ali thanked him graciously, but the other boys teased him mercilessly.

"It's okay," Chase told Matt. "I agree with you completely." This time, Ali turned red.

Kat joined the group and so did Jake and Eric. The bonfire grew warm, and the kids at the party were getting louder and more rowdy as they consumed too much beer. Ali stood there, watching everyone, feeling like an outsider no matter how nice they were to her. At home, she would have never gone to a beer party. She'd had too much experience watching the consequences of alcohol at home. Megan and her other friends weren't into partying, either. Their idea of a fun time was shopping at the mall or hanging out at the pizza place and watching the cute delivery boys. Standing here, in the deep woods, by a lake with a bonfire blazing while everyone drank beer was just too new to Ali, and she didn't really like it. It reminded her too much of how her mother acted when she was drunk—silly and stupid— and it brought back too many bad memories.

After a while, Chase looked down at Ali and quietly asked her if she'd like to go home. She nodded. They were just turning to leave when Jake came stumbling over to them with three beers in his hands.

"Hey guys, don't leave yet. The party's just started," Jake said. Suddenly, he tripped, and the beers went flying out of his hands. Ali jumped back, but it was too late. Beer spilled all over the front of her new sweatshirt and jeans. Everyone in the group stopped and stared with wide eyes.

"You idiot!" Chase yelled at Jake. "Look what you've done."

Jake righted himself and ran up to Ali. "I'm so sorry," he said, swaying. "I didn't mean to, I swear. I'm so sorry." He reached out as if to brush the beer off of Ali's sweatshirt but Chase ran interference.

"Don't touch her. Geez, Jake. What were you thinking?" Chase said, exasperated. He took Ali's hand and pulled her away from the group toward the truck. Everyone in the group looked at them for another moment before they went back to drinking and talking.

Chase reached inside the truck and pulled out a clean rag. "Come on. Let's see if we can wipe some of that off of your sweatshirt." Ali silently followed him to a quiet place by the lake. There was only enough moonlight for them to see where the shore ended and the water began. Chase dipped the rag into the water, squeezed out the excess moisture, and turned to Ali. "Here," he said, handing her the rag.

Ali wiped at the beer stain with the wet rag, but it was no use. The beer had soaked through her sweatshirt and nothing short of a full washing was going to take the beer smell out of it. Her jeans weren't as wet, but she knew they'd also stink of beer. She looked up at Chase and shrugged. "I'll just have to wash it," she said quietly.

"I'm sorry," Chase said. "We should have left earlier."

"No. It's not your fault. I can wash it."

They stood there beside the lake, the light from the half-moon reflecting off the water and onto them. The water was calm, lapping gently against the shore. It was chilly out, but it was quieter here, away from the party, and it felt peaceful and intimate.

"Do you want to go?" Chase asked.

Ali looked up at him. "We could just sit here for a while."

Chase smiled. "Wait here a moment." He ran off toward the truck again and came back with a big, heavy blanket. Chase opened it up, placed half of it on the ground for them to sit on and then wrapped it around their shoulders like a small tent as they sat close together inside it.

"What don't you have in that truck?" Ali asked, laughing.

Chase shrugged. "It's Minnesota. We all carry warm blankets and winter emergency kits in case we get stuck in the snow. I've never had to use this blanket before. I kind of like using it like this, though."

"Me too," Ali agreed.

"Are you warm enough?" Chase asked.

"Yes."

"I never come to these parties," Chase said. "Everyone acts so stupid and immature. I don't care that they want to drink and have fun, most kids our age do. But I don't want to act stupid, then black out and wonder what I'd done the night before. It just seems like such a waste to me."

Ali nodded agreement.

Behind them, they heard the party going in full swing. But around them the frogs chirped and croaked and the water made soft rippling noises. Ali felt Chase's warmth beside her, and it felt good. She hugged her half of the blanket closer around her, thinking about the party, and how that awful girl, Emily, knew who she was. It bothered her that everyone in town knew who she was, who her grandfather was, and where she came from, but she didn't know who any of them were.

"You're awfully quiet," Chase said. "Is something the matter?"

"Why is it everyone knows who I am, even before I tell them? And they know I'm Ben's granddaughter, and that my mother died."

Chase sighed. "It's a small town. News travels fast when someone new comes to live here."

"It's creepy," Ali said.

Chase chuckled. "Yeah, it probably is to you. I've been around it all my life, so I'm used to everyone knowing my business."

Ali dropped her eyes. "Does everyone also know how my mother died?" she asked quietly.

Chase looked over at her, a serious expression on his face. "I don't. No one in town has ever said anything to me about it, either. I think Ben and my mom do, though. But that's about all."

Ali looked up at Chase. She hadn't talked much about her mother since coming here, and she hadn't planned on talking about her tonight. But all the drinking and partying going on around her had stirred up old memories, and she thought she'd burst if she didn't confide in someone.

"I found her," Ali said softly. "She was laying on the sofa, on her side, one arm hanging over the edge. She was so still, I thought she was just passed out again. But when I touched her to wake her up, I knew. She felt, different."

"Oh, God, Ali. I'm so sorry," Chase said. He wrapped his free arm around her waist and pulled her closer to him. "What had happened to her?"

Chills traveled over Ali's body despite the warmth she felt sitting beside Chase. Two tears ran down her cheeks. "She'd been drinking, and she'd taken some of her sleeping pills, too. No one knows if she took too many by accident, or on purpose. But it was too much, and it killed her."

"That's so sad," Chase said. "I'm so sorry, Ali. It must have been terrible."

Ali dropped her head onto Chase's shoulder, the tears now running freely down her cheeks. She'd been strong the night her mother had died. She'd been strong at the funeral, unable to allow the tears to flow. But now, sitting here with Chase, the tears came easily, and he held her close as she cried for her mother.

* * *

Ben looked over at the clock on the nightstand. Eleven thirty-five p.m. Quietly, he rolled over and started to rise from bed.

"Hey. Where are you going?" Jo asked in a sleepy voice from the other side of the bed.

Ben smiled and rolled back over toward Jo. He kissed her gently on the cheek. "The kids will be back soon," he said. "It won't look good if they find me in bed with you, now will it?"

Jo chuckled. "You know, it's not as big a secret as you think. I can almost bet Chase is onto us, and it won't be long before Ali figures it out, too."

Ben sighed, slipped out of bed, and began dressing. "I have to be careful not to give Ali the wrong message."

"I think Ali's smart enough to understand the difference between teens having a relationship and us old people having one. Our situation is different, Ben. We've both been married and now we're both single. It might gross her out to think we're 'doing it,' but I doubt if it will confuse her."

Ben shook his head. "You have such a way with words."

"Thank you," Jo said, laughing.

Dressed now, Ben leaned over the bed and kissed Jo lightly on the lips. "Let's just get Ali safely through this next year, and Chase off to college, then you can tell them anything you want. They'll be grown up and no longer our responsibility."

"Oh, Ben. Do you really believe that? Chase will always be my responsibility, as long as I live. And Ali will be yours. Kids may grow up, but they'll always need their parents."

"I'm not Ali's parent," Ben said.

"No. But you're all she has left. So you're responsible for her whether you like it or not."

Ben sighed. He leaned down and kissed Jo again. "Goodnight," he said softly. Then he headed out of the lodge and up to his cabin.

# Chapter Twelve

At a minute to midnight, Chase pulled his truck into Ben's driveway and stopped, leaving it to idle. "Looks like Ben didn't wait up for you. It's dark inside."

"Well, you know Ben. Lights out at nine, that's his motto," Ali said, and both kids chuckled. Ali bit her lip. "I'm sorry for crying. It was your night, your graduation celebration, and I ruined it for you."

Chase shook his head. "I didn't mind. And you didn't ruin my night. The party wasn't fun anyway. I liked sitting with you by the lake. And I'm glad you confided in me."

Ali smiled at him. "Thanks. I guess I should go in." She slowly opened the truck's door.

"I'll go with you and open up the garage door for you," Chase offered.

"You don't have to. I can open it."

"I know, but I want to. How will you see, going up to your room?"

"There's a flashlight by the washing machine I can use," Ali told him.

They both left the truck and stood by the garage door. The night air was cold, and Ali shivered after leaving the warmth of the truck's cab. Chase stood close to her, placing his hands on her arms. Ali looked up into Chase's eyes. In the light of the headlights, their shadows stood tall above them against the garage door. Just as Chase lowered his head to touch lips with Ali, the garage door flew open with a bang, making both kids jump back.

"Are you coming in or are you both going to stand there all night?" Ben asked. His shirt was half tucked into his jeans and his hair was mussed.

"Geez, you scared me to death," Ali said. "I thought you were asleep."

"Well, I would have been if that blasted truck hadn't come roaring up the driveway and those headlights weren't in my eyes," Ben said, sounding gruff as ever. Ben sniffed the air. "Do I smell beer? Geez, it's strong. Were you drinking?" he asked Ali.

"No," Ali said defensively. "Jake tripped and spilled beer all over me, that's why it's so strong."

Ben crossed his arms. "And you expect me to believe that? You went to a drinking party and didn't have any beer?"

Ali glared at her grandfather. "Yes. I do expect you to believe that. I don't drink. You, of all people, should know why."

Ben turned to Chase. "And I suppose you didn't have any beer, either?"

"I had one, but Ali didn't have any. She's telling the truth. Jake dumped beer all over her by accident," Chase told him.

"Humph," Ben said. "Well, go on home, Chase. Morning's going to come fast."

Chase smiled over at Ali, then got into his truck and left. Ali turned on her heel and walked over to the washing machine, pulled her sweatshirt off, and threw it in the machine. She glared one last time at her grandfather before grabbing the flashlight next to the washing machine and heading up the stairs.

Ben shrugged and headed back into the cabin and to bed.

\* \* \*

The next morning in the boat, Ali and Ben barely spoke a word to each other for the first half hour. Ali was tired. She was physically tired from being up late the night before and mentally tired from being angry at her grandfather for accusing her of drinking. It made her so mad that he treated her like an irresponsible teenager. She'd been the one who'd held her and her mother's life together for years back in California, yet her grandfather treated her like she was incapable of doing anything. Finally, trying not to sound irritated, she spoke up.

"When I tell you I didn't do something, I expect you to believe me."

Ben looked at her, his expression guarded. "What?"

"Last night. I told you I didn't drink any beer, and you didn't believe me. I don't lie. If I say I didn't, I didn't. I'm not irresponsible, and I certainly would never drink. If you knew me, you'd understand that."

Ben sat a moment without responding. He reeled in his line, then cast it out into the water again. Finally, he spoke. "Okay. You're right. I have no reason to distrust you."

Ali sat there, dumbfounded. She couldn't believe he'd given in this easily.

"Can I ask you a question?" Ben asked.

"Okay."

"What did you mean when you said that I, of all people, should know why you wouldn't drink alcohol?"

Ali sat silent. She didn't want to have this conversation with her grandfather. She'd said it in a moment of rage last night, without thinking. Now, she had to explain herself. She took a deep breath, trying to hold her emotions in check.

"You know how my mother died," Ali said steadily. "I know Megan's mother told you. Knowing that, you should realize that I wouldn't want to touch alcohol."

Ben nodded. "Okay. I understand." He returned to fishing in silence and didn't probe for more details. Ali relaxed and was finally the first one that morning to catch a walleye.

* * *

The first week of June hit with a heat wave. Ali's grandfather kept saying how unusual that was, how June was generally cool and wet. Instead, it was hot and muggy, and the mosquitoes and biting flies came out with a vengeance. Ali learned quickly that staying out after dusk or walking in the woods during the day wasn't possible without a coating of mosquito repellent. And to top it off, the humidity brought with it flies that looked harmless but would snack on you if given the chance.

"Crap," Ali yelled one day after another nasty fly took a bite out of her arm. She swatted at it, killed it, and was rewarded with her own blood smeared all over her arm. "Gross. How do you stand these things?" she asked Jo, who was helping her clean out one of the larger cabins.

Jo shrugged. "I guess you get used to it. Don't you have flies and mosquitoes in California?"

"Flies, yes, but not ones that bite you. Mosquitoes, no. At least not in southern California. Ouch!" Another fly bit her on the shoulder. "These things bite right through clothes. It's terrible."

Jo chuckled. "Sorry, Ali. You'll have to put the bug spray on pretty thick. You must be new meat to them. If I were you, I'd stay out of the woods, too. If you don't like mosquitoes and flies, you really won't like the ticks."

Ali shivered. She'd seen Chase pull a tick off of his ankle after he'd been in the tall grass. She didn't want to even think about how nasty those creatures were.

June also brought more guests to the lodge and the cabins were full most nights. Ali worked hard each day, cleaning cabins, doing laundry, and helping with breakfast and supper.

Now that the families were arriving, Jo served breakfast from six to nine each morning, so that meant extra time in the kitchen. Ali didn't mind the work, she was used to working hard, but she missed spending time with Chase, who was also busy working around the lodge.

One morning in the boat, as Ali enjoyed the cool morning breeze before the heat of the day set in, Ben sniffed the air and said, "It's going to rain soon. Hopefully, it will break this heat wave."

Ali quietly sniffed the air. She didn't smell anything different. "How do you know it's going to rain?"

"I can smell it in the air. The maple and poplar tree leaves are flipped over, too. All signs of a storm brewing," Ben told her.

Ali sniffed the air again. "All I smell is bug spray," she said.

That night, just as Ali and her grandfather walked up to the cabin a little before nine o'clock, Ben pointed out the dark clouds rolling in. "Thunder clouds," he said. "We're in for a big storm tonight." And he was right. By nine thirty, just after Ali had snuggled down in her bed, exhausted from her busy day, she heard the wind outside pick up and the first roll of thunder echoing across the sky. She lay there awhile, waiting, and then jumped when her room lit up from a flash of lightning and the thunder rumbled louder. Rain began to pound on the roof with such vengeance that Ali thought for sure it would come right through. Then the sky lit up and rumbled so loud, Ali swore the room actually shook. She wasn't sure if lightning could strike the attic roof or not, and she didn't want to find out, so she grabbed her flashlight, slipped on a pair of pajama pants, grabbed a sweatshirt, and ran downstairs where she hoped it would be safer.

Another roll of thunder ripped through the sky just above the cabin when Ali entered through the kitchen door. She saw light coming from the living room, and when she entered, she saw her grandfather in his favorite chair, a lit oil lamp at his side.

"Couldn't sleep through all this racket?" Ben asked with a grin on his face.

Ali sat down on the sofa opposite of him, and shook her head.

"I figured if you were anything like your mother, you wouldn't like this storm, especially up in that attic room," Ben said, chuckling. "Your mother used to sleep on the sofa during storms like this. Of course, that was at the lodge. We were living there, then."

"We don't have storms like this in California," Ali said in her defense. "It just startled me. I suppose I'll get used to them."

"Well now, I can't blame you. Couldn't blame Jen, either. I'm sure the rain and wind is much louder upstairs than down here. It would scare anyone. Jen's bedroom was in the loft room at the lodge. She loved being up high, looking down at everyone. She said it was like living in a bird's nest. She just didn't like it much during a storm."

Ali cocked her head. "Loft room? I didn't know there was an upstairs in the lodge."

Ben nodded. "Yep. Where did you think those steps in the living room led to?"

Ali shrugged. "I didn't really think about it. I suppose I thought it was an attic room."

"Well, it kind of is. Jo doesn't use it for a bedroom, never has. She stores stuff up there. As a matter of fact, some of your mother's stuff is stored up there still. Lizzie boxed up some of the important things she thought Jen might want someday and left them up there."

Ali's eyes grew wide. "You kept some of my mother's stuff?"

"Yep. I'm not sure what all is there. Some photo albums, I

suppose. School yearbooks, mementos, that sort of thing. Maybe even a few of her favorite books and stuff." Ben looked over at Ali. "You seem surprised. Why?"

The thunder continued to rumble above them as the rain pelted against the windows. Ali studied her grandfather, the flickering oil lamp casting shadows across him and around the room. He didn't look angry, just curious.

"I guess I just figured that when you threw her out of the house, you probably got rid of all her things, too," Ali said.

Ben sat straight up in his chair and stared hard at Ali. "Threw her out? Who said I threw her out of the house? Did your mother tell you that?"

"No," Ali said, crossing her arms. "I told you, Mom never talked about you or living here. I just figured she was thrown out for being pregnant with me because we never came to visit, and you and grandma never came to see us."

Ben sat forward in his chair. "I never threw your mother out. Never. We had words, yes, and I'm not proud of some of the things I said to her, but I never told her to leave. She had gone up to her room after we fought and the next morning, when I went up to talk to her and tell her that we'd make it all work out, she was gone. She'd left in the middle of the night in her car, and we had no idea where she'd gone."

Ali frowned. She'd always thought her mother had been told not to come home because she was unmarried and pregnant. Because of her. "Then why didn't you go after her? Why didn't you try to find her?"

Ben sighed and sat back in his chair. "I did. It took a while, but I tracked her down and found her in California. You had already been born, and Jen was living in a small apartment and was working as a secretary in an office. I asked her to come home so we could help her, but she refused. She said she'd already started a new life and didn't want to come back. She told me to never come see her again. So, that was the end of it. I didn't."

Ali heard the sadness in her grandfather's voice and she felt sorry for him. He was a man who was used to getting his own way, but he couldn't control his own daughter. The daughter he had loved so dearly that he'd called her "my Jen".

Ben looked over at Ali. "I never meant for her to leave or stay away. I've paid for it over and over again for the past seventeen years, believe me. But I never sent her away. I couldn't have done that. She was my Jen."

Quiet fell between them as the storm rumbled on outside. Ben finally stood after a long moment. "You know, if you ever want to look through your mom's things, you're certainly welcome to. They're your things now. Jo will know where the boxes are. Take what you like."

Ali nodded. "Thanks," she said softly.

"I'm going to bed," Ben said. He went over to the small closet in the hall and pulled out a pillow and blanket and laid them on the edge of the sofa. "You can sleep out here if you like. The storm should pass over soon. Goodnight."

Ali said goodnight and watched her grandfather walk into the darkness to his room. He'd looked sad, like the past had unexpectedly crushed him. Ali made up a bed on the sofa and curled up on it. The storm was moving away, but she continued to hear thunder in the distance. As she slowly fell to sleep, she thought of her mother, her grandmother, and her grandfather, and of all the pain that could have been avoided if they'd just talked to one another. She would have had a family then, instead of growing up alone as she had. And maybe her mother would still be alive and happy, instead of spending years drowning in depression and alcohol. Instead of dying unhappy.

\* \* \*

The storm did clear away the muggy air as Ali's grandfather had predicted and the weather became mild and beautiful again. Ali couldn't help but feel that she and her grandfather had also cleared the air a little in their relationship. Even though it made her sad that her mother and grandfather never had the chance to settle their differences, Ali was happy to learn he hadn't forced her to go. Somewhere, deep inside that grumpy exterior was a man who did know how to love, and Ali hoped she could find a way into his heart so they could be more like family and less like two strangers living together.

Another thought occurred to Ali as she did her work around the lodge. She'd never dared even wonder who her father was, because she had no idea where to start looking for him. But now, living here, she realized that her father might also live around here and maybe even went to school with her mother. She hoped she would find some clues to who he was in her mother's things, so she wouldn't have to ask Ben. She had a feeling that Ben wouldn't tell her even if he did know, so she hoped to find out herself.

The lodge was buzzing with guests all week so Ali didn't have a chance to ask Jo if she would show her where her mother's belongings were stored. On Thursday, the food truck came with Jo's order for the week and Ali and Jo began unpacking and putting the items away. Jo had told Ali that having the food delivered was so much easier than going shopping every week, plus, because of food safety laws, she felt safer buying the food from the service.

"Years ago, they used to raise their own chickens for eggs and purchased their milk, butter, and cheese directly from a local dairy farmer," Jo told Ali as they worked. "Nowadays, that wouldn't work since we're considered a public kitchen. Everything has to be on the up and up, thank goodness," Jo said, wrinkling her nose. "I hated getting eggs from the chickens. They were mean old buggers."

Ali laughed. Ben had come into the room at that point. "The fresh eggs and milk were wonderful," he said. "I miss everything being fresh. What I don't miss is the two mile trek all year round my brother and I had to walk three times a week to get milk, butter, and cheese from the dairy farm."

"You have a brother?" Ali asked. It was the first she'd heard of him.

"Yep. Jeremy is his name. He lives down south in Florida now. He hated the lodge and all the outdoor stuff. Became an engineer and has worked inside his entire life."

"Ben. You should take Ali to the old farm where you used to get the milk," Jo suggested. "The barn is still standing and it's a nice hike. She can see firsthand where you used to go."

Ben shrugged. "Maybe we can squeeze in a walk there. We'll see."

Ali saw a look pass between Jo and Ben, one that reminded her of when her mother had a boyfriend and her mother would tell her boyfriend to do something he didn't want to do.

"It's okay. You don't have to if you don't want to," Ali told her grandfather.

"I didn't say I didn't want to. I just have to find the time, that's all," Ben said gruffly. He headed out the back door, into the June sunshine.

"Why's he always so mad?" Ali asked Jo.

Jo chuckled. "He's just a grumpy old man, that's all. He doesn't mean anything by it."

Ali sighed. Then she remembered the attic. "Grandpa mentioned that some of my mom's things are in the loft room here. He said I could look through them if I wanted. Could you show me where they are when we get a chance?"

"Oh, sure dear," Jo said. "I forgot all about those things up there. It was nice he thought of them. There are two or three boxes. We can grab Chase after we're done here and he can help us move stuff so we can get at them."

Ali and Jo each picked up a ten pound bag of flour and carried it to the pantry. Once they'd set down their bags, Ali turned to Jo. "Can I ask you a question about my mother?"

"Of course, dear," Jo said.

Ali bit her lip. "Do you know who she was seeing before she got pregnant with me? I mean, does anyone know who my father is?"

Jo looked over at Ali with tenderness in her eyes. "I'm sorry, dear. I don't know who he was. I was working here at the time it all happened, but no one ever said anything about who your father could be. Your mom wasn't dating anyone seriously at the time, that's why it came as such a surprise. She was a good student and hung out with a nice crowd of kids. But as far as I knew, there was no one special."

Ali's eyes dropped. She didn't want Jo to see her disappointment. "I just wondered, that's all."

"Have you asked Ben?" Jo asked.

"No, and I really don't want to. I'm sure he would blow a cork if I did. Please don't mention to him that I asked. I was just curious, that's all."

Jo nodded. "I won't. Let's finish up here and we'll go up and find those boxes, okay?"

A little while later, Jo found Chase and the three of them headed up the stairs to the attic room. At the top of the staircase was a small landing with a railing where a person could see everything that was happening down in the living room. Ali now understood why her mother had compared this spot to a bird's nest. It would be fun for a child to sit up here and spy on all the grownups. Beyond that was a door, and through that they entered into a room much like Ali's attic room, long and narrow with a sloped roof on both sides.

Jo pulled a string in the middle of the room and the light came on. It only took moving a few big boxes, Christmas decorations Jo told her, before finding three small boxes marked "Jen's Things".

"Do you want to go through the boxes up here, or do you want Chase to take them up to the cabin?" Jo asked.

Ali decided she'd rather have them in her room at the cabin so she could go through them in private. The three of them each carried a box downstairs but before they made it to the kitchen, Jo was waylaid by a guest who had questions about signing up for a fishing trip. She set down the box and told the kids to go ahead without her.

Ali and Chase loaded the two boxes into the back of his pickup truck, then Chase ran back inside to get the third box. As he closed the tailgate on the truck, Ali looked up to the top of the hill and saw her grandfather talking to another man. Actually, it looked like he was arguing with the stranger. After studying the man a moment, Ali realized it was the guy who'd stared at her in town and who her grandfather had said to stay away from.

"Who's that guy my grandfather's yelling at?" Ali asked Chase as she pointed up the hill.

Chase looked up, shading his eyes against the glare of the sun. "Oh, that's Jared Halverson. He owns a real estate business in Grand Rapids, but he sells homes around here, too. He's into developing land around lakes, too."

"What do you think they're arguing about?" Ali asked.

"Halverson comes around here every once in a while to try to talk Ben into selling some of his land. He wants to plot off lots around the lake and sell them to people who want to build lake homes. Ben always refuses, even tells him to not come back, but he keeps coming back anyway."

Ali's brows furrowed. "My grandfather owns a lot of land on the lake?"

"Oh, yeah," Chase said, looking at Ali. "Didn't you know that? Ben's family has owned the land around here for decades.

He owns about a thousand acres of land, most of it around this side of the lake and the rest heading back into the woods toward the old dairy farm."

Ali's mouth dropped open. "You mean, he's rich?"

Chase laughed. "Yeah, I guess he is. At least the land is worth a lot of money. But Ben refuses to sell any of it to Halverson. He has sold a plot of land here and there to certain people who he didn't mind having live nearby, and he sold the resort and land to our family, but other than that, he won't sell out. He likes the lake undisturbed, and that's good for the resort, too."

"Wow, I didn't know that. He's so cheap. I thought he didn't have much money," Ali said. She remembered how he'd handed her money in town without even blinking. She had thought at the time he was just being nice. She never realized he could afford to give it to her.

"Ben is cheap," Chase said. "But he can be generous, too."

Ali watched as the man Chase called Halverson got into his truck and drove away. Her grandfather turned and walked back into the house.

"Why does my grandfather hate this Halverson guy so much? When we ran into him in town, Grandpa said I should stay away from him, and he called him trash."

Chase shook his head. "I don't know why he hates him, but he does. I always figured it had something to do with his wanting to buy up Ben's land. I don't really know Halverson, so I'm not sure."

Ali thought it was strange, but decided to brush it away for now. They got into the truck's cab and headed up to the cabin to unload the boxes.

# Chapter Thirteen

June weather in northern Minnesota, Ali soon learned, was a rollercoaster of temperatures. Some mornings she'd wake up to air so cool she could see her breath, and she'd have to dress in warm clothing when she went out on the lake with her grandfather. By afternoon, the temperature could rise up to the eighties, and she'd find herself taking off layers of clothes that she'd then have to put back on as evening approached. One day could be unbearably hot and muggy, then a rainstorm would erupt and the next day would be cool and comfortable. Ali got used to wearing layers and always having a sweatshirt close at hand in case the temperature dropped quickly.

One morning it was warmer than usual, so after Ali came into the lodge's kitchen, where it was hot from the stove and dishwasher running, she hung up her sweatshirt and changed into a pair of jean shorts before helping Jo serve breakfast to the guests. When Ben came in for breakfast, he eyed Ali up and down, frowned deeply, and asked, "What are you wearing?"

Jo, Chase, and Ali looked at him with confused expressions. Ali had on a hunter green T-shirt with the Willow Lake Lodge logo on it that Jo had given her, jean shorts, and a pair of sneakers. She looked down at herself, then back at her grandfather, her brows furrowed.

"Clothes," she replied.

Ben huffed. "You weren't wearing those tiny shorts in the boat. Why are you wearing them here?"

Ali rolled her eyes. She couldn't help it. "Tiny? These aren't tiny. These are just normal shorts. Jo said it was okay to wear shorts on hot days. I get too hot cleaning cabins in jeans."

Jo piped up. "She looks fine, Ben. I've seen much shorter shorts on girls who are guests here. Besides, I wear shorts all summer, so why shouldn't Ali?"

Ben's gaze went from Jo's khaki walking shorts that went halfway down to her knees, then back to Ali's shorts that were up much higher on her thighs. Ali's legs were long and lean, so there was a lot more leg showing. "Not the same thing. If Ali wants to wear shorts while she's working, she can get a pair like yours."

Jo sighed. "Don't be silly, Ben. Ali's young and cute. She doesn't want to wear old lady shorts like mine. Now sit down and eat your breakfast before it gets cold."

Ben scrunched up his face, but he sat and ate.

Later, Ben and Chase helped Ali clear and reset tables in the dining room as groups of people ate and left and others came in. A family of four came and sat down, and Ali brought out the coffee pot and started telling the family their choices for breakfast. The teenage son in the group kept staring at Ali, which didn't go unnoticed by Ben or Chase.

"Chase will serve that table," Ben said abruptly when the three were back in the kitchen.

"I can serve them," Ali said as she started stacking fresh pancakes on a platter and asked Jo for a bowl of fruit.

"No, it's okay. I'll serve them," Chase said firmly, taking over as Ali and Jo stared at him in disbelief. "That kid out there was staring just a little too hard at you, Ali." Chase grabbed the tray of food and drinks and headed out the door.

"Well, I'm glad to see Chase has the good sense to step in when necessary," Ben said, then headed outside.

Ali looked at Jo and sighed. Jo shook her head.

"Men," Jo said, disgusted. "Don't worry. They'll get used

to boys staring at you. They'll have to. You're a pretty girl. You're going to be stared at."

Ali sighed again. She thought her grandfather and Chase were being stupid, but she decided the best thing to do was ignore them.

In the afternoons, when Ali had some time off of work, she'd go up to her attic room for an hour or so and look through her mother's boxes. She'd turn on the generator so she could run a fan in the room to cool it off, sit on her bed, and sort through the many things that once belonged to her mom.

Ali had opened up all three boxes to see what was in them, and then slowly took her time looking through each box, one at a time. One box was filled with her mom's favorite books as a teenager. There were a few steamy historical romances that Ali laughed about, some Judy Blume books, and some classics like *The Great Gatsby* and *Catcher in the Rye* that Ali assumed her mom had read for English class. Ali thumbed through each book to see if her mother had left any scraps of paper, notes, or anything that would tell her more about her mother as a teen. Finding none, Ali carefully packed the books away and started searching through the next box. This one was more interesting. There were yearbooks from her junior high and high school years. Ali pulled out her mother's seventh grade yearbook and slowly went through it. Kids had written messages on the inside of the cover and beside pictures. It looked no different than Ali's own yearbooks that she'd left behind with Megan for safe keeping. Ali wanted to read everything so she could get to know her mother better. She decided to read them a little every night. It would be a good way to remember her mother before she fell asleep each night.

Ali made a point of going into town at least once a week to sit in the coffeehouse and talk to Megan on her phone. School was now out and Kat worked there almost every day, so Ali was able to visit with her, too. Ali missed her California friends. Every time she talked to Megan, she felt more homesick. Chase always asked her how Megan was, and each time Ali told him how distant she felt from her best friend. Megan was working at the mall, hanging out with their group of friends, and had even started going out with a new boyfriend that Ali had never met. Ali felt disengaged from her former life, yet not quite fitted into her new one. As much as she enjoyed Chase's and Jo's company, and she was getting along fairly well with her grandfather, she still felt disconnected from what she once knew and where she was now.

One afternoon, Kat and Jake drove out to the lodge and joined them for lunch, and Chase suggested they take the bigger motorboat out for a while to swim, tube, and enjoy the sun. Jo thought it was a great idea and even packed snacks and soda in a cooler for the kids. Ben was out fishing with a tour group and wouldn't be back until supper, so Ali didn't have to hear him grumble about her skipping a few hours of work.

Ali was the first one ready to go and waited on the dock by the boat for the others. She'd changed into her swimsuit and wore a tank top and shorts over it. She couldn't even imagine what her grandfather would say if he saw her in a bikini, after the shorts incident. But what was she supposed to swim in? Jeans and a sweatshirt?

As she stood on the dock, staring out at the lake, Ali was surprised by a deep voice that came up behind her. "Hi."

Ali turned, and there stood the boy from the other morning who her grandfather and Chase had complained about staring at her. He was as tall as Chase and had sandy brown hair that was long and shaggy. He wore light-colored board shorts and a white T-shirt with a surfer design on it.

"Hi," Ali replied.

"I was surprised to see you down here," the boy said. "It seems like you're always working."

Ali smiled. "Usually, I am. It's a nice day today, though. I thought I'd get some sun."

The boy smiled back at her showing perfect white teeth. "I'm Aaron," he said. "You're Ali, right?"

Ali nodded.

"I've heard that older man call your name, that's why I knew it," Aaron told her. "So, does your mom own the resort?"

Ali shook her head. "No. Jo is just a friend. I live up the hill in that cabin with my grandfather and work for Jo." She pointed up at their cabin.

Aaron looked disappointed. "Oh. I thought maybe she was your mother and that blonde guy was your brother. You all seem like a family."

Ali laughed. "No. Chase isn't my brother, he's just a friend. I just moved here in May, and Jo was nice enough to give me a job."

"Where are you from?" Aaron asked.

"Southern California. Torrance, actually."

Aaron's face lit up. "Really? We're from Monterey, up in northern California, but we have relatives we often visit down near Torrance."

"That's neat," Ali said. She looked around for the others, but didn't see them coming yet.

"Are you waiting for someone?" Aaron asked, a look of disappointment spreading across his face again.

"My friends and I are going out on the lake this afternoon," Ali said, then silently admonished herself for saying it. What if he wanted to tag along? She wouldn't know how to say no, and Chase might not like having him along.

"So, what do you guys do for fun around here?" Aaron asked. "There's literally nothing in town to do, unless you want to go to an old movie or hang out at that coffeehouse wannabe. All there is around here is the lake and woods."

"Hey. Who's this?" Kat had come down the dock and

stared at Aaron warily. Ali wondered if she'd heard what he'd said about her parent's coffeehouse.

"This is Aaron. He's staying here at the lodge with his family," Ali said.

Kat slowly looked him up and down. She didn't look impressed.

"Kat's parents own the coffeehouse in town," Ali said. "Next time you go in there, you can say hi to Kat."

Aaron's face reddened, but he didn't say anything.

Chase and Jake came down the dock then, Chase carrying a large, round, blown up raft. After looking at Aaron a moment, Chase turned to Ali. "Sorry it took me so long. I had to blow up the tube."

"This is Aaron," Ali said. From the look Chase gave him, she knew right away he didn't like him there.

"Hi. Everyone ready to go?"

Jake and Kat stepped into the boat. Ali turned to Aaron. "Maybe we'll see you later," she said, then stepped down into the boat, too.

Chase started the boat and backed it away from the dock, then turned it around and sped off. They rode over to another cove, away from the resort and where they wouldn't disturb any fishermen. Ali was sitting in the seat next to Chase, and Jake and Kat were sitting on the bench seat behind them.

When the boat was idling, Ali said to Chase, "I feel bad leaving Aaron behind and not inviting him. Was that rude? Should we have asked him to come along?"

Chase didn't look like he felt bad about it. "Don't worry about him. We don't even know him. Today is for just us friends."

Ali glanced at Jake and Kat and thought that she didn't really know them, either. But it made her feel good that Chase considered them all to be friends.

The boat had an inboard motor, so it was perfect for

waterskiing and tubing. Chase turned off the motor and hooked up the rope for the tube. "Who wants to go first?" he asked.

"We will," Kat and Jake said together. The tube was large enough and had enough hand grips for both of them to ride it. Kat and Jake slipped on their life jackets and carefully crawled out onto the tube. Chase gave them a push away from the boat then went and started up the motor again.

The day was warm and still, and the water was smooth as glass. It was a perfect day to go flying around the lake on a tube. Ali hung on tightly to the side of the boat and watched as Chase sped the boat one way and then another, making crazy circles and causing the tube to jump over the waves the boat made. Kat and Jake were laughing and screaming with excitement, and Ali laughed, too, at the sight of them struggling to hang on and not fall off into the water.

After a time, Chase slowed down and cut the engine. "Want to try it?" he asked Ali.

Ali bit her lip. "It looks like fun, but it looks scary, too."

"It's not so scary. I'll tell Jake not to drive too fast. He's so afraid of upsetting you after the beer incident, he'll do whatever I say."

Chase pulled Kat and Jake in and they exchanged places. Soon, Chase and Ali were hanging onto the tube's handles and being pulled around the cove. The cool water splashed up around them, but since Jake was driving slower than Chase had, they didn't get drenched.

"Ready to go faster?" Chase yelled over to Ali. Ali nodded. Chase gave the thumbs up to Jake and off he went, doing circles like Chase had, causing the tube to bounce over the waves made by the boat. Ali laughed so hard, it made it difficult to hang on. Then, the tube hit one wave too fast and flew up out of the water, falling down hard. Ali lost her grip and went flying off of it into the water. Chase flew off, too, and landed nearby.

"Are you okay?" Chase asked once he'd righted himself in the water and swam over to Ali, who was bobbing in her life jacket.

Ali laughed. "Oh, my God! That was so much fun. We were flying for a moment."

The foursome took turns tubing for a while, then they ate the snacks that Jo had sent along. They talked and joked and laughed in the afternoon sun. Their arms were sore from hanging onto the tube, but they didn't mind. They were young and having fun.

Ali and Chase eventually went to lie on the tube as it floated gently in the water while Jake and Kat lay out on the bench seats to dry off and suntan. It was so peaceful and calm, floating in the water, that Ali fell asleep. She was awakened by a nudge from Chase.

"Hey, look up there," he told her.

Ali opened her eyes, shading them with her arm, and looked up at the sky. Directly above her was a large bird, circling.

"What is it?" she asked, fully awake now.

"It's a bald eagle," Chase told her. "You'll see it better when it comes closer to the water. See how it's circling? It's looking for fish. Any minute now he'll swoop down and pick one up. Watch."

Ali sat up carefully so as not to tip the tube and followed the eagle with her eyes. The contrast of the dark feathered bird against the brilliant blue sky was striking. It wasn't long before it stopped circling and suddenly headed down toward the water about twenty feet away from them. Quick as a wink, the eagle captured a large fish in its talons and, flapping its long, powerful wings, started rising up from the water again. The majestic bird flew higher and higher with its heavy load until it reached a nest up in the treetops.

"That was amazing," Ali said in a hushed whisper. She was in awe of what she'd just witnessed so close to her. "I've never seen an eagle in the wild before," she told Chase. "They're so big. So impressive."

Chase nodded. "He probably has eaglets in the nest up there, and the mama eagle is up there, too. It won't be long before we see all of them hunting around the lake. Baby eagles grow up fast."

Ali turned to Chase. "You're so smart about all the animals and birds that live around here."

Chase smiled. "It's nothing. They just interest me. I'm thinking of majoring in Environmental Sciences in college."

Ali lay back again on the tube. "It's so beautiful here. In the morning, when I go fishing with my grandfather, it's calm and peaceful. I can understand why he likes going out so early. I kind of like it, too. And today was great. I've never had so much fun on the water as I have today."

Chase looked at her, surprised. "Really? You lived near the ocean. Didn't you go out in the water a lot there?"

Ali chuckled. "No. I'd lay on the beach and suntan, but we never went out in the water. I was scared to death of the undertow and being sucked under and drowning."

"Weird," Chase said.

They lay there under the clear sky as the tube drifted silently in the water.

"Thanks for today," Ali said softly. "I know you asked Jake and Kat to come out and you took us all tubing to help make up for how I feel about missing my old friends. It was nice of you to do that."

"I felt bad for you. I just want you to feel like you belong here now," Chase said, reaching for Ali's hand and holding it gently in his.

"I know it will take time to get used to it here. Today was great."

"Are you happy now that we didn't ask Aaron to come out here with us?" Chase asked, emphasizing Aaron's name in an unflattering tone.

"I was just being nice to him. I'm sure he's bored up here. It's not what he's used to. He said he was from California, too," Ali said.

"He's kept himself pretty busy stalking you for the past two days, waiting for a chance to get you alone," Chase said.

"Don't be silly. He hasn't been stalking me. On the dock is the first time I've seen him all day."

"Well, I've been watching him and I've seen him following you around. I wanted to tell him to leave you alone."

Ali turned and looked at Chase. "Are you jealous of Aaron?"

Chase turned slightly red. "Maybe. Just a little."

"That's so cool. I've never had a boy be jealous of someone because of me before," Ali said, grinning.

"Oh, I don't believe that. You must have had a ton of boys trying to get your attention back in California," Chase said.

Ali shook her head. "Nope. I was too busy all the time with school, going to work, and taking care of my mom. I didn't have time for boys. I barely had time to spend with my girlfriends."

Chase rose up on his elbow and looked down at Ali. He reached over and brushed a strand of her hair away from her face. "The boys in California must be idiots for not noticing you," he said softly. They lay there like that, looking into each other's eyes.

"Just kiss the girl and get it over with? You're making us sick over here," Jake yelled at them from the boat. His words echoed across the lake.

The moment was over. Ali rolled her eyes and Chase sighed. They both sat up on the tube.

"Just pull us back to the boat, smartass," Chase yelled at Jake.

# Chapter Fourteen

The summer days flew by for Ali. She and Chase went to town occasionally to visit his friends at the coffeehouse or to a movie on a Saturday night. After the movie, most of the town kids hung out at The Loon's Nest Bar & Grill and played foosball or pool in the back of the bar. Ali always felt uncomfortable there. She couldn't believe that underage teens were allowed to hang out in a bar at night, but it seemed normal to everyone else. Despite her discomfort, she did learn to be a pretty good pool player with Chase's guidance.

Days were warm but luckily nights cooled down and a breeze almost always came off the lake. Ali's attic room stayed fairly comfortable at night if she left the windows open wide. Before bed most nights, she'd pull out one of her mother's yearbooks and study it. They had the normal teen-aged writings in them, like "Have a cool summer" or "See you in the fall", and it was always the same kids writing in them year after year. Since the school was so small, Ali soon recognized the names of the kids in each yearbook. She knew who the jocks were and who the cheerleaders were. She could tell who the smart kids were and the popular kids. Even with the school's small classes, there were cliques, just like any other school. What Ali couldn't quite tell was where her mother fit in. She had been a cheerleader starting in the ninth grade, but she had also been on the volleyball team and made excellent grades. She sort of fell in with all the groups, yet she didn't seem to be one of the popular kids.

Ali enjoyed learning more about her mother's past. She remembered her mother as being a kind, sweet person who had trouble dealing with difficulties in life. When things got tough, her mother broke down and headed for the bottle and pills. Her mother wasn't a bad person, she just hadn't been a strong person. But through the photos from her teen years, Ali saw that her mother was happy then, and it made Ali feel better knowing her mother had been happy once.

Aaron and his family left the resort but other families came and went in their place. Cute girls in bikinis swam out to the floating dock to sunbathe and flirted with Chase as he worked around the lodge. Muscular teen boys followed Ali around and even asked her out, but she always declined. She and Chase made a pact not to be jealous of any attention given to them by the guests, because they both understood that the guests would leave eventually. Ali wished she could have made the same pact with her grandfather. Any time he caught a young boy staring in her direction, he practically snarled at him. Once, when Ali was serving supper to a table of rowdy teens who had their eyes on Ali's long legs, Ben had actually told them, "You'd better keep your eyes on your plates if you know what's good for you." Chase couldn't help chuckling over this, but Ali had blushed a deep red and hadn't gone back to serve that table.

Late one morning in the last week of June, Ben came in from cleaning a fishing group's morning catch and approached Ali. "Let's go for a walk," he said.

Ali and Jo had been busy scheduling the food order for the Fourth of July week, which Jo had told her would be their busiest. Ali turned to Jo, her brows raised in question.

"Go ahead," Jo said. "It'll be good for you to get outside for a bit."

Ali followed her grandfather outside. It was a beautiful day with a light wind and cool air, although the sun was shining brightly. Ali had on a pair of jeans since it wasn't too hot out and one of her scoop necked T-shirts. She followed her grandfather up the gravel road to their cabin where he stopped a moment.

"You should put on some bug repellent," he said. "They shouldn't be too bad with this breeze, but better safe than sorry. I'll be right back."

Ali sprayed on some bug repellent, all the time wondering where they were headed. When her grandfather came back out from the house, he had a shotgun in his hand.

Ali's eyes grew wide. "What do you need that for? Are you going to shoot me?"

Ben gave her one of his sardonic looks. "Of course not. We're going out in the woods. Around here, it's smart to have a gun along, just in case."

"Just in case of what? What's going to attack us?" Ali asked. *Who in the world wanted to go walking in the woods if they were going to become some animal's meal?*

"Nothing, I hope. But we've got bear around here, wolves, and cougars. Generally, they're just as afraid of us as we are of them. Well, except for cougars. But don't worry, we probably won't see anything. Come on, this way."

"Generally they're afraid of us?" Ali said under her breath. Reluctantly, she followed behind her grandfather.

Ben led her down the gravel road for a distance, then turned onto a narrow trail that he called a "deer path" and after a short walk, they came to an open field. The grass was about ankle high and there was a narrow, worn down dirt path that grass grew along both sides of. There were patches of pine trees here and there, but mostly it looked like farmland that had gone to seed.

"Where are we headed?" Ali asked now that she was able to walk beside her grandfather.

"To the old dairy farm. You can see where your old

grandpa used to walk to in order to bring back pails of fresh milk, butter, and cheese," Ben told her.

Ali walked along, looking around her. There was a dense wooded area on the left where she supposed all the wild animals that were going to attack them lived. On the right was open land for a distance before it hit a line of trees. As she looked around her, she saw a large bird fly overhead and off to the trees on the right. To her, it looked like an eagle.

"Is there a lake or river around here?" Ali asked.

"Yep. There's a small lake about a quarter mile off beyond those trees. Why?"

"I just saw an eagle fly that way, and Chase said they usually build their nests by a body of water," Ali said.

Ben's brows rose. "Hmmm. That's smart of you to notice," he said.

"Well, I'm not dumb, you know," Ali said defensively.

"Nope. Never thought you were dumb. Just didn't think stuff like that interested you, that's all," Ben said.

Ali turned to her grandfather. "Why? I'm interested in fishing. I'm interested in the loons. Why wouldn't you think I'd be interested in other animals and birds?"

Ben shrugged. "You got me there. Okay. If all that interests you, I can talk your ear off. Take a deep whiff of the air around here."

Ali frowned at her grandfather but did as he said. "Okay, now what?"

"Do you smell anything?"

"Yeah. It sort of smells like one of those old hope chests people used to store their valuables in."

"Yep, you got that right," Ben said, smiling. "It's cedar. It rained last night and it brought out the scent of the cedar trees. If you really pay attention, you can smell the wet pine, too, although the cedar masks it."

Ali took another strong whiff of the air. "You're right,"

she said, excited. "I can smell pine, faintly. It sort of smells sweet, like those scented cardboard pine trees people hang in their cars."

"You got it."

Ben continued pointing out different types of trees to Ali and also some wildflowers. He showed her a milkweed plant with blooms that looked like stars, pink wild roses that grew on a vine up a tree trunk, and a large group of prickly-looking purple flowers that he called milk thistle. There were so many different plants that her grandfather showed her, it was impossible for Ali to remember them all.

"How do you know what all of these are?" Ali finally asked, amazed.

"My mom taught me when we went on walks. My grandfather, too. Way back when, people used some of the plants around here to make medicines. I couldn't tell you what they are used for, only what they are."

"Do you own all the land back here, too?" Ali asked, now interested in his family history.

Ben stopped a moment and stared at her. "What do you know about the land I own?"

"Chase said you owned a lot of the land around the lake and out toward the old dairy farm. He told me that the day that Halverson man came to the cabin," Ali told him.

"Humph. Halverson. Can't stand the guy." Ben grumbled. "But yes, Chase is right. My family has owned the land around here for years. My grandfather bought a lot of the land around here back in the 1920s, then my father inherited it and built the resort in the 40s. He never sold off any of it because he wanted the resort to have primary access to this lake. He liked that the resort was exclusive on the lake. It makes the fishing better, too. This is one of the few resorts people can come to without there being rows of houses all around the lake. And we don't have those damned jet skis flying around on the water, disturbing the wildlife."

"That's cool, owning so much land. How far back does the land go?"

"Oh, we're already off my property," Ben said. "Someday, I'll take you on a long hike and show you where the property lines are."

Ali nodded and smiled. She thought it would be neat to see all the land.

"You know, owning a lot of property only means I have money invested in it. It doesn't mean I'm rich or anything. Most people get that confused," Ben said.

"Oh, I know that. I just wondered about the land," Ali said.

"Hmmm. Well, I'm not exactly poor, either," Ben said. "I have enough for my needs. I don't really need that many material things, although I like having a nice truck and a good boat. Other than that, owning a lot of things doesn't mean that much to me."

Ali shrugged. "I've never really had all that much. Almost everything I own is either used or a gift from someone. Money is nice, but I wouldn't know what it felt like to have a lot of it."

Ben glanced at her but didn't reply.

They continued to walk. Soon, far ahead, Ali saw a faded red barn. "Is that the old dairy farm?" she asked.

"Yep. We're almost there."

As they neared the barn, a bellowing sound came from the woods on the left. Ben reached out his arm to stop Ali. "Did you hear that?"

Ali nodded. She looked around but didn't see anything. "What was it?" she whispered.

"Shhh. Listen."

A moment later, another bellowing sound came from the edge of the trees. Ben pointed, and Ali looked in that direction. A large, black bear stood on all fours, staring warily at them.

Ali's heart pounded. "Should we run?" she asked, keeping her eyes trained on the bear.

"Nope," Ben whispered.

"You're not going to shoot it, are you?" Ali asked, afraid he'd use the gun he'd brought along.

"Of course not," Ben whispered back. "It's not bear season, yet. Just hold on a moment and watch."

Ben and Ali stood still as the bear stepped farther out of the woods and into the clearing. The bear looked huge to Ali. She'd seen one in a zoo before, but never this close up.

The bear raised its light brown snout, opened its mouth, and bellowed once more, its large teeth glinting in the sun. Ali thought she was going to faint.

Slowly, Ben moved his arm and nudged Ali. He pointed in the direction of the old barn. She looked, and then she saw what he was pointing at. Two round, roly-poly bear cubs came bounding out from around the side of the barn and over to their mother. When the cubs were safely by their mother's side, she looked one last time at Ben and Ali, then turned and walked with her cubs back into the cover of the forest.

When the bears were out of sight, Ali let out the breath she'd been holding. "That was scary."

"Oh, it wasn't so bad," Ben said as they started walking again. "Just don't ever get yourself between a momma bear and her cubs or she will attack you."

"Good to know," Ali said. She didn't intend to go this deep into the woods alone, ever.

They approached the barn and walked around it. It still looked sturdy, it just had a few missing boards on the sides and there was ivy growing up the walls in places.

"So this is where the dairy was?" Ali asked. "Was it big? Like, lots of cows?"

Ben shook his head. "Nah, they didn't have a lot of milking cows, just enough to have milk to sell to a few of the local people. I guess, years before I was born, it was a larger farm with cattle and dairy cows, but through the years, the demand for fresh milk waned and they eventually closed up."

Ali looked around. "Where's the house?"

Ben pointed over to an open area a distance from the barn. A few trees shaded the space. "It used to stand there, but it finally fell down and the owners of the land burned what was left of it. All that's left of the house is the root cellar."

"How come no one lives here anymore? Does the same family still own it like you own your family's land?"

"There's not much money in farming these days, at least not for a small farm. This place only has about three hundred acres. As far as I know, the family still owns the land, but no one ever comes here anymore. So it just sits here, deserted."

Ali looked around and thought how sad it was that a place like this had been deserted. It was a pretty spot, and it held history. Except the history of it would be gone one day when no one remembered it anymore. Ali smiled over at her grandfather, happy that he'd shared this place with her.

"So, you really walked all this way to get pails of milk and carry them back?" she asked, and he launched into stories of his childhood when he and his brother used to make the trek for milk for the lodge. Ali listened, soaking it all in. The memories wouldn't die with her grandfather because they'd go on with her.

After a time, they turned and headed back home. Ben pointed out more wildflowers to her along the way. They eventually grew quiet, until Ben broke the silence.

"So, is everything going okay with you here? I noticed you and Chase were going to town every so often. Are you meeting other kids?"

Ali nodded. "Yeah. We've gone to a couple of movies and play pool with his friends at The Loon's Nest afterward. Kat's been nice, too. I still think it's weird that kids are allowed in a bar at night. My friends and I would never have been able to do that back home."

"Yeah, there's really no place for kids to go in this small town. The owner there is pretty careful about who he serves alcohol to, so it's safe. He doesn't want to lose his license." Ben hesitated a moment. "How about around here? Is your room okay? Do you need anything?"

Ali tilted her head and gazed at her grandfather. She could tell he wasn't used to having to worry about anyone else's needs, but his questions seemed sincere. "I like my room. I've got everything I need," she told him. "Well, except electricity whenever I need it," she teased.

Ben slid his eyes over to her. "Just let me know if you need something. I'm not such a grouch that I would have you go without." He grinned. "And you get all the electricity you need."

Ali laughed.

"Have you been going through your mom's things?" Ben asked.

Ali nodded.

"Anything interesting in those boxes?"

"Pretty much what you said there would be. Some old books, a few school yearbooks. I've been looking through those to see what she was like in school. I didn't know Mom was a cheerleader in school or that she played volleyball. I guess there's a lot I didn't know about her early years."

Ben beamed. "Yep. She made good grades, too. She never had too many friends though. Guess she was too busy with her activities and helping out at the resort. Most kids around here back then worked in their parents' businesses, so it wasn't unusual. She was a good girl, never going out to parties or getting in trouble."

Ali grew silent as the unsaid truth floated between them. *Never in trouble until she got pregnant with me.*

Ben cleared his throat. "Tell me about your mother. Was she happy? Sad? From the sounds of it, you didn't have an easy life. I'd like to know what she was like after she left here."

Ali kept her eyes on the ground. She didn't want to say anything that would make her mother sound terrible. She'd loved her mother, despite her problems. "I really don't want to talk about her right now," she said.

"Okay," Ben finally conceded. "But when you're ready, I'll listen. And I won't judge her."

Ali heard him but didn't respond. His last words, 'I won't judge her', spoke volumes to her. That was her biggest fear, him judging how *his Jen*, her mother, had turned out.

"Can you just tell me more about the plants and trees?" Ali asked.

Ben nodded, and began telling her names of flowers and showing her how to distinguish different varieties of trees.

# Chapter Fifteen

The Fourth of July holiday came and went in a blur. Jo had been right, the resort, as well as the surrounding resorts and the town, had been bustling with activity over the entire week. People were everywhere. The night of the Fourth, there were fireworks in town so Chase and Ali went to watch them. Ben and Jo stayed back at the resort, even though most of the guests were in town. The tiny town was packed, and street venders were selling popcorn, mini-donuts, sodas, hot dogs, and a variety of other foods along the street. The bars were hopping with activity, and a group of Girl Scouts were selling plastic glow-in-the-dark necklaces, bracelets, and rings as a fundraiser. Ali couldn't believe how crazy it was in the small town. The people of Auburn, young and old alike, all came out for the fun, and the tourists mingled among them.

The next week, it was a relief to be back to a normal busy for Ali. On Thursday in the late afternoon, Ali and Chase played hooky, with Jo's permission, and lounged around the lake in the canoe. Ali hadn't seen her grandfather all morning since breakfast, and thought he might be out on a fishing trip with guests. She didn't really give it much thought the rest of the day.

Ali and Chase checked on two of the loons' nests and found them both abandoned. Chase explained that meant the eggs had hatched and now the family of loons would be on the lake and not return to the nest. Ali was excited, hoping she'd see a baby loon, but they never came near any all day.

Ali and Chase came in to help serve supper and Ali was surprised that her grandfather wasn't there. "Is grandpa out with a fishing group?" she asked Jo. Jo told her he was busy with a project and he'd probably be by later to grab a bite. After supper, Ali and Jo cleaned up and then Ali and Chase took a walk to the point where they sat on the boulders and enjoyed the end of the day. Guests were milling about, heading to and from their cabins, so it wasn't the quietest place to be, but the view was always beautiful.

Sunset came late in July and Ali and Chase headed back to the lodge by nine o'clock before dusk fell. Ben had been keeping the generator running a little later since the days were longer, so Ali was surprised to see the cabin was still dark. Chase walked with her up to the cabin as dusk settled in.

"Looks like no shower tonight," Ali told Chase. "Grandpa must have come up early to bed."

The two said goodnight and Chase left as Ali went inside. She'd had a wonderful day spending time with Chase out in the canoe, and she felt happy and carefree. Even though Chase hadn't tried to kiss her again after Jake had teased them that day on the boat, she knew he cared about her and she anticipated their first kiss. She knew it would be dreamy and romantic, either out on the lake or at their favorite place on the point. She was flying high with these thoughts as she quietly entered the house to use the bathroom before going up to bed.

Ali was startled by the dark figure slumped in a chair at the dining room table in the nearly darkened house. After a moment, she recognized it was her grandfather sitting at one end of the table, his head in his hands.

"Grandpa?" she asked hesitantly. "Are you okay?" As she drew nearer, she saw what sat in front of him on the table. A half-empty bottle of whiskey.

"Just go on to bed," Ben said, sounding hoarse and tired.

He didn't even look up at her when he spoke.

Ali stood there, stunned. She hadn't seen her grandfather drink one ounce of alcohol the entire time she'd been here, not even a beer. And here he sat with a bottle of whiskey. Anger rose inside her. All the years of watching her mother drink herself into oblivion. All the nights of having to help her to bed. All the unpaid bills because drinking and drugs got in the way of her mother working. It bubbled up inside of Ali until she couldn't hold it in any longer.

"Oh, my God," Ali exclaimed. "You're just like her. You're a drunk, too. She got it from you!"

Ben raised his head a little and in the fading light, Ali saw his bloodshot eyes and the dark circles surrounding them. "Just go on to bed," Ben told her again. "Leave me be."

Tears formed in Ali's eyes despite her anger. She wouldn't do this again. She'd had enough. "I won't live with a drunk, do you hear? I won't. I can't do this again. I won't do this again!" Before Ben could reply, Ali turned on her heel and ran out of the cabin with tears streaming down her face. She ran all the way down to the lodge and in through the kitchen door.

Jo was kneading bread dough at the island when Ali burst into the kitchen. Ali ran to her and Jo folded her into her arms.

"What happened?" Jo asked. "Are you okay?"

Ali pulled away. "He's drunk. He's sitting up there in the dark, drinking whiskey. There's only half a bottle left. I can't do this, Jo. I can't live with a drunk. I won't!" Tears spilled down Ali's cheeks as she spoke. She was shaking in Jo's arms.

Jo sighed. "It's okay, dear. I promise you, everything's okay." Jo wiped the flour off her hands on her apron and led Ali to the table.

"No," Ali insisted, wiping away her tears with the tissues Jo had handed her. "He's just like my mom. I don't know how he's hid it all these weeks, but he is. I just can't live with him." Ali broke down in sobs and Jo comforted her, rubbing her back and telling her everything would be okay. Finally, when Ali's tears subsided, Jo looked at her with compassion and spoke.

"What you saw up there, dear, wasn't what it looked like. I had hoped that this year would be better, but when Ben didn't come down here at all today, I'd feared he'd locked himself away for the day, and apparently, he had."

Ali frowned. "What are you talking about? What do you mean it isn't what I thought? I saw him sitting in front of a bottle that had been drunk down halfway and he had red eyes. He was drinking."

Jo sighed. "Ali. Today is the anniversary of the day your grandmother Lizzie died."

Ali sat still a moment, letting this new information seep in. "But that doesn't excuse the drinking," she said.

Jo nodded. "I agree. But I also know that Ben hasn't had a drink of alcohol in seven years. Not since he stopped after a six week binge the year Lizzie died."

"But he had the bottle right there!" Ali insisted.

"Did you see him take a drink out of it?" Jo asked.

"No. But it was half-empty."

"Ali. What you saw was Ben sitting with a bottle of whiskey, staring at it, not drinking it. He does that every year on this day. That bottle has been half-empty since the day my husband told Ben he could no longer mourn Lizzie by losing himself in a bottle. He hasn't taken a drink from that bottle ever since."

Ali stared at Jo, confused. "I don't understand."

Jo ran her hand down Ali's hair, smoothing it in a comforting gesture. "I'm sorry, dear. I should have told you about today. I had hoped that Ben wouldn't fall into his grief this year, now that he had you here. You see, the day his Lizzie died was the worst day of his life. Actually, the second worse day of his life. Losing his Jen was the first. But Lizzie, why, he loved her so much, he couldn't bear to lose her. Even though he knew that day was coming, it still hit him like a brick. The very day he laid her to rest, he started a drinking binge that we thought for sure would kill him, too.

"You see, long ago, when Jen was young, Ben used to drink quite a bit. It never got in the way of his running the resort, and he was never a mean drunk, like his father had been sometimes, but he drank just the same. That's what men did in those days when they were stressed. They drank. Then, finally, Lizzie told him that he had to choose between his alcohol and his family, and he chose them. Lizzie had seen how Ben's father had behaved all those prior years and she wasn't about to have Ben end up that way. So, until the day Lizzie died, Ben hadn't had a drop of liquor."

Jo took a breath and continued. "Then Lizzie died, and it was more than Ben could take. He sat up in that cabin he'd built for her and drank. Every day my husband, Rick, would go up and check on him and bring him supper. And every day Ben had a fresh bottle of whiskey that he drowned his sorrows in. We had no idea how he got all that booze, he just did. Finally, Rick went up there and told him it was time to stop. Surprisingly, Ben did, and that's when he slowly started helping out around the lodge and started up his fishing and hunting tours again. That bottle you saw was the last bottle he'd opened. Now, every year, he sits up there and stares at it, but he doesn't touch it. Because he knows if he does, he may not be able to stop again."

"But his eyes were bloodshot," Ali said.

"Oh, sweetie. His eyes are red and swollen from crying. Yes, believe it or not, he sheds tears for his Lizzie. I know he seems like a crotchety old man to you, but he loved her so much. He lets out his pain of her loss in tears now, not by sinking into the bottle."

Ali sat there a moment, absorbing everything Jo had told

her. She looked up into Jo's kind eyes and saw something there that she'd never before acknowledged. Ali's eyes widened and she gasped. "You love him, don't you?"

Jo sat back and stared at Ali, stunned. "Why do you say that?"

"I saw it just now, in your eyes. The way you talk so kindly about him, the way you tease him, even the way I've seen you brush your hand over his arm or back as you pass by him. I just never put it together before. Geez, you even do his laundry. You're in love with him," Ali repeated.

A smile spread across Jo's face and she chuckled softly. "Yes, sweetie, I do. Don't ask me why, I just do. He's a good man, deep down inside."

"Does he love you back?" Ali asked, unable to believe her grandfather could truly love anyone.

"Yes, Ali. He does. But he seems to think we have to keep it a secret until Chase is off to college and you are through high school, so it's best if you don't say anything to him."

Ali sighed. So many secrets. It made her tired. "You're sure he doesn't drink, though? Are you positive?"

Jo nodded. "I believe him when he says he doesn't. Sometimes, you just have to believe in a person no matter what."

Ali wasn't sure of that. She'd believed in her mother, had hoped she'd be able to one day climb out of the dark hole she'd created for herself, but it had never happened. But if Jo believed in her grandfather, Ali would try.

Jo rose from the table. "Why don't you stay here tonight in one of the guest rooms? You can talk to Ben tomorrow with a clear head."

Ali agreed. She didn't want to go up to the cabin and confront him just yet. As she slipped into the snug bed in the small guest room after Jo had hugged her goodnight, she thought about her grandfather, sitting up there in the dark cabin, all alone, grieving for the woman he'd loved. Ali fell asleep with tears trickling down her cheeks.

* * *

The next day was chilly and damp as Ali made her way through the darkness to her grandfather's boat dock. She wasn't sure if he'd go out fishing this morning, but just in case, she went down to find out. They had a lot to talk about.

Sure enough, Ali found him just getting into the boat with a bucket of minnows in his hand. She didn't say a word, just stepped into the boat, slipped on her life jacket, and sat down. They took off at a fast clip across the lake and soon they had their fishing rods out, baited, and their lines in the water.

The morning was silent. Ali watched as the sun rose through the gray clouds, barely giving off light or heat. The damp day made no difference to the wildlife. One loon flew overhead, singing its crazy song, and another appeared in the distance, gliding gracefully through the water. Ducks flew in, as well as geese, and soon the world around the two silent figures in the boat came to life.

"I won't live with an alcoholic," Ali announced, her tone determined.

Ben looked her way and nodded slightly. "I can't blame you for that. You shouldn't have to."

"I mean it," Ali continued, annoyed by his answer. "I can't live with a drinker. Not again. Ever."

"I understand," Ben replied.

Silence ensued. Ali wasn't sure if he understood her completely. She thought about her mother, and how she'd struggled so hard with addiction.

"She got it from you, didn't she? My mom. She got her alcoholism from you," Ali said in a small voice.

Ben looked directly at her with sad eyes. "Yes, she did.

Like I got it from my father, and he from his. It's a family gene you don't want to pass down to your child, and I regret that deeply."

Ali felt bad that she'd accused him of something he couldn't control. "I didn't mean to say it was your fault."

"No. I know it can't be helped. But I wish with all my heart that my Jen had been spared that problem," Ben said. "And my biggest hope is that I didn't pass it down to you, too."

"I don't ever plan on finding out if I'm like that," Ali said. "I don't ever want to drink. Ever."

Ben nodded. "You're a smart girl."

"Please, just promise me you won't drink, okay?" Ali asked, her tone softer.

Ben nodded. "You don't have to worry about me. But if it makes any difference to you, I never took a drink from that bottle yesterday."

"Then why?" Ali asked. "Why do you sit there and stare at it?"

Ben took a deep breath. "It reminds me of how painful it was, losing my Lizzie. It helps me remember her, and how much I loved her."

Ali frowned. "That's how you honor her memory? Most people honor their loved ones by visiting their grave and leaving flowers, not by staring at a bottle of whiskey."

Ben looked at Ali as if she'd thrown cold water on him. "I never thought of it that way. I guess that is how I've been honoring her memory."

"Well, maybe you should change that. Geez, do you think Grandma Lizzie would like it if she knew you were remembering her that way? It's terrible." Ali knew she was pushing him, and she expected him to get angry, but he didn't. He only looked defeated.

"I don't have a grave to go to," Ben said. "Lizzie insisted

that she be cremated and have her ashes scattered across the lake. So I honored her wishes."

Ali sat there, aghast. *Was that even legal?* She didn't say anything though. She didn't want to upset him any more than she already had. "You could spend the day on the water. Or stare out at the lake, remembering the good times. Or you could sit with others who knew her and talk about her. But you don't have to sit in a dark cabin, brooding, staring at a bottle of booze."

Ben didn't reply. Looking at him, Ali could tell he was thinking about it. She just left it at that. She knew she'd said enough already.

The next morning, Ali came to the boat with a bundle in her arms, wrapped in newspaper.

"What on earth do you have there?" Ben asked after she'd climbed into the boat and was seated.

"You'll see," she said.

They took off across the lake to a new fishing spot. The morning was warmer and dryer than the morning before, and the sun shone through puffy white clouds as it made its way up into the topaz blue sky. Once they stopped, instead of pulling out her fishing rod, Ali carefully unwrapped the bundle. Inside the newspaper was a large bouquet of pink and white daisies.

Ben stared at the flowers warily. "Where did you get those?"

"I picked them yesterday along the road and down the trail we took to the dairy farm." When she saw the frown on his face she added, "Don't worry. Chase went with me. He brought along a gun so we'd be safe."

Ali picked up one of the pink daisies, pulled the flower from its stem, then carefully laid the flower face up in the lake. She watched as it slowly floated away from the boat.

"What are you doing?" Ben asked.

"I figured since the lake is where Grandma Lizzie's ashes

were spread, this is where she was the happiest, so I'm leaving flowers for her," Ali told him.

Ali continued pulling the flowers from their stems and setting the blooms in the water to drift away as Ben watched her. Soon, she had a lovely line of flowers decorating the surface of the lake. Ali handed a single flower to Ben. "Do you want to help me?" she asked.

Ben hesitated, but then reached for the flower, pulled off the bloom, and leaned over the side to drop it in the water. It floated along to join the rest. "How did you know that daisies were my Lizzie's favorite flower?"

"Jo told me. She said Grandma loved white roses, but I knew I wouldn't be able to get any of those. But then she told me her favorite wildflowers were daisies. I knew I could find those easily."

Ben lifted another flower from the pile and dropped the daisy bloom into the water. Then another. "You know, the very first bouquet of flowers I ever gave your grandmother was a bunch of pink and white daisies. I was young and poor and couldn't afford to buy flowers in a store. But she liked them all the same. She said she liked them even more because I had picked them myself."

Ali smiled. It was a sweet story.

Ben's expression softened as he looked at Ali. "This was a nice idea, Ali. Thank you."

"Maybe we can do this every year for Grandma," Ali said as she set the last flower in the water. "It can be our way of remembering her."

"I'd like that," Ben said. And the two sat and watched as the flowers spread out over the lake.

# Chapter Sixteen

As the summer days slipped by, Ali thought more and more about the possibility of her father still living somewhere around Auburn. She searched through her mother's possessions for clues to her father's identity, but found nothing. She thought the yearbooks might tell her something of his identity, so she scoured through each of them carefully from her mom's ninth grade year through her senior year. Ali paid particularly close attention to the senior yearbook. Ali's birthday was in January, so that meant her mother became pregnant in April of the previous year. From what Ali could tell, her mom hadn't realized she was pregnant until July, and that was the month she'd run away. The question was, who had she been seeing in April that year?

Ali's birth certificate didn't list the name of her father, so even though she had a copy of it, it told her nothing. It was as if her father had slipped into her mother's life for only a moment, then slipped away again. But Ali was determined to find out his identity.

In the box with the yearbooks, Ali had found a dried wrist corsage that was so old and brittle she didn't dare move it lest it fall apart. There was also a light blue bow tie in the box. These were obviously mementos from a prom night, but Ali didn't know for sure if it was her mother's senior prom or an earlier one. Chase had told her that since the school was so small, grades ten through twelve were allowed to go to the prom.

One Thursday afternoon while Ali and Jo were putting away that week's food delivery, Ali brought up the subject of her mother. Since Ali rarely spoke of Jen, Jo look up at her curiously.

"What do you want to know?" Jo asked as she stacked cans of vegetables in the panty.

"Was she popular? Did she have a lot of friends?" Ali asked while she busied herself with pouring a bag of sugar into an airtight container.

Jo stopped a moment, thinking. "I'm not sure if she was popular in school or not. There were only about two hundred kids in the entire school and that included sixth through twelfth grade. Everyone knew everyone. She rarely brought any friends out to the lodge. I remember your mother mostly being busy with homework or working around here. I guess she did attend school activities when she was older, like basketball and football games. She played a sport, too, but I don't remember what it was."

"It was volleyball," Ali said. "And she was a cheerleader, too. I saw it in her yearbooks."

Jo smiled. "I'm sorry. I don't remember much. It was a long time ago, and I was older than Jen and we didn't really talk much. I just remember her being a quiet girl who loved being out in the boat with her dad and going on long hikes in the woods."

Ali was disappointed that Jo didn't know much about her mother, but she didn't let that discourage her. That afternoon, she studied her mother's senior yearbook again. She looked through the prom pictures in the yearbook, then realized that they were from the year before. There were no pictures of her mother in the prom photos, and since the pictures were in black and white, she couldn't tell what color the tuxes or dresses were.

One thing Ali did notice was that a select group of kids showed up in the majority of the photos throughout all of her mother's yearbooks. These were the popular kids, the ones who ran the student council, participated in several sports and activities, and who put together the yearbook. One boy's face in particular kept popping up. He was the captain of the basketball team, the football quarterback, and the lead runner on the track team. He also had the lead in the senior play. He was cute; tall, slender, with dark, wavy hair, and piercing eyes. When Ali saw his name, however, she couldn't believe it. Jared Halverson. That was the same last name as the man her grandfather hated so much, but she couldn't remember if his first name was Jared. After all, there were six Halversons in the eleventh and twelfth grades, so it might not be him. And the Halverson she'd seen in town and at the cabin hadn't been cute. She decided she'd ask Chase what his first name was again.

Another thing in her mother's senior yearbook caught her eye as well. There were autographs with well wishes all over the front and back pages, just like her other yearbooks. All were written in blue ink. Ali assumed her mother carried around a blue pen when she had her friends and teachers sign the book. Except one passage written in the bottom corner of the back cover had been scribbled out with black ink. And not just scribbled as if someone had made a mistake. It was scribbled over with hard-pressed lines indented into the cover. It was as if her mother hadn't wanted anyone to ever read this passage. Ali looked at it under the light, but try as she might, she couldn't make out the words under the scribbling.

That evening, Ali and Chase went out on the lake in the canoe and floated near the shore across the lake where the cliff rose above them. A set of loons drifted by them, and Chase smiled and pointed for Ali to look.

"See there?" Chase whispered. "Look on that loon's back."

Ali stared at both loons. After a moment, she saw what Chase was pointing at. "Is that a baby on its back?" she asked excitedly.

"Two," Chase replied. "The males generally carry the chicks on their backs."

Ali watched as the downy gray chicks rode on their father's back like a float in a parade. They were so cute and cuddly looking, they made her smile. "They're adorable," she told Chase, who grinned back at her.

"They'll grow fast. We're lucky to have seen them this small," Chase said.

The two teens watched as the loons floated away. The evening was peaceful, and the lake was calm. The only ripple in the water was from the loons swimming by, and their canoe.

"We still have to find a day to go hiking on the old Indian Trail over here," Chase said, pointing to the cliff. "The view from the cliff is incredible."

Ali looked up to the top of the cliff. "It looks kind of scary."

Chase laughed. "It isn't. The trail goes up behind it. It's steep, but it's not like rock climbing. It's beautiful in the fall, but I'll be at school then."

Ali sighed, a sad expression crossing her face. "I keep forgetting that you're leaving for school this fall. Maybe I just try to forget because then I have to start school here, too. I'm not looking forward to that."

"You'll do fine. Kat will make sure you meet all the nice kids, and you can ignore the nasty ones like Emily and her little gang." Chase pretended to shiver, making Ali laugh.

"When do you have to leave?" she asked.

"The end of August. College starts the last week of August, and freshmen have to be there a week earlier for orientation."

"Wow. That's coming up fast. Are you excited?" Ali asked.

Chase shrugged. "I've wanted to go for years, but now that it's almost here, I'm not as excited as I thought I'd be. Maybe I'm afraid of going to a new school, too. Or maybe…"

He paused and leaned closer to Ali. "Maybe I'm sad about leaving you behind."

Ali moved in closer, too. "Remember," she said in whisper. "I'm not allowed to muck up your life."

Chase shook his head slightly. "Don't worry. I won't let you," he said with a wink. He leaned in even closer. So close, their noses almost touched. Ali's blue eyes stared into the depths of his baby blues. Just as their lips were about to meet, a loud motor went off across the lake and startled them. Both teens looked over to the dock where the lodge boats were kept. They saw Ben standing in one of the older motor boats, pulling on the engine's starter cord.

Ali and Chase both sighed and pulled apart. Chase started lazily paddling the canoe back toward the lodge.

The sight of her grandfather reminded Ali of a question she had for Chase. "What's the first name of that Halverson guy my grandfather hates so much?"

"Jared. Why?"

Ali told Chase about how she'd seen him in her mother's yearbooks and how he'd been one of the popular guys who were involved in everything. "You know. The annoying type in school."

Chase grinned. "Hey, I was like that. Good grades, sports, homecoming king, school yearbook committee. In a small school, everyone is involved in a lot of different things."

"Yeah, I suppose so. My high school was so big there was too much competition to be in everything. So, if you were part of the yearbook committee, tell me why prom pictures were always from the previous year."

"The yearbook was already off to the printers by the time prom came around. We didn't have enough time to get it in." Chase cocked his head and looked curiously at Ali. "Why?"

Ali bit her lip. She was afraid Chase might think her ideas were silly. "I wanted to see who my mom went to prom with in her senior year. There's a dried up corsage and a guy's bow tie in one of her boxes, but no prom picture."

"Why don't you just ask Ben? He'd know."

"I can't. I have a feeling he wouldn't tell me anyway."

Chase stopped paddling. "What are you thinking, Ali?"

Ali took a deep breath. "Prom was in April. I was born the next January. From what I've found out so far, my mom wasn't dating anyone in high school. It just seems logical to me that the person who took her to prom is my father."

Chase let out a low whistle. "Wow, that's big. Did you ask my mom?"

Ali nodded. "I just asked her general questions about my mom. She says she doesn't remember all that much though. I have a feeling she wants to stay neutral because of my grandfather."

"Yeah, I'm sure you're right. If Ben knows who your father is, he's probably told my mom, but she'd never tell you." Chase looked over at the dock where Ben was still working on the motor, then back at Ali. In a whisper, he said, "Have you figured out that Ben and my mom are involved?" Chase raised both hands and made quotation marks in the air when he said 'involved'.

Ali nodded, then giggled. "Eww, right? I just figured it out the other day. How long have you known?"

"A while. They think they're hiding it, but they're not doing a very good job of it."

"Does it bother you?" Ali asked. It used to bother her when her mother had a new boyfriend, but her mother never allowed her boyfriends to sleep over or live with them. Ali just hadn't liked sharing her mother with someone else when she was younger.

Chase shrugged. "No. I like Ben, and my mom's been alone for a long time. At least I know Ben is good to her and she'll have someone to take care of her when I leave for college. Well, now she'll have two people because now she'll have you, too."

'Now she'll have you, too.' Ali thought about those words as Chase guided the canoe to shore. It was nice feeling like she was part of a family. It had been just her and her mother for so long, that being part of a bigger family felt good.

"You kids have fun out there?" Ben asked as Chase and Ali walked past the dock after leaving the canoe on the beach. Chase nodded, but Ali noticed a grin on her grandfather's face. That same grin that he used when he was teasing. She wondered if he'd started that motor on purpose at the exact time Chase was going to kiss her. She wouldn't put it past the grouchy old man.

* * *

Ali sat next to Kat on the bench outside of the coffeehouse. Kat was taking a break from work and she and Ali were eating sandwiches and drinking sweet tea. It was afternoon and it was another warm day, perfect for sitting outside. The lunch rush had just subsided at the coffeehouse, and the new girl they'd hired and Kat's mom were finishing up with the last of the customers.

The small town was quiet with only a few people milling around. Two older women were folding towels in the Laundromat at the end of the block. The grocery store had three cars in front of it, and Chet's Hardware store's parking lot was empty. Across the way, music from the jukebox was drifting out into the street from The Loon's Nest, and every now and then someone walked in or out of the bar. Ali thought the town had a lazy, Mayberry feel to it. She wouldn't have been surprised to see Andy and Opie walk by.

"So, did Chase finally kiss you?" Kat asked, grinning at Ali.

Ali rolled her eyes. "What makes you think he wants to?"

"Don't be silly," Kat said, sipping her tea. "I saw the way he looked at you out there on the lake. He looks at you like that all the time, all gooey and lovey dovey. I figured by now you two would be an item."

Ali sighed. "I'm not looking to be an item with anyone. Chase is a really nice guy. And cute, too. But he's leaving in less than a month and I don't want to end up heartbroken."

Kat looked at her seriously. "Chase would never break your heart. He's too nice. If he wasn't serious about you, he wouldn't start anything."

Ali turned and studied Kat's face. "You really mean that, don't you?"

"I know Chase. I've known him since he was five years old. He doesn't take anyone for granted, and he never leads a girl on if he isn't serious about her. And to tell you the truth, I've never seen him look at anyone else the way he looks at you." Kat poked Ali's shoulder. "You're the real deal. He's got it bad for you. And I can tell you have it bad for him, too."

Ali smiled and looked away. She'd underestimated Kat when they'd first met. Kat was nosy and loved to gossip, but she was also observant, intuitive, and loyal. "I'm happy I have you for a friend, Kat. Being your friend has made living here easier."

"Thanks," Kat said, returning back to her light, cheerful self.

Both girls looked up and saw Jared Halverson standing across the street in front of The Loon's Nest, staring at them. Ali felt his eyes boring into her.

"Eww," Kat said quietly to Ali. "That guy gives me the creeps." Kat turned up the volume, put on a fake smile, and waved animatedly. "Hello, Mr. Halverson," she yelled.

Halverson stared at her a moment, nodded, then walked inside the bar.

Ali threw Kat a shocked look. "Why did you do that? You

just said you didn't like him."

"It made him go away, didn't it?"

Ali looked at the door to The Loon's Nest, wondering why Halverson always stared at her when she was in town. She'd run into him two other times, and both times he'd openly stared at her. It gave her the creeps, too.

"What is it about him that seems so sinister?" Ali asked Kat.

Kat shrugged. "I don't know. He's just kind of greasy and smarmy. He walks around town acting like he's some big shot, but no one really likes him. My dad says he's having money problems and that's why he hangs out in the bar a lot. A friend of my mom's says he hangs out in this town because he can't stand his wife and kids. He supposedly lives in a big house outside of Grand Rapids and lives a high lifestyle, yet he's always here. He gives me chills. And not in a good way."

Ali laughed. "Who gives you chills in a good way?" she teased.

"Wouldn't you like to know?" Kat said, smirking.

Kat got up and sighed. "I should go help with dishes or baking. My mom has to make up a few new batches of baked goods since we ran out this afternoon. The tourist season has been busy this year. We're always selling out of cookies and brownies."

"I'll come in before I go home," Ali told her friend as Kat went inside.

Ali sat a while longer, waiting for Megan to call her back. She'd called Megan earlier to talk, but she'd been busy at her mall job and said she'd call back during a break. It had been over an hour and Ali hadn't yet heard from her friend.

Ali sighed. She missed Megan and her other friends, but they seemed to have forgotten all about her. They were busy working at their summer jobs, hanging out at the beach, and with their boyfriends. Ali couldn't blame them. She'd been busy, too. But they didn't even email or text her anymore. Ali felt as if she'd fallen off the planet. She had never thought anything would ever come between her and Megan, but the miles between them had proven to be too much.

As Ali was about to stand up, Halverson came out of The Loon's Nest and stood there, staring at her again. Ali quickly picked up her empty plate and cup and headed into the coffeehouse.

Karen came over to the counter to take Ali's plate and refill her to-go cup with sweet tea. "Kat had to run an errand for me," she told Ali. "She said to tell you goodbye, and that she hopes you and Chase will be in town Friday night for the movie."

"Thanks," Ali said. She studied Karen a moment. Karen had said she was two years behind her mother in school. Maybe she'd know something about her mother's prom.

Ali took a deep breath for courage. "I was going through my mom's yearbooks and things," she said, trying to sound casual. "I saw she had some mementos from prom, but I didn't see any pictures. Were you at her senior prom?"

Karen smiled and handed Ali a full cup of tea. "Yes, I was. I was in tenth grade that year. It was my first prom. Your mom was so beautiful that night. I'm surprised you didn't find a picture, though. Everyone had one taken as they came into the gymnasium."

Ali's heart began to beat faster. Karen knew the answer to her question. But Ali didn't want to sound too desperate so she skirted around the only question she wanted the answer to and kept up the conversation. "I'd love to see a picture of my mom's dress. She had a blue bow tie with her things, so I figured her dress must have been blue, too."

"Oh, yes it was," Karen said, her eyes dreamy. "It was a beautiful topaz blue. She looked like a princess. You know, it was the nineties and everyone wore those puffy, shiny dresses, but not your mom. She had on a long, sweeping, blue satin dress that looked like something out of an old movie. I think Lizzie had made it for her. She took your breath away."

Ali couldn't believe she was this close to finding out the answer to her question. She was just about to ask Karen who her mom had gone to prom with when she heard footsteps behind her. Ali saw the dreamy look leave Karen's eyes as they narrowed slightly.

"Oh, hi Jared," Karen said in a flat voice. "We were just talking about Jen's and your senior prom. Jen was so beautiful that night, wasn't she?"

"Yes, she was," Jared said evenly. "Can I have a cup of black coffee to go please, Karen?"

"Sure." Karen picked up a cup. "Ali. Jared might have a picture from prom night. He was your mother's date."

A chill ran up Ali's spine. Jared. He was the owner of the blue bow tie. Ali slowly turned and looked up into the piercing, dark blue eyes of Jared Halverson. He looked down at her, no smile on his face.

Ali had to escape. "Thanks, Karen," she said as she made a hasty retreat. "I'll see you later." Ali all but ran out of the coffeehouse to the truck, climbed in the cab, and drove out of town as fast as she dared, tears filling her eyes.

# Chapter Seventeen

Ali sat in the boat with her fishing rod hanging over the side but her mind wasn't on the task at hand. It had been three days since she'd learned that her mom had gone to her senior prom with Jared Halverson, and even though she'd had time to digest that news, she still couldn't believe it. That day after leaving the coffeehouse, she'd felt physically ill and had stopped by the side of the road to throw up her lunch. The idea that Jared Halverson, creepy, greasy Jared Halverson, might be her father made her stomach churn. It was all she could do that afternoon and evening to go about her duties without breaking down in tears. But she had, and now, days later, her mind was still having trouble accepting the truth. There was no other explanation. No one knew of any other guy her mother had dated or been seeing. He was the obvious person. He was her father.

Ali hadn't told anyone what she'd found out, not even Chase. She didn't even know if she could get the words to come out of her mouth, it disgusted her so much. She'd gone through the days and nights feeling like she was in a trance, holding this terrible secret inside her.

"You've been awfully quiet. Something going on?"

Her grandfather's deep voice broke the silence and made Ali jump. "No. I'm just concentrating on fishing, that's all," she told him.

"You're not concentrating very well. I saw the end of your

rod jiggle a bit and you didn't even notice. That's not like you. Are you sure everything's fine?"

Ali frowned. Since when did her grandfather pay enough attention to her to actually ask her how she was feeling? "Everything's fine," she insisted.

"Humph," was Ben's only answer.

Ali stared out at the lake as the sun came up. In the distance, she saw a dark object moving awkwardly in the water. She pointed it out to her grandfather. "What's that?"

Ben squinted and stared, then shrugged. He pulled a pair of binoculars out of the glove compartment, uncapped the ends, and then put them up to his eyes. After a moment, he swore under his breath. "Dammit. Looks like a loon is tangled up in something. Pull in your line and we'll see if we can get a closer look."

Ali quickly pulled in her line and rod and turned in her seat. Ben turned the boat in the direction of the loon and moved slowly through the water so as not to scare it. As they neared the loon, Ali saw the bird was struggling to open its wings, and its head was down at an odd angle. The loon rolled in the water, tried unsuccessfully to flap its wings, then rolled again, stopping for a moment before trying again.

Ben cut the boat's engine about ten feet from the loon. "He's tangled in fishing line. Must have gone through a snarl underwater and now he can't get it off."

Ali leaned over the side of the boat, watching the poor bird struggle. "What can we do?" she asked.

"Nothing we can do. That loon won't let us near him, let alone cut fishing line off him," Ben said.

Ali's eyes grew wide as she stared at her grandfather. "We can't just let him die that way. We have to help him," she insisted.

"There's no helping him, Ali. Even if you could get close enough to hold onto him while I try to cut the line off, a wild bird like that will peck your hands bloody with that sharp beak."

Tears filled Ali's eyes as she watched the beautiful bird struggle to break free. Just last week she and Chase had seen one of the loons with baby chicks on his back. This could be that very one. Ali turned to her grandfather as the tears rolled down her cheeks. "We have to help him. We have to!" she insisted. "He might have a family. They need him. We can't let him die."

"Ali, listen to me. Things like this happen. I'm sorry, but there's nothing we can do."

Angry now, Ali stood and tightened her life jacket. "Hand me the scissors. If you won't help him, I will." She sat on the edge of the boat, one leg hanging over the water.

Ben reached out and grabbed her arm, his face creased with anger. "Whoa! You're not jumping into that water to help that stupid bird. Are you crazy?"

"Then help him!" Ali said, pleading. "Help him!"

Ben stared at Ali a moment, then looked over at the loon. He rolled his eyes and sighed heavily. "Dammit. Fine. Get back in this boat and sit down." He reached into his toolbox and pulled out a pair of heavy work gloves that he wore when he handled large fish with spiny fins. He handed them to Ali. "Put these on."

Ali did as he told her, tears still falling down her cheeks. She watched as her grandfather slowly moved the boat closer to the loon. The bird didn't try to move away. It looked as if it had spent all its energy trying to get free and was sitting on the water, resting, before it began wrestling with the line again.

Ben cut the engine and pulled out a pair of needle-nosed cutters. "Okay. Try grabbing around his wings from up behind. Hold your hands under him and just steady him. If he doesn't fight you, I'll try cutting the line."

Ali carefully leaned over the side of the boat, feeling it tip under her weight. She took a breath, then reached for the loon. After two tries, she was able to grasp him from underneath and around the back part of his wings. The loon squawked, but didn't move. Its upper neck was also tangled in the line, so he wasn't able to peck at Ali's hands.

Ben leaned over, which made the boat tip even farther down toward the water. He studied the line a moment. "I'm looking for a spot to cut that might make the whole line unravel," he told Ali quietly so as not to scare the loon more. He reached over the bird and snipped line that went directly across his back. The sound of the cutters made the bird jump and Ali lost her grip on it. She would have fallen in the lake head first if her grandfather hadn't grabbed her by the back of her life jacket.

They both watched the loon struggle with the line. It still didn't come loose.

"It didn't work," Ali said. "We have to try again."

Ben looked over at her, sighed, but didn't say a word. He turned on the engine again and moved close to the loon, then shut it off. Once again, Ali grabbed the loon around its underbelly and wings and held it firm. Ben didn't waste any time. He snipped the line in several places, being careful not to cut the loon. The bird struggled in Ali's grasp and slipped away again.

Ali held her breath and watched as the loon wiggled and rolled, then tried to open its wings. After a moment, the loon raised his head high and his wings opened wide. He flapped them wildly as he rose to a standing position on the water and called out his laughing tune.

Ali turned to her grandfather, her eyes glistening with tears. "We did it! We saved him." She reached out and hugged Ben hard. "He's going to be okay."

Ben smiled wide and wrapped his arms around Ali in return. "By God, we did it," he said, surprise filling his voice.

Ali pulled away and looked up into her grandfather's deep blue eyes. They looked warm and kind and happy.

"Hey, we saved him. Why are you still crying?" Ben asked.

"Because I'm so happy," Ali said, wiping at her tears. "He can go back to his family. They won't have to live without him."

Ben smiled down at her again and Ali reached out and hugged him once more. Ben folded her into his arms, bringing her close to his heart.

\* \* \*

Ben stood on the back porch of the lodge and watched as Ali and Chase walked around toward the front. He wondered where they were headed. It was evening, after supper, and the warmth of the day was cooling off. It had only been this morning that he and Ali had saved the loon tangled in the fishing line. They'd told the story to Chase and Jo during breakfast, and again at supper, still amazed they were able to save the majestic bird. Ben readily admitted that if Ali hadn't been there, he'd have never tried to cut the line off of the loon.

"I'm surprised you didn't just shoot it," Chase had said, grinning at Ben.

"Oh, geez. Don't give him any ideas," Ali had responded, rolling her eyes.

"Hey. I'm not that cold hearted. Besides, it's illegal to shoot the state bird," Ben had said. Groans from the others at the table had followed.

Ben had been proud of Ali. She'd stuck to her guns and insisted they help the silly loon. Then she'd held onto it without even flinching. Ali had grit. She was a true Jenson. And for reasons he couldn't even fathom, the incident had made him feel closer to her.

Now, Ben turned from the window and headed back into

the kitchen. Jo was standing at the island, stirring batter for brownies in a large bowl.

"Where do you think those kids head off to in the evening?" Ben asked, sitting down on the bench at the table.

Jo shrugged. "Just walking, I suppose. Maybe out to the point. Why?"

"No reason," Ben said. "Don't you wonder, though, about them spending so much time together? I mean, they seem to be getting closer, and they are teenagers, after all. Anything could happen."

Jo sighed. "Ben. We've been over this before. They're both smart kids. We just have to trust them. I highly doubt that Ali is going to do anything that would jeopardize her future. And Chase wouldn't either."

"Humph," Ben grunted. "My Jen was a smart girl too, remember? Things happen in the heat of the moment and all sense flies out the window."

Jo grinned and walked around the island and over to Ben. She sat down on his lap and wrapped her arms around his neck. Ben's arms encircled her waist. "Tell me about it," she said, her eyes sparkling, teasing.

Ben leaned toward her and kissed her gently on the lips. Jo responded. After a moment, they pulled apart. "See what I mean?" Ben said softly. "All sense just flies out the window."

Jo laughed, pulled Ben closer, and kissed him again.

\* \* \*

Once Ali and Chase were out of sight of the lodge, they clasped hands and headed through the woods to the point. Chase helped Ali up on one of the large boulders and they sat there together, her in front and him behind her so she could lean back into him. Chase wrapped his arms around her waist, holding her close. They sat this way for a time, quietly watching as loons flew to and fro and ducks and geese swam and searched for food. High above, an eagle circled in search of dinner.

Ali sighed and snuggled deeper into Chase's embrace. This was the first time in days she'd felt calm. She was happy that they'd forgone the movie in town and decided to stay here and spend time alone together at the point.

"That was quite an adventure you and Ben had this morning. I wish I had seen it," Chase said.

Ali nodded. Saving the loon with her grandfather had been incredible. Yet, she felt that more happened in that moment than just saving the loon. She felt they had connected, in a way they hadn't been able to before. It had felt good, like she was a real part of the family. Family. That one word brought back all she'd been feeling before saving the loon. Ali turned to face Chase, her eyes sad.

"What's wrong?" Chase asked, looking confused.

"Something happened this week at the coffeehouse," Ali said.

Chase frowned. "What?"

"I was talking to Karen about my mom and her senior prom. Karen said she remembered who my mother had gone to prom with, but before I could ask her, Jared Halverson walked in."

"What happened?"

Ali took a deep breath. "Karen mentioned to Jared that we were talking about his senior prom. Then she told me that Jared might have a prom photo of my mother because he was her date that night."

Chase's mouth dropped open. "Jared Halverson? He took your mother to prom?"

Ali nodded as tears began to form in her eyes. "Jared Halverson is my father," she said in a whisper. As soon as the words spilled from her lips, she began to cry.

Chase held Ali close as she cried on his shoulder. "No, Ali. That doesn't mean he's your father. We have no proof. It could have been someone else."

Ali pulled away, swiping at her tears with her sweatshirt sleeve. "I looked right into his face that day. He was only inches away from me. He has dark hair and those dark blue eyes. Just like mine. He has to be my father, whether I like it or not."

Chase shook his head. "That doesn't mean a thing. Ben has dark hair and blue eyes, too. That's where yours come from. Not Jared."

"But what if he is? I can't stand the thought of him being related to me, but maybe he is," Ali said.

"I don't know," Chase finally said. "You should do more checking. And you should just ask Ben. Maybe your mother knew another kid that spring. Maybe it was someone she met here at the lodge. It could have been anybody."

"No, Chase. By everyone's accounts, my mom wasn't like that. I don't dare ask my grandfather. And if I did, he wouldn't tell me anyway. I don't know what to do."

Chase held Ali close as the sun dropped low in the sky. Ali didn't know how she was going to find out for sure if Halverson was her father, but she knew she had to find out, somehow.

# Chapter Eighteen

Ali found herself drawn to town more often as the summer days slipped by. If Ben or Jo needed an errand run, she offered. If she had an hour or more of time off, she asked Ben if she could use the truck to go to town. She used the excuse that she wanted to talk to Megan in California and they believed her. But talking to Megan wasn't the real reason she wanted to go. She went to sit in front of the coffeehouse and try to catch a glimpse of Jared Halverson. She thought if she could watch him, she might find some familiar trait about him that might prove or disprove her theory that he was her father. But every time she saw him, she couldn't help but cringe at the idea of being related to him.

One afternoon as Ali sat outside the coffeehouse with Kat, sipping a caramel cappuccino and eating a brownie that Kat had brought out for her, Halverson walked down the sidewalk on the opposite side of the street and entered The Loon's Nest. Ali saw nothing in the way he moved or walked that hinted at the fact that they were related.

"Hard to believe he was considered a hunk back in his day, huh?" Kat asked, wrinkling her nose at the sight of Halverson.

Ali turned and looked over at Kat. "Really? How do you know that?"

"My mom told me that the other day after he'd been in for coffee," Kat said. "He always gets a cup of black coffee after sitting all afternoon in The Loon's Nest. I guess he thinks it will sober him up before he drives home."

Ali could care less about his coffee drinking habits. She wanted to know more of what Karen had said. "What about the hunk thing?"

Kat shrugged. "Guess he was the cutest guy in high school back then. All the girls wanted to go out with him. My mom said that your mom was thrilled when he'd asked her to the prom and all the other senior girls were jealous. She figured your mom had a big crush on him like all the other girls did."

Ali stared at The Loon's Nest as she thought about this. She'd seen pictures of him in the old yearbooks, and she guessed that he was okay looking for his time. She'd never thought that he was that special, though. "Did your mom say anything else?"

"Just that he never dated anyone for very long. One or two dates. She said he wasn't really that nice to the girls. He was too cocky. Too full of himself. As far as I'm concerned, he still is. He's nothing like Chase is. Everyone wants to date Chase, too, but he's always nice to all the girls and honest, too. Chase never takes advantage of his good looks and sweet personality to use girls. That just makes girls like him even more."

Ali thought about what Kat had said all the rest of that day and that evening as she sat in her bedroom, the yearbooks spread out around her. Had Halverson used his charm on her mom to get her to have sex with him, then dumped her as fast as he had all the other girls? Was that why her mother had never told her about him?

Ali opened her mother's senior yearbook again and looked through the pages, reading all the words her friends had written. She found the back corner where the words were scribbled out, held it up to the light but couldn't read through the scribbling. If only it had been written on one of the pages, she might have seen what was written from the other side when held up to the light. She sensed that the scribbled out words had been written by Halverson, and her mother had blocked them out after she was betrayed by him. No other explanation made sense.

Using her thumbnail, Ali scraped at the corner of the yearbook cover to see if the paper would peel off a little so she could look at the back of it. To her surprise, the paper peeled off easily and from behind it a five by seven photo fell out. Ali gasped. There, in full color, were her mom and Jared Halverson dressed up for prom, standing in a typical prom photo pose. Her mom wore the wrist corsage and Halverson wore the blue bow tie.

Ali stared at the young woman who only nine months later would become her mother. She was beautiful. Karen had been right, her mother's topaz blue dress shimmered under the lights and swept to the floor like a Hollywood starlet's gown. Her mom's light blond hair was up, showing off her creamy shoulders, and her blue eyes sparkled in the light. To Ali's surprise, Halverson looked handsome in his black tux with a topaz blue vest, cummerbund, and bow tie. Her mother looked so young and innocent, standing there in front of the black wall with gold stars on it, that it brought tears to Ali's eyes. This was before life had worn her mother down, when her mother's eyes were clear and bright instead of dulled from drugs and alcohol. This was before her mother became fragile and could no longer handle reality. Before Ali was born and changed everything.

Ali brushed away tears and turned the photo over. These words had also been scribbled over, but Ali could still read them. It said, "Prom, 1996, Jen and Jared". Surrounding the words, her mother had drawn hearts and stars, but then had scribbled over it all with a heavy, black pen.

"He broke her heart," Ali said aloud. "He'd taken her to

prom, made her feel special, then used her and threw her away." Ali could only imagine how devastated her mother had felt when she found out that the boy she'd crushed on hadn't really cared about her at all. She'd just been another girl. Except that her mother hadn't turned out to be just another girl. She'd ended up being the mother of his child.

Ali lifted the yearbook up to the light from the oil lamp to try and read the words that were scribbled out. It was a short passage, and she was reading it backwards, but she could make it out just the same. "It was a blast! JH."

"Jerk," Ali said. "What an obnoxious jerk." Ali imagined her mother had been so distraught, she'd scribbled over the words in the yearbook and on the photo, and hidden the photo away so no one could see evidence of who she'd been in love with.

Ali slipped the photo back into the lining and gently closed the yearbook. She packed it away in the box and closed the lid, then slipped back into bed and curled up under her mother's quilt. Outside, the sounds of night drifted in her open windows. The flame from the oil lamp flickered, causing shadows to bounce around on the ceiling and walls. Ali just lay there, thinking. Halverson knew she was his daughter. He had to. That's why he stared at her every time he passed by her. He knew, but he wasn't going to acknowledge her. She could almost bet her grandfather knew, or at least suspected, that Halverson was her father, too. Why else would he hate the man so much? Well, she decided, Halverson wasn't going to get away with ignoring her so easily. As she lay there in bed, she decided that it was time Halverson met his daughter, and at least acknowledge her existence.

* * *

The next day Ali asked her grandfather if she could use the

truck to go into town and visit with Kat for a while. She brought it up casually at breakfast, thinking it would be like any other day and he'd just agree to let her go. What she hadn't counted on was Chase offering to take her to town instead.

"I have to go in and get a few things at the hardware store for Mom," Chase said between bites of pancakes. "You can ride with me."

Ali didn't dare say no or else it would look suspicious. So she agreed, and they were off to town later in the afternoon. With any luck, Chase would drop her off at the coffeehouse and she'd finish her errand before Chase was done with his.

Ali spoke very little as she fidgeted with her phone on the drive into town. When they arrived, Chase pulled into Chet's parking lot and stopped the truck.

"Want to come in? I won't be long," Chase said, smiling.

"I think I'll just walk down to the coffeehouse and see Kat," Ali replied as she climbed down from the truck's cab.

Chase's smile faded. "Is everything okay?" he asked.

Ali put on a fake smile. "Sure. Why wouldn't it be? I'll see you in a few minutes." She turned and walked down the street at a fast clip.

Once there, Ali went inside and ordered sweet tea from Karen. Karen told her that Kat wasn't working that day and was at home, but she could call Kat to let her know Ali was in town.

"Oh, no, that's okay. I'm waiting for Chase anyway," Ali told her. Ali was actually relieved that Kat wasn't there. The fewer people who knew what she was about to do, the better.

Ali went out and sat on the bench swing in front of the coffeehouse, waiting for Halverson to go into The Loon's Nest. She hoped she wasn't late. Halverson usually went there every day about this time, so Ali was counting on him sticking to his usual schedule. With any luck, he'd show up before Chase did, and she'd be able to approach him without Chase knowing.

Unfortunately, Ali's luck didn't hold. Chase's truck came

down the street a few minutes later and parked in front of the coffeehouse. Ali pulled out her phone and pretended she was texting Megan so it would look like she'd been busy instead of scoping out Halverson.

"Want anything?" Chase asked when he walked up to Ali. "I'm going to get a cookie."

Ali shook her head and Chase went on inside. Ali heard Chase say hello to Karen. It was past two o'clock, and Halverson still hadn't come down the street. Ali was worried. What if he didn't come today? What if he was actually working and wasn't anywhere near Auburn? She'd built up her nerve to approach him today and she wasn't sure if she could make herself do it another day instead.

"What'cha looking at?" Chase asked as he came out the door and sat down beside Ali.

Ali jumped. She turned and looked at Chase. "What?"

Chase chuckled. "It looked like you were boring a hole through that wall across the street with your eyes. I was wondering what you were looking at."

"I was just spacing out, I guess," Ali said.

They sat there a while as Ali sipped her sweet tea and Chase ate his cookie. The day was cloudy and breezy, not exactly a beautiful day but at least it wasn't hot and humid. Ali kept searching the sidewalks for Halverson, but he hadn't shown up yet.

"Ready to go home?" Chase asked.

"No!" Ali blurted out. She realized how desperate she sounded, so she added, "I just want to sit here a while."

Chase sat back and folded his arms. He looked directly at Ali. "Okay. What's going on?"

Ali tried to look contrite. "Nothing."

"I may not have known you long," Chase said, "but I know you pretty well. Something is going on with you. Just tell me, okay?"

Ali bit her lip. She realized that if Halverson did show up and walk into The Loon's Nest, Chase would know what she was doing anyway. "Okay," she finally said. "But this is just between you and me." Chase nodded and Ali took a deep breath. "I'm waiting for Jared Halverson to go into The Loon's Nest."

Chase frowned. "Why?"

"I'm going to tell him he has a daughter."

Chase slumped back on the bench, his eyes wide. "Are you kidding me? Or maybe I should ask, are you crazy? You can't just go up to him and say that. You don't even know if it's true."

"I know enough to believe it's true," Ali told him. "I have to do this, Chase. I have to do this for my mom."

Out of the corner of her eye, Ali saw Halverson walking down the street. She turned her head and so did Chase. They watched as he turned into The Loon's Nest. Ali set down her cup and started to rise.

Chase grasped her hand. "Don't Ali. Please. Talk to Ben first. Make sure it's really Halverson. Don't go in there. You may not like what you hear."

Ali wavered a moment, then slipped her hand from Chase's. "I have to do this, Chase. No matter what happens." She took off across the street. Without hesitating, Chase followed her.

Ali stepped into The Loon's Nest and stopped, letting her eyes adjust to the darkened room. She'd been in here countless times with Chase to play foosball or pool after a movie. To the right was the bar that ran along the side of the room. Booths lined the other wall and tables sat in the middle. The game tables were off in the back room. A flat screen television hung up over the bar. Today, it was playing an old movie without the sound on. Luke, the owner, smiled over at Ali as she entered. He was tall and heavyset with unruly black hair and a goatee, but he was a teddy bear of a man. The only other person in the room was Halverson, sitting at the end of the bar with a mug of beer in front of him.

Behind her, Ali heard someone enter the door and she turned to see Chase standing there, slowly shaking his head at her. But Ali couldn't stop now. It was now or never.

Ali approached the bar and stopped to stand beside Halverson who was sitting on a tall barstool. Halverson turned and looked at her. Sitting on the stool, he was at eye level with Ali. His eyes were dull and uncaring.

"Hmmm. I was wondering how long it would be before you showed up," Halverson said without emotion. "So, did your grandfather send you to see me?"

Ali frowned. She hadn't expected him to talk first, much less accuse her grandfather of instigating their meeting. "No," she said evenly. "I came here on my own."

Halverson took a drink of his beer then turned back to Ali. "Well, say what you have to say then and get it over with."

Ali stared at him, unsure if she even wanted to continue. Despite his dress slacks and button down shirt, he looked almost ragged. His hair was mussed, his face was already sprouting a five o'clock shadow, and his breath smelled of alcohol. For sixteen years she'd wanted a father, but not this man. He was the exact opposite of what she'd pictured as her father.

"Well?" Halverson said, staring at her with those dark, piercing eyes.

"You went to the prom with my mother. Nine months later I was born. Are you my father?" Ali asked, plain and simple.

Halverson grunted. "Did Jen tell you I was?"

Ali shook her head slowly. "She never told me who my father was."

"Good. Then I can deny it all I want." Halverson turned

away and stared down into his beer.

"Are you my father?" Ali asked again.

Halverson sighed. "Listen, kid. If you want something from me, you're too late. You're not going to get a damned thing. I already have a wife and three kids who have sucked the life and money out of me. Besides, I gave up any claim to you the day I told Jen I'd pay for the abortion to get her off my back. I told her then that if she kept the kid, she was on her own."

Ali's mouth dropped open. "You wanted her to kill me?"

Halverson's lips became a thin line. "You weren't a person yet. You were just a mistake that was going to ruin my life. Don't you get it? I had a college basketball scholarship and I was going places. The last thing I needed was some pregnant girl insisting I take care of her and a kid."

Ali stood there, stunned. She couldn't believe the cold words coming from this man. How could anyone be so heartless? "Didn't you ever even wonder about me or what had happened to my mom? You had a child out in the world somewhere, and you never even wanted to know who she was or what had become of her?"

Halverson leveled his gaze on Ali. "No. I never gave it another thought until you came back here. And once you walk out that door, I'll never think about you again."

Ali hadn't expected anything from this man, but the cruelty of his words was more than she could take. Tears filled her eyes as anger rose inside her. "I'm glad I never knew you," she spat at him. "My life was better off without you in it. You're a cruel, cold, heartless creep that nobody likes or wants to be around. I hope you enjoy the rest of your miserable, drunken life." Ali turned on her heel and stormed out of the bar as Halverson's laughter followed her outside.

Chase followed her back to the truck and once inside, Ali immediately broke down in tears. When he tried to comfort her, Ali only brushed him away and told him to take her home.

* * *

Ben was pulling fishing gear out of a boat and Jo was weeding her flower garden by the porch when Chase pulled up alone in his truck.

"Oh, good, you're back," Ben said. "The group I took out caught a few good ones, so I'll need help cleaning them before supper. Where's Ali?"

"I left her up at the cabin," Chase said.

"Well, go on up and tell her to come help Jo. She just got a call from a family that wants to rent a cabin for the week so the Moose cabin needs cleaning before tonight," Ben said.

Chase looked between Ben and his mother. "I can go clean up the cabin, then I'll help you with the fish," he told Ben.

Ben and Jo both stared at Chase.

"Don't be silly. That's Ali's job. Go on and get her," Ben said.

Chase was about to protest when Jo stepped in. "Is Ali okay? Did something happen in town?"

Chase stood there a moment as if debating what to say. Finally, he spoke. "Ali talked with Jared Halverson in town today. He was awful to her."

Ben's face creased with anger. "Why in the hell would Ali talk to Halverson?"

"She figured out that he's her father," Chase said. "She wanted to confront him about it. He didn't deny it. In fact, he pretty much said he was her father. Then he said some pretty nasty things to her, like he didn't care that she was his daughter, and he had wanted Jen to abort the pregnancy. It was terrible. Ali cried the entire way home and said she wanted to be alone for a while."

Ben held in his rage the entire time Chase talked, but his face was red and his eyes sparked with hatred.

"That God damned son of a bitch," Ben growled. "He doesn't deserve to walk the same planet as my Ali." Ben dropped what he'd been carrying and pulled the truck keys out of his pocket. "Where was he when this happened?" he asked Chase.

"Ben, what are you going to do?" Jo asked.

"What I should have done years ago," Ben told her with certainty. He turned back to Chase. "Where?"

"The Loon's Nest," Chase told him.

Ben headed over to his truck with Jo right behind him. "Ben, stop. Don't do anything you'll regret."

Ben turned and looked at Jo, his expression a cross between anger and sadness. "Sweetie, I already have too many regrets. This is one thing I won't regret." He hopped up into the cab and took off.

It wasn't long before Ben was in town and parked outside The Loon's Nest. He stepped out of his truck and headed with purpose into the bar. Luke saw him first.

"Hey Ben, how's it going?" Luke asked.

Ben nodded but didn't answer. There was only one person in this place he had business with and that man was sitting at the end of the bar.

Halverson turned around as Ben approached him. "Well, Ben Jenson, imagine seeing you here. Just had a nice little talk with your granddaughter."

Ben walked right up to Halverson and punched him in the face so hard he flew off his barstool and onto the floor.

Halverson lay there a moment, stunned. He sat up and wiped his jaw with the back of his hand. Blood smeared over his hand. "What the hell, Ben? Are you crazy?"

Ben stood over Halverson. "I should have done that seventeen years ago."

Halverson got up slowly, lost his balance, then regained it and leaned against a barstool. "I could sue you, you crazy old man. I could put you in jail for hitting me. Luke, call the Sheriff. I'm pressing charges."

Ben took a step toward Halverson. Halverson backed away closer to the bar. "Yeah. You should call the Sheriff," Ben said. "Have him arrest me. Then it will be in all the papers why I hit you, you lousy excuse for a man. Wouldn't your wife and children love reading all about why I hit you? How you got my daughter pregnant. How you've ignored the fact that you've had a daughter all these years. In fact, I bet the law will get involved and make you pay years and years of overdue child support. Yup. Go ahead and call the Sheriff. I'll enjoy every minute of running your name through the mud."

Halverson sneered at Ben.

Ben moved his face closer to Halverson. "Now listen to me, you weasel. Don't you ever talk to my granddaughter again. Don't walk past her, don't even look at her. If you see her heading in your direction you'd better cross the street to avoid her. Cause if I ever hear that you even breathed the same air as her, I'll come find you and finish this once and for all."

"Hey. She came to me. I didn't go search her out," Halverson whined.

"You can bet she'll never do that again," Ben told him. "Cause after today, you're dead to her. You aren't worth the dirt on the bottom her shoes, you scumbag. If I were you, I'd stay away from Auburn entirely, because you aren't welcome here."

"Did you hear that, Luke?" Halverson asked. "Did you hear him threaten me?"

Luke shook his head. "I didn't hear a thing."

Halverson threw a disgusted look at Luke, then at Ben, and then he got up and walked out the door.

"See you later, Luke," Ben said, waving as he left the bar.

When Ben got back into his truck, he looked at his right hand and winced. His knuckles were swollen and bleeding from hitting Halverson's jaw so hard. "Shit that hurt," he said under his breath, then turned the truck toward home.

# Chapter Nineteen

When Ben arrived home, he pulled into the cabin's driveway, walked inside the garage, and headed up the steps to Ali's room. Gingerly, he knocked on her door. "Ali? Are you in there?" From where he stood outside the room, he heard her shuffling around.

"I was just getting ready to come down to the lodge," Ali said, her voice sounding strained.

"Can I come in?" Ben asked.

"Okay," Ali replied in a small voice.

Ben entered Ali's room. She was sitting on the trunk at the foot of her bed. He noticed her eyes were red and swollen, even though she'd applied makeup to conceal it. But no amount of makeup could cover up the sadness that shone in her blue eyes.

"Are you okay?" he asked, standing in the center of the room. He was nervous. Not more than thirty minutes before he'd punched out a man almost half his age without a qualm. But this teenage girl in front of him had a way of turning his bravado to mush. Anger had fueled his reaction to Halverson. Anger was an emotion he could deal with. But a crying teenage girl was something that he had little experience with, especially when it came to saying the right thing.

Ali nodded her answer to his question, but it was apparent she was anything but fine.

Ben pulled out the chair at the desk and sat down across

from Ali. "Chase told us what happened with Halverson," he said gently.

Ali covered her face with her hands. "I'm such an idiot," she said, choking back tears. "I should have listened to Chase. I never should have talked to Halverson. He's a jerk. No, he's more than that. He's an asshole!"

"Well, we can both agree on that," Ben said with a grin.

Ali dropped her hands and looked at her grandfather with serious eyes. "You knew, didn't you? You knew he was my father. Is that why you hate him so much?"

Ben nodded. "I suspected he was, but I didn't know for sure until today. Jen never told us, and I'm assuming she never told you, either."

Ali wiped the tears from her eyes with the back of her hand. "She never told me anything about him. I guess I can understand why now. He must have been as coldhearted then as he is now. Mom was protecting me by not telling me."

Ben reached out and took both of Ali's hands in his. "I'm sure my Jen understood that he wasn't good enough for you to call your father. And you don't ever have to worry about him again. I made sure he'll leave you alone from now on."

Ali frowned and looked up into her grandfather's eyes. Chase had been right. She'd inherited her eyes and hair color from him, not that creep Halverson. "What did you do?"

"I just had a few words with him, that's all," Ben said.

Ali looked down at her grandfather's hands holding hers. The knuckles on his right hand were red and swollen. Her eyes grew wide. "What happened to your hand?" She looked up at him. "What did you do?"

"My hand had an accident with Halverson's jaw," Ben said sheepishly. He sat there, waiting for a lecture from Ali. Instead, he saw her grin.

"You know, violence never solves anything," she said, her eyes twinkling.

Ben grinned back at her. "You're absolutely right. But it sure makes a person feel better sometimes."

Ali laughed, but then her smile faded and her eyes turned sad again. "It would have been nice to have a father," she said. "I've wanted one for so long, I guess I just hoped that when he saw me, he'd be nicer, knowing I was his daughter. But it didn't turn out that way. I guess I just wanted the happy ending."

Ben's tough heart softened for his only grandchild. He reached over and tilted up Ali's face to look into his eyes. "You don't need him for a happy ending. Why, your story is just beginning and you have the power to create your own happily ever after. Plus, for what it's worth, you have me, Jo, and Chase. We're your family now."

Ali looked at her grandfather and slowly smiled. "You're right. I have you guys and a lot to look forward to."

Ben stood up and offered his hand to Ali. She took it and rose.

"Let's get back down to the lodge before Chase starts fidgeting and comes looking for you," Ben said, teasing.

Ali looked at Ben's hand. "Um, you'd better do something with that hand before Jo sees it. She's not going to be very happy with you."

Ben grinned and winked. "Nope, she won't. But she'll get over it." Together they went down the stairs and inside the cabin where Ali helped her grandfather bandage his hand.

* * *

August proved to be the busiest month for the resort, and the hot, humid weather made cooking and cleaning unbearable. Thunderstorms were becoming more frequent, and by now Ali was used to them and even looked forward to them so they would wash away the sticky heat and cool down the air. She slept right through even the most violent of storms now, since she was exhausted from working all day in the heat.

Without air conditioning, the kitchen was like an oven when she and Jo were cooking breakfast and supper. Ben had brought in fans, and they helped a little, but weren't enough to stop the sweat from dripping beneath Ali's clothes. She and Chase cooled off in the evenings by swimming in the lake or lazing around in the canoe out on the water. She was used to heat in California, but the humidity made the heat here unbearable. If she hadn't been able to cool off on the water, it would have driven her crazy.

After Ali's disastrous confrontation with Halverson, she decided it was best to let go of her desire to have a father figure in her life once and for all. She'd carefully packed up her mother's belongings and stored them back in the attic room at the lodge. She wanted to remember only the good times she'd had with her mom. It was time to put to rest the bad memories, the ones that she had somehow understood, even from an early age, her mother just couldn't control. Her grandfather was right. She now had him, Jo, and Chase as her family, and that was all she needed.

The time for Chase to leave for college was drawing near and Ali dreaded the day he drove away. Jo had sent them on a shopping trip to Grand Rapids to pick up items he needed for living in the dorms at school. It was fun helping Chase pick out necessities like sheets, towels, pillows, and blankets, even though she knew this meant their time together was growing short. They also picked out a new laptop for him since he'd need it for his classes. Ali had looked at all the shiny, new laptops and tablets with envy, wishing she could afford a new one. But she knew she should save her money and wait until she went to college to buy a new computer.

One Sunday after breakfast Chase grabbed Ali's hand and pulled her outside toward the canoe. He was carrying a backpack in his other hand and wore a sly grin.

"What are you doing?" Ali asked, laughing. "I have to help Jo with the breakfast dishes and we have three cabins to clean for new guests tomorrow."

"Don't worry about that. Mom's going to enlist Ben's help with your chores today," Chase said. They arrived at the canoe and Chase handed Ali the backpack so he could flip it over.

"Where are we going?" Ali asked.

"To the old Indian Trail. It's cooler today, so it's the perfect day for a hike. And if we don't go now, we won't get a chance until next summer. Mom even packed us a lunch." He pointed to the backpack.

Excited now, Ali helped Chase slip the canoe into the water. They hopped inside and rode off across the lake. They both paddled the canoe in rhythmic motion and once they crossed the lake, they maneuvered it around the point to the other side. They found a sandy spot to land on shore and pulled the canoe up out of the water.

Ali had worn shorts and a T-shirt that day and her sneakers without socks. She'd taken off her shoes when they pulled the canoe up onto shore so as not to get them wet because she thought there was nothing worse than wearing soggy shoes while hiking. Chase had done the same, and once they'd pulled their shoes back on and Chase had slipped the backpack up onto his shoulders, they were off in the direction of the trail.

"Why do they call this 'the old Indian Trail'?" Ali asked as she followed behind Chase. The trail was nothing more than a narrow, dirt path with tall grass on each side. It looked more like one of the deer trails her grandfather had shown her in the woods, the trails that the white-tailed deer frequented enough to stomp down the grass.

"There's a whole story that goes with it," Chase told her as they slowly started making their way up an incline. "I'll tell you about it when we get to the top."

They hiked up the narrow trail and into the thick forest of pine trees that covered the side of the cliff. The trail steadily became steeper with switchbacks occurring more often, and they had to carefully pick their way over tree roots and loose rocks. About halfway up, Chase stopped and asked Ali to pull out a bottle of water for each of them from the backpack, and they both drank thirstily.

Ali closed her eyes and inhaled deeply. "I smell cedar," she told Chase. "I love that scent."

Chase smiled. "You're correct. You're on your way to becoming a true northern Minnesotan," he teased.

Carrying their water bottles, they began the ascent once more and after nearly thirty minutes of hiking, they were rewarded by stepping up onto the top of the cliff.

Ali's eyes grew wide with wonder when she looked all around her. The cliff top was long and wide, with a smooth rocky surface where patches of grass grew. Pine trees sprouted here and there. She had to walk several feet so she could see out over the cliff toward the lodge. The sight was incredible. If she made a circle, she could see everything all around her for miles.

"It's so beautiful," Ali exclaimed as Chase came to stand beside her. Ali slowly turned in a circle. She saw the cove the lodge sat on, the gravel road that led to town, her grandfather's house, and the point where she and Chase enjoyed sitting in the evenings. To her left, she saw the cove on the opposite side of the lodge, and as she circled she saw each cove that made up the lake. From her vantage point, she felt like she was skimming treetops, just like the loons and eagles did. "It feels like flying," she told Chase as she completed her circle and looked up at him.

Chase smiled down at her, his eyes twinkling. They were as blue as the lake. "Just don't go crazy on me and jump, okay?" he teased.

Ali laughed and they both began looking for the perfect spot to set up their picnic. Chase pointed out a patch of grass that grew under a huge blue spruce.

"Here's a good spot," he said. He slipped the backpack off his shoulders, opened it, and pulled out a plaid blanket. He flicked it open and spread it out on the ground in one smooth motion.

"Another emergency blanket?" Ali asked with a grin. "You Minnesotans are always prepared."

They sat down beside each other and Chase began pulling out plastic containers that held their lunch. Jo had packed two turkey sandwiches, a huge baggie of chips, apples, and chocolate chip cookies. There were extra bottles of water in the backpack, too.

"How on earth did you carry this up that trail?" Ali asked, looking at everything laid out on the blanket. "It must have weighed a ton."

Chase flexed his arm. "Don't you see how strong I am," he asked.

Ali shook her head at him, then they both dug into their lunch, hungry from their long hike.

The day was cooler than it had been in weeks and there was a lovely breeze up high on the cliff. After eating, Ali made a pillow out of the backpack and lay back, looking up into the clear, blue sky. Not too far up an eagle flew by and swooped down toward the water.

"So tell me now. Why is it called 'the old Indian Trail'?" Ali asked.

Chase was sitting crossed-legged beside Ali, looking down at her. "It's been said that long before white people came to this part of the country, native Indians climbed this trail up to the top of the cliff for spiritual rituals. Of course, no one knows for sure, it's just a story that Ben's grandfather passed down, supposedly from an elder of a local tribe. All we know for sure is the trail has been here since before the lodge was built."

Ali's eyes sparkled. "So, is this cliff magical?"

Chase smiled, stretched out beside her, and propped himself up on one elbow. "I don't know. Do you believe in magic?" he asked, his face close to hers.

Ali looked up into Chase's eyes. She'd never felt this way about a boy before, had never felt any desire to find a steady boyfriend like all her other friends had. But Chase had taken her by surprise. He was sweet, caring, intelligent, and adorable. Looking up at him now, she couldn't help but believe in magic.

In the distance, far below the cliff, a loon sang out its laughing song. Ali smiled.

"I want to kiss you," Chase said softly, his face only inches from hers. He reached over with his free hand and tucked a loose strand of her hair behind her ear. That simple gesture melted Ali's heart.

"Just kiss the girl and get it over with," Ali said softly with a grin, mimicking what Jake had said that day on the boat weeks before.

Chase lowered his lips to hers, brushing them softly. Ali raised one arm and ran her fingers through Chase's hair at the nape of his neck. The kiss was soft, gentle, warm, and lovely, just as Ali had imagined it would be, with all the magic a first kiss should hold.

\* \* \*

Ali and Chase reluctantly left their cozy spot on the cliff and headed down the winding trail, back to the canoe. Chase paddled slowly around the back cove as they watched for families of loons. Close to shore, they saw four loons swimming together, two larger and two smaller ones. "That must be a family," Ali said, excitedly. "Look how big the babies are already."

They sat and watched as the loons dived for food, came up, then dived again. Soon, their canoe had drifted away in one direction while the loons had made their way to deeper water in another direction.

"Do you think one of those is the loon we saved?" Ali asked, hoping one was. It warmed her heart to know that she'd kept a family together by saving the loon's life.

"Certainly could be," Chase said, slowly paddling the canoe in the direction of home. "The loon should be your talisman. Once you saved him, you connected with him for life."

Ali's eyes grew wide. "I love that idea. I feel like the loons have connected with me since the first day I was here and one scared me then laughed at me. I've been fascinated by them ever since."

Chase chuckled. "That was funny, you have to admit. But you were just a greenhorn then. Now you're becoming a real North Country lady."

Ali grimaced. "That doesn't sound very flattering."

"Don't worry. Once you bag your first moose and bear, you'll be a Minnesotan for sure."

Ali shook her head vigorously. "That will never happen."

Chase laughed, bent over, and kissed her, then proceeded to paddle the canoe home.

* * *

Ben stood on the screened-in porch glaring out at the lake. It had been six hours since the kids left and he'd been wrangled to do Ali's work for the day. Six hours. What in tarnation could they be doing on a cliff for that long?

"What are you grimacing at?" Jo asked as she came through the porch door. She'd been cleaning the last of the cabins and had a carrier of cleaning supplies in one hand and a mop in the other. Ben automatically took the cleaning supplies from her and followed her into the kitchen to put them away.

"Just wondering why it's taking those kids six hours to climb a cliff, eat lunch, and climb down. That's two hours max," Ben said, frowning.

"Oh, don't worry about them. Here," Jo handed him the mop. Ben grudgingly took it and the cleaning products to the supply closet and put them away.

"How can you not worry about what they're up to?" Ben asked, narrowing his eyes at Jo. "Chase is leaving in less than two weeks, and those two are thick as thieves. You know what happens when two people think something's coming to an end."

Jo raised her brows. "What happens?"

"You know damned well what happens. They start getting desperate and do things they might otherwise not do."

"Like what?" Jo asked innocently.

Ben waved his hand through the air as if brushing Jo away. "Ah, you're just being difficult 'cause you don't believe me. Situations like this are how boys talk girls into doing things they shouldn't, and you know that."

Jo frowned. "I trust Chase. And so should you. You've known him his entire life. He doesn't play games like that. And he certainly wouldn't be disrespectful with Ali."

"Ah, you just don't get it. This isn't about Chase being a gentleman or not, it's about two teenagers all hot for each other."

Jo sighed. She walked over to Ben and placed a hand on his arm. "What makes you think there's anything going on between those two? Have you seen them kiss?"

Ben drew his lips into a thin line. "No."

"Have you seen them hold hands? Hug? Whisper sweet nothings into each other's ears?"

"No."

"Then stop being so hard on them. Now, come help me peel potatoes for supper." Jo headed to the pantry for a bag of potatoes.

"You know, just because I haven't seen anything doesn't mean it isn't happening," Ben said, crossing his arms.

Jo came out of the pantry and set the bag of potatoes on the counter by the sink. She grabbed two peelers from the drawer. "Come peel potatoes, please."

Reluctantly, Ben walked over to the sink and took the peeler from Jo. She reached up on tiptoe and kissed him on the cheek.

Ben looked at her smugly. "See? Case in point. Has Chase or Ali ever seen us hold hands, kiss, or whisper sweet nothings in each other's ears?"

Jo rolled her eyes. "No. Probably not."

"There you have it. Just because no one sees it doesn't mean it isn't happening. Right?"

Jo sighed. "Just peel potatoes, smartass."

# Chapter Twenty

After that first kiss on the cliff, all Ali wanted to do was kiss Chase. They snuck kisses in secret at the point, out in the canoe in the evening, and even in the panty after breakfast. They were careful not to be seen because neither one of them wanted a lecture from Ben, but they couldn't help but want to kiss. They were young and slowly falling in love, and they both dreaded the day that Chase would have to leave for college. So they made up for it by kissing every chance they could get.

Ali opened up to Chase about her life with her mother in California and how difficult it had been as she'd grown older. She knew he'd understand and not judge her mother like she felt her grandfather would. Chase would listen quietly, and tell her how sorry he was about the past. In turn, Chase shared stories about his dad and how much he missed him. Ali listened, happy she could be as sympathetic an ear for him as he was for her. With each passing day, Ali felt closer to Chase, and it felt good to have someone she could confide in completely.

The heat came back with a vengeance, as did the thunderstorms that tried to sweep the heat away. Cleaning cabins and working in the kitchen was hot and uncomfortable, and Ali actually wished for cooler weather. But she knew that the cooler weather meant Chase would be gone and she'd be in a strange school, and that saddened her.

One morning after breakfast, Ben stood up and instead of

helping to clear away the dishes, he told Chase to come and help him for a few hours. "It's time to bait for bears," Ben said. "I've got two hunting parties booked for bear season and I need to have sites ready for them."

Ali stopped picking up plates and stared at her grandfather. "Bait for bears? What do you mean?"

"We set up bait stations to draw in the bears," Ben replied. "We also set up trail cameras to see what's eating the bait. Then we know where we're likely to get bears during the hunt."

Ali looked crossly from Chase to her grandfather. "That's not fair. I mean, if you're going to hunt something, then you shouldn't be allowed to set traps for it."

Ben raised his hands, palms up in defense. "Hey, I didn't make the laws, the DNR and state did. I'm just following them. How else do you think we'd be able to find a bear?"

Ali crossed her arms. "Where are you going to put these bait stations?"

"Out in the woods, of course. Where else would we put them? We'll put one over by the old dairy farm, then one in the woods near that, and another one farther out. Our family has had permission to hunt that land for ages."

Ali's eyes grew wide. "The dairy farm? You can't hunt for bear there. That's where our bears are."

Chase looked up at this. "Your bears?"

"Yeah," Ali said. "The mom and two cubs Grandpa and I saw when we went walking out that way." Ali turned to her grandfather. "You're not going to kill that mother bear and cubs, are you?"

"Of course not," Ben said. "I wouldn't let anyone kill a female bear that I know for sure has cubs. And it's illegal to kill baby bears. But you can bet if there's a female bear around, a male bear is around somewhere."

Ali's eyes grew sad. All she could think about were the

adorable little bear cubs bounding up to their mother. *What if someone shot their mother? How would they survive?*

"Listen, Ali. I know you're not used to all this hunting, but that's what people come up here to do," Ben told her gently. "It's just something you'll have to get used to."

Ali looked away, picked up a few dirty plates from the table, and mumbled to herself, "I'll never get used to killing animals."

Ben sighed. Jo brought out a pail of old cooking grease she'd saved over the summer for this very purpose and two huge buckets of stale cookies. Ben grabbed the pail and Chase took the buckets and they headed outside.

"What were those for?" Ali asked Jo, scrunching her nose.

"That's what they use for bait. Bears will eat just about anything this time of year since they're fattening up for hibernation. Chase and Ben will dig holes to place the cookies in, then cover the holes with heavy logs that only a bear can move. Then they'll pour the grease over the logs to bring in the bears. They'll hang up a trail camera to get photos of what comes to the bait station."

Ali shook her head. "I'll never get used to people hunting animals for fun."

Jo patted Ali on the back. "It'll take some getting used to, but believe me, if you live here long enough, you will."

Ali and Jo cleared away the dishes from the dining room tables and from their table in the kitchen. Ali stacked the dishwasher trays while Jo scrubbed pans and large platters in the sink. After that, Ali started a load of dishtowels and aprons in the washing machine.

Jo came into the laundry room as Ali finished up folding a load of towels from the dryer. "It's only a few more days before we take Chase to college. Is that going to be hard for you?" Jo asked.

Ali looked over at the older woman. "You know about me

and Chase?"

Jo smiled. "It's pretty hard not to see that you two have become close. The way you two look at each other, it's pretty obvious."

A worried look crossed Ali's face. "Do you think my grandfather has noticed?"

"Ben's suspicious of everyone and everything. But no, he doesn't know for sure," Jo said.

"We've been trying to hide it from him because he gets so crazy about stuff like that. What about you? Does it bother you?" Ali asked.

"Oh, sweetie, I don't mind a bit," Jo told her. "As long as you two are not going too fast and are being careful, that is. I'd hate to see anything happen that would abruptly change your lives. You're both so smart and have so much ahead of you, I just want you both to have a chance to finish college first."

"Oh, you don't have to worry about that," Ali assured her. "We're haven't taken it that far."

"That's good to know," Jo told her. "Taking Chase off to college in Duluth will be hard but at least you and I get to stay the night to help him get settled in. Plus, Ben said to take you shopping in the mall there so you can buy new clothes for school. That'll be fun, won't it?"

Ali looked up at Jo, a surprised expression on her face. "Grandpa said that? Why didn't he tell me?"

"Oh, you know how Ben is. He just told me to take you shopping and get you everything you need. You know what else he said to have you pick out? A brand new computer. He realizes it's important nowadays to have one for schoolwork."

Ali's mouth dropped open. "I can't let him buy me something like that. It's too expensive. I can just use my old one."

"Honey, if Ben's willing to buy you one, then take him up on it. Chase mentioned that your old one doesn't work all that well and you were practically drooling over a new one when he bought his. Ben said for us to go get a new one for you. Isn't that exciting?"

Ali stood silent a minute, taking it all in. She wasn't used to buying new things, or having anything bought for her. She'd become used to buying used items and was comfortable with them. She wanted to be excited about her grandfather buying her things, but it was hard.

Jo looked at her with a worried frown. "What's the matter? Did I say something wrong? I thought it would make you happy."

"It does, sort of," Ali said. "It's just that I'm not used to getting something I want so easily, and it seems strange to me."

Jo came over and gave Ali a big hug. "Oh, sweetie. You've been through so much this year between losing your mother and moving here. You've become so much a part of our lives that I forget about all the changes you've had to get used to. And now with Chase leaving, I'm sure it will be even harder for you. But don't worry about spending your grandfather's money. He wouldn't offer if he didn't want you to have nice things. You know he's not so good with words, this is how he shows he cares."

Ali nodded. It was true. It was difficult for her grandfather to express his feelings. "Doesn't it ever bother you that he hides his feelings about you from Chase and me? Especially since Chase and I know there's something going on anyway."

Jo grinned. "I figured Chase already knew. Ben is so old fashioned. He thinks we have to be married before we can show that we have a relationship otherwise you two kids will get the wrong impression."

"Then why doesn't he marry you?"

Jo's expression turned serious. "I'm sure you've noticed that Ben has trouble letting go of the past. He's still struggling with Jen running away all those years ago, and I know he struggles still with losing Lizzie. I don't mind waiting for him to come around. I know he cares about me, and that's all that matters."

The rest of the day while she cleaned cabins, Ali thought about what Jo had said. Jo was right. Her grandfather still hadn't let go of the fact that her mother had run away, and he was still getting used to her living with him. She knew he still loved her Grandma Lizzie, too, even though she'd been gone a long time. Ali hoped that over time, her grandfather would see that she wasn't at all like her mother, and accept her for who she was. And also that he'd realize it was time to put aside the past and spend his life with Jo. Ali hoped for a happy ending.

The next morning in the boat, Ali thanked her grandfather for offering to buy her a new computer when she and Jo went to Duluth.

"Ah, it's nothing," Ben said, shifting in his seat. "It's something you need, and I'm happy to do it."

"I bought mine second hand from a kid at school," Ali told him as she slowly reeled in her line. "We never had enough money for new things. It works okay. It's just really slow and out of date. It will be nice to have a new one."

Ben cleared his throat. "Why don't you ever talk about your life in California, or your mom? I'd like to hear about it, good or bad."

Ali bit her lip. "Some of it I'd like to forget," she said in a small voice. "I also don't want to give you the wrong impression about mom. She tried really hard, but she just never could get her feet on the ground for long. It was like…" Ali hesitated.

"Like what?" Ben asked gently.

"I always thought of mom as being too fragile for this life. It never took much to bring her down. She was always so sad."

Ben sat back in his seat, staring out at the lake. "My Jen always seemed so strong when she was growing up. And stubborn, too." Ben chuckled. "Sometimes she'd get set on something and her jaw would tighten and you knew you were in for a fight. Sort of like when you get angry," Ben teased.

Ali rolled her eyes at him.

"I wonder what happened to her out there to change her so much," Ben said. "I always believed she'd do well in life."

Ali shrugged. She knew little about her mother's life before she was born and she didn't remember much as a child, but as she grew older, she began to notice changes in her mother. "She wasn't a bad mother," she told her grandfather. "She just couldn't seem to help herself. Sometimes she'd be happy and hold down a job and we'd do things like go to the park or beach for picnics or go walking through the mall and look at all the beautiful things in the windows. She'd tell me, 'We're going to own nice things someday, Ali. You just wait and see.' But then she'd fall down into a depressed state again and the drinking would start up. I never understood why."

"She should have done better by you, Ali," Ben said gruffly. "My Jen should have tried harder."

Ali looked away. "She did the best she could."

Ben took a deep breath. "I'm sure she did," he said, softening his tone.

As the sun came up and the loons and ducks flew in to feed, Ali sat quietly, hoping she hadn't said too much. She didn't want to tarnish her mother's memory with angry words, and she didn't want her grandfather judging her mother too harshly. Ali just wanted to remember the good times with her mother and bury the bad memories. She believed her mother was in a happier place now, maybe even with her Grandma Lizzie, and she hoped she was finally at peace.

# Chapter Twenty-One

The day of Chase's departure was drawing near, and Ali took every opportunity to spend time with him. When he wasn't helping Ben clean fish or checking the bait stations, and when he wasn't cleaning out boats or mowing lawn, Ali found things for him to help her with in the cabins so they could just be together while she cleaned. She knew she shouldn't make up excuses for him to help her, but she just wanted to spend as much time as possible with him.

One hot, humid day, late in the afternoon, Ali had asked Chase to come help her move a stove in one of the cabin's kitchens so she could mop behind it. People were always dropping food between the counters and stoves, which was tempting for mice and other small animals. The last thing they needed was to scare guests with skunks looking for a snack in their cabins.

Chase readily agreed to help and followed Ali into the Moose cabin. Once he pulled the stove out, he grabbed Ali around the waist and drew her to him. "I get paid in kisses," he said, grinning.

Ali was only too happy to oblige. Every time they kissed, tingles went up her spine. She ran her fingers through his silky, blonde hair and loved the feel of his arms around her waist. Their kissing was beautiful and magical to Ali, and although she never wanted to stop, she knew they had to. It would have been so easy to keep going, but she knew she didn't dare. She didn't want to end up like her mother had, and she didn't want to put Chase in the position to choose between her and his future. When she pulled away, Chase groaned.

"I know how you feel," Ali told him, wanting to pull him close again. "But we have to be careful."

Chase reached for her hand. "I know," he said, caressing her hand. "But sometimes I just want to hold you and never let go."

Ali loved hearing that. She kissed him quickly on the lips and jumped back. "I have to finish cleaning," she said with a giggle.

"Tease," he said, pretending to reach for her as she jumped back again.

Chase helped Ali with the cabin by changing the sheets and blankets on the beds while she scrubbed down the kitchen and mopped the floor. He pushed the stove back into place and together they stacked the cleaning supplies into the carrying tray. He carried it outside onto the small porch while she carried the mop and broom. Just as Ali turned from closing the cabin's door, Chase pulled her to him and gave her one more kiss. Ali giggled again and they turned to walk back to the lodge.

* * *

The heat was driving Ben crazy. He couldn't remember when an August had been this hot for this long. He stood up in the boat he had been wiping down on the inside. "Damn tourists," he said under his breath. "Spilling pop all over the inside of a boat and leaving it."

Ben wiped his brow with the back of his arm. In the distance, he heard thunder rumbling. He looked to the west. The sky was turning black as pitch. He finished up with his cleaning and stepped out onto the dock. "Looks like we're in for a hell of a storm," he yelled up to Jo who was shaking out a kitchen rug behind the lodge on the porch steps. Jo looked up to the sky and nodded. Ben watched her, smiling, then turned, and his eye caught sight of the kids as they were stepping out of Moose cabin. Ben frowned. He watched as Chase pulled Ali to him, and they kissed. Then they smiled at each other and headed toward the lodge.

Ben stood there, processing what he'd seen. They had been in a cabin alone. They were kissing. "What the hell?" he said aloud.

Ben dropped the bucket of water he'd been carrying and stormed up the dock, his pace quickening as his face turned red with anger.

Jo looked over at him curiously as he passed her. "What's going on, Ben?" she asked. But Ben either didn't hear her or ignored her. He just kept walking.

Ben made it to the front of the lodge at the same time the kids did. He reached out and grabbed Chase by the front the shirt and shoved him against the wall. Chase dropped the cleaning supplies and they fell to the ground.

Ben's eyes bulged with rage. "What the hell were you doing in that cabin?" he bellowed into Chase's face.

Ali stood, frozen in shock.

Jo ran around the side of the lodge and up to Ben and Chase. "What's going on here? Ben, let go of Chase right now."

Ben didn't even notice Jo. He pulled Chase away from the wall then pounded him up against it again, all the time twisting Chase's shirt in his fist. "Tell me now. What were you doing in there? I saw you two kissing. God dammit. What the hell is going on?"

Ali found her voice. "Let him go!" she screamed. "You're hurting him. Let him go!"

Chase struggled to get free of Ben's grasp, but it was

fruitless. Although Chase had youth on his side, Ben was taller, weighed more, and held on firm.

Jo's face grew angry but she stayed calm. She walked up to Ben and placed her hand on his arm. "Let go of my son, Ben. Now."

Ben blinked. Jo's calm words hit him hard. He looked straight at Chase, who was turning red from the tight grasp Ben had on him. Slowly, Ben loosened his grip on Chase and took a step back. He looked from Chase to Jo. Then he narrowed his eyes.

"You said nothing was going on between these two but you were wrong. I just saw them coming out of that cabin. They were kissing. I told you they were getting too close. I told you we'd be sorry." Ben's voice was rose in anger.

Chase took a breath. "Nothing was going on," he told Ben.

Ben's eyes blazed at him. "You call that nothing? God dammit boy! You're leaving in a few days and she's going to be left behind." Ben pointed to Ali who was standing there, dumbfounded. "I'll be damned if I'll be stuck with some bastard child to take care of when you leave," Ben yelled. "You get her pregnant, it's on you. It's not going to be my problem."

"Ben," Jo said, shock covering her face.

"Oh, my God," Ali said, finally finding her voice. Ben turned and faced her. "Nothing's changed. After everything we've been through together. After everything I've confided in you, you still think I'm just like my mother." Ali took a step back, away from her grandfather. Her voice turned shrill as tears fell down her cheeks. "I thought we were getting closer, but we're not. You're the same mean, angry man you were when I first came here. You won't give up the past. You won't listen to anyone but yourself. You won't even let Jo inside your heart, let alone me. You just want to wallow in your lonely, loveless life and keep it that way. I can't live like this. I won't live like this. I'm going home. I don't need you. I can take care of myself. I've always taken care of myself." Ali took another step back as Ben reached out to her but before he could say anything, she turned and bolted up the road to the cabin. Above them, thunder rolled across the sky.

Chase started to move past Ben. "I'm going up to her. She needs someone," he said, glaring at Ben.

Jo touched Chase's arm. "No. This is Ben's mess. Let him clean it up."

Chase glanced between Ben and his mother, looking unsure.

"I'll talk to her," Ben said, all the fight gone from him now. He looked at Jo with mournful eyes. "I'm sorry," he said softly. He turned and walked up the road with heavy steps.

The sky was dark and raindrops started to fall as Ben walked into the garage. He started the generator, looked up toward Ali's room, then headed into the cabin. He splashed water on his face at the kitchen sink and wiped it away with a dishtowel.

What had he done? He'd gone completely insane down there without even letting them explain. It had felt like a bad flashback, like he'd been transported back in time to when Jen had told them she was pregnant. All the anger he'd felt then had come rushing back at him before he could control it. And now he was going to lose his Ali. She was probably up there packing her things to leave at this very moment.

Ben stood there, listening for any sounds coming from upstairs. He heard nothing. Maybe she was lying on her bed, crying. That thought tore at his heart even more.

Another shot of thunder ripped through the sky and Ben heard rain falling lightly on the roof. This storm was going to be a doozy. Ben took a deep breath, straightened his shoulders, then headed out the door and up to Ali's room.

He knocked softly on her door. "Ali? Can I come in?" He

listened, but there wasn't a response. "Ali, please. I know you're mad at me, but can we talk?" Still, no answer.

Worried now, Ben opened the door. There were no lights on in the room. "Ali? Are you in here?" When no answer came, Ben walked to the middle of the room and pulled the string on the light. Ben looked around. Ali wasn't here.

Ben's eyes scanned the room. Ali's phone was on the desk. Her computer sat there, too. Her suitcase was tucked away in the back corner. All her clothes hung on the rod. Nothing had been taken, yet she wasn't here. Where was she?

Ben ran out of the room and down the stairs. He searched the small cabin for Ali, but she wasn't downstairs either. He hurried outside and hopped into his truck as the rain pelted against him. Maybe Ali had turned around and headed back to the lodge. As he drove down there, he hoped he was right.

Running into the kitchen, Ben found Jo and Chase busy serving supper to the guests. "Is Ali here?" he asked, trying to keep calm.

Chase stopped filling a platter with mashed potatoes and Jo stopped in mid-step on her way out to the dining room. The both looked at Ben with wide eyes.

"No," Jo said. "I thought she was up at the cabin with you."

"She isn't there. It doesn't even look like she stopped there," Ben said.

Chase moved away from the table and headed toward the door. "I'm going to look for her," he said as his hand grasped the door handle.

"No," Ben said. "You stay here. I'll go look for her. Maybe she's on the road heading for town."

"In this rain?" Jo asked. "It's starting to pour out there."

Ben looked at Jo as a worried crease formed between his brows. "I don't know where else to look. If she's not here, and she's not at the cabin, where else would she be?"

"There are two empty cabins," Chase said. "I'll go check those first." Chase grabbed a coat and ran outside into the rain.

"What have I done?" Ben said hoarsely, looking at Jo for answers.

Jo came over and Ben folded her into his arms. "She's going to be fine," Jo assured him. "She's a smart girl. Wherever she is, she'll find a safe place to wait out this storm."

Ben hoped Jo was right.

Chase came in dripping water on the kitchen rug. "She's not in either cabin. We should go check the road."

"I'll go," Ben said. "You stay here and help your mother."

"No." Chase held his shoulders rigid and stared directly at Ben. "I'm going with you. I have to know that Ali's all right."

Ben narrowed his eyes at the boy, but seeing the determination in his eyes, he relented. "Okay." Ben turned to Jo. "Can you handle serving by yourself?"

Jo nodded. "You two just go. Find Ali and bring her home safe."

The rain beat mercilessly against the windshield of Ben's truck as he slowly drove down the muddy, gravel road toward town. Lightning lit up the sky at intervals as thunder exploded. Ben quietly prayed that Ali wasn't outside in this violent storm, but the alternative would be that some stranger may have picked her up on the road, and that thought didn't sit well with him either.

The rain was falling so hard it was washing out sections of the gravel road, causing Ben to drive even slower. They could barely see anything because of the dense rain and the dark sky. Ali could have been standing right beside the road, and they probably wouldn't have seen her.

"This wouldn't have happened if you hadn't flown off the handle," Chase said angrily.

Ben looked over at Chase in surprise. Never in his life had Chase talked to him with anything but respect. "What would you have thought if you were me? Seeing you come out of that cabin, kissing, looked damned suspicious."

Chase glared over at Ben. "If I were you, I'd have trusted Ali enough to know she wouldn't do anything wrong. Geez, Ben. The last thing Ali wants is to end up like her mother. She's already paid a high price for her mother's mistakes. She took care of her mother, not the other way around. Why do you insist on making her continue to pay for her mother's mistakes by putting them back on her?"

The question hit Ben hard. He realized that Chase was right. He'd been transferring Jen's mistake onto Ali, when all along, she'd already been the one to suffer the consequences of those mistakes.

"I'm not going to do anything to ruin Ali's life," Chase continued. "I care about her. I'm not some jerk like Halverson. I want Ali to be happy."

Ben turned to Chase. "I'm sorry, Chase. Of course you'd never do anything to hurt Ali. I've known you your entire life, and I should know that better than anyone. I'm sorry."

Chase looked straight at Ben. "I'm not the one you need to apologize to. Ali is."

Ben nodded. He knew Chase was right.

Once they arrived in town, they split up and checked all three bars to see if Ali was in one of them. The theater and coffeehouse were both closed, so that ruled them out. Inside The Loon's Nest, Ben asked Luke if he'd seen Ali, but he shook his head no. Ben asked the kids playing pool in the back, but they hadn't seen her either. When Ben and Chase met back inside the truck, Chase didn't have any good news to report either.

"No one has seen her, so she can't be in town. Now what?" Chase asked.

Reluctantly, Ben headed the truck home. "We'll call the Sheriff when we get back to the lodge. I'm hoping that by some luck, Ali's waiting for us at home."

* * *

After yelling at her grandfather, Ali had run up the hill toward the cabin with tears streaming down her face. She ran past the cabin, not thinking about where she was headed. All she knew was she had to get far, far away from her grandfather.

Ali couldn't believe what he had accused her of. His words had ripped her apart. 'I'll be damned if I'll be stuck with some bastard child to take care of.' It didn't matter how much she'd opened up to him, he still believed she was going to end up just like her mother.

After a time, Ali stopped running to catch her breath. Thunder pounded across the sky and raindrops began to fall on her. Ali stood there, unsure of what she should do. She could walk into town, but that would take a long time, especially in a storm. She could go back to the lodge and stay with Jo and Chase, but then she'd eventually have to deal with her grandfather. And going back to the cabin wasn't even a choice.

"I want to go home," Ali wailed as tears blurred her vision. Lightning lit up the darkening sky and then a crash of thunder hit right above Ali. She jumped in fright. Behind her, Ali saw the headlights of a vehicle coming down the road from the direction of the lodge. She ran off the road down a trail and hid behind a tree as the truck drove past. Through her tears she couldn't tell if it was her grandfather's truck or a stranger's.

Ali wiped her eyes with her now soaked sweatshirt sleeve. She had to find a place to wait out the storm. She needed time to think. As she stood there, she realized she recognized the trail. It was the one that went to the old dairy farm. She'd only been on it twice, once with her grandfather and once with Chase when she picked daisies for her grandmother. But she knew where she was, and the barn at the dairy farm was her best bet to get out of this storm. With renewed energy, Ali ran down the trail as the storm rumbled on.

* * *

Ben and Chase returned to the lodge as Jo was cleaning up after supper.

"Did you find her?" Jo asked, hurrying over to them.

Ben shook his head. "I was hoping she'd come back here," he said, disappointed. "We need to call the Sheriff and get some help looking for her."

Jo sighed. "I already did. They said they couldn't risk anyone getting hurt or lost searching for Ali in this storm, but he'd come out first thing in the morning and start searching. He also said he'd drive around town and be on the lookout for her or any strange vehicles."

"Well, I'm going out looking for her. I'm not waiting for morning," Ben said with determination.

"Me, too," Chase said, already changing out of his soaking wet coat and putting on a dry one. "Where to first, Ben?"

"Now wait a minute, guys," Jo said firmly. "The last thing we need is to lose you both out there, too. You have no idea where to even look for Ali, and for all we know, she could have made it to town already and is somewhere safe. As mad as she is, it's unlikely she's going to call us and tell us where she is."

Ben sat heavily on the bench next to the table and dropped his head in his hands. Chase hovered by the door, still determined to go searching.

"I can't just sit here while Ali's out there somewhere," Ben told Jo. "I have to find her."

Jo came over and knelt down in front of Ben, taking his hands in hers. Ben looked at her with sad, tired eyes. "You know I'd be the first one out there helping you find her, Ben. I love her, too. But I'm not about to let you go out in this storm looking blindly for her. I can't bear to have something happen to you, too. Please." Her eyes begged him. "Please wait until first light and we'll all go searching."

Ben saw the fear in Jo's eyes. The last thing he wanted to do was hurt her, too. "Okay," he told her. "Okay. I'll go up to the house and wait until light. You're right. You always are. There's no way I could track her or find her in this pouring rain."

Jo looked relieved, but Chase protested. "We can't just wait. We have to go find Ali now."

Ben shook his head. "No, Chase. Your mother's right. You stay here with your mother and wait until morning. We don't want you lost out there, too."

Chase reluctantly agreed to wait.

Ben stood and headed toward the door.

"Ben. Promise me you'll just go home and wait," Jo pleaded.

"I promise," he told her, then headed outside in the pouring rain and drove home.

* * *

Ali fell twice on the muddy trail as she ran through the rain to the dairy farm. When she finally saw it in the distance, she let out a sigh of relief. The rain was pelting down on her and she was soaked to the skin. The storm had relieved the hot temperature and the air was cooler. Normally, she would have been thrilled to feel the cool air after a hot day, but right now, soaking wet, it chilled her to the bone.

Wiping her eyes again, despite her hands and sleeves being sopping wet, she made her way to the side of the barn and entered, relieved to finally be out of the downpour outside. It was dark inside the barn, and she had to wait a moment for her eyes to adjust enough so she could see. She looked around, getting her bearings. The place smelled like manure, even though animals hadn't inhabited this barn for years. It was musty smelling, too. Ali shivered. She was suddenly aware of just how cold she felt.

Ali's eyes adjusted enough for her to see that the layout of the barn consisted of two big sections on each side that ran the length of the barn with a narrow aisle running down the middle. The floor looked to be either mud or years of caked-on manure. Ali decided she didn't want to find out which it was. She carefully picked her way to the other side of the barn and saw some hay bales stacked up with a large pile of loose hay that was smashed down next to the bales. The smell of excrement was even stronger here.

Ali moved on down the aisle toward the back of the barn. Outside, the rain was hitting heavily against the wood siding. Inside, it was eerily quiet. At the back of the barn was a ladder built onto the wall that led up to what Ali assumed was the loft. To her right, she saw a door that was slightly ajar. Cautiously, she pushed the door in a bit farther and saw it was a small room that probably once held supplies. She walked inside and looked around. On the wall hung an old leather horse bridle and bit. Looking further, Ali squealed with delight. There, hanging over a sawhorse, was a heavy, wool horse blanket. Gingerly, she lifted it up to make sure nothing was living inside it. When nothing fell out, she opened it up some more and shook it. Once she was sure no creepy crawlies were hanging onto it, she wrapped it around her, immediately feeling its warmth. Ali didn't care that it smelled moldy, dusty, and like a wet horse. It was warm, and that was all that mattered.

Ali stepped out of the room and looked around. It was so dark in the barn, she couldn't see from one end to the other. Suddenly, she heard a rustling sound, like something was burrowing in the hay at the other end. Her heart skipped a beat. What if some wild animal had come in?

Feeling panicky now, Ali looked around. She saw the ladder again. If she climbed up to the loft, would she be safe? Once again, she heard rustling. That made up her mind for her. Keeping a tight grasp on the blanket, Ali pulled herself up the ladder and through the hole that led to the loft.

Once up there, Ali looked around. There were more hay bales up here, stacked on one side of the floor. Across the barn at the other end was a large opening. Wind was coming in through it, and Ali couldn't see if there was a door to close it off. She wasn't about to go near it. If she fell out that door, it was a long way down to the ground.

Below her on the first floor came a snorting sound. Ali frowned. "It sounds like pigs," she whispered to herself. But then she heard a sound that made her blood run cold. It was the deep, bellowing sound that the mother bear had made the day she and her grandfather had walked here. Ali froze. Hadn't they seen the baby bears coming out from around the barn that day? Maybe they were the ones that had smashed down the hay. Maybe that was where they slept.

Ali pulled the blanket tightly around her, wondering what she should do. There was no way she was going down to investigate. But what if the mama bear smelled her scent? Didn't her grandfather say bears could climb? Could a bear climb up a ladder?

Slowly, Ali moved over toward where she'd come through the floor. She saw a trap door lying beside the hole. Holding her breath, she quietly lifted the wooden door on hinges and set it down to close off the hole. There was no lock or latch, but it made her feel safer.

Ali went back over to the hay bales and sat down against them on the side away from the open door at the end of the loft so she didn't feel the wind. She pulled the blanket tightly around her for warmth. Below, she heard rustling, but no more bellowing. She sat there, shivering under the blanket, angry with herself for running off in the storm, angry with her grandfather for saying those awful words, and most of all, angry with her mother for dying and leaving her in this terrible mess.

# Chapter Twenty-Two

Ben did as he promised Jo and drove back to the cabin. The generator was still running, so he took off his soaking wet clothes and took a hot shower, then dressed again in dry clothes. There'd be no sleeping tonight. His every moment was going to be spent worrying about where Ali was and if she was okay. He left lights on all over the cabin so it would glow as if it were a beacon in the night. If Ali was out there somewhere, he wanted her to be able to see the cabin to find her way home.

Ben sat in his chair in the living room, letting the day wash over him, reexamining every word he'd said. How could he have done this again? How was it possible that a man could be so stupid not only once, but twice in his life?

He remembered the day he'd found out that his Jen was pregnant as if it were only yesterday. He'd felt anger, sure, but most of all, he'd felt betrayed. He had taken it personally. Instead of feeling compassion for his daughter and asking her what he could do to help, he'd turned on her. And he'd been paying for it ever since. He and his Lizzie. They'd both paid for his angry words that day.

"And I did it again today," he said aloud to the empty room. "Lizzie. I did it again."

Ben dropped his head in his hands and closed his eyes tight, trying to conjure up his Lizzie. She'd know what to do. She'd know how to fix this. The last time, she'd been unable to bring Jen back, but this time, she'd know how to bring Ali home. No matter how hard he tried, the vision of his Lizzie would not appear. All he saw in his mind was Ali's tear-stained face looking back at him.

'You're the same mean, angry man you were when I first came here,' Ali had screamed at him. 'You just want to wallow in your lonely, loveless life and keep it that way.' Ali was right. He'd held onto his pain like a trophy, and it had made him angrier and meaner through time. He'd let Jo into his heart only so far, but he'd failed to let her in completely. He hadn't wanted Ali to come and live with him in the first place. In fact, he hadn't ever expected to meet her at all. But here she was, and she'd found a place in his heart, too. Yet he'd refused to trust her completely. Refused to believe that maybe she'd be different from his Jen. Now he might lose her.

Angrily, Ben stood up and stomped into the kitchen. He reached up into the highest cupboard, pulled down the half-empty bottle of whiskey, and set it on the counter. Ben stared hard at the bottle. Just one drink, that was all he needed. One drink to get him through this terrible night. He'd stop at one because he couldn't risk Ali coming home and finding him drunk. He'd promised her.

He unscrewed the lid and raised the bottle to his lips. He could smell the sweet liquid inside. It called out to him. Slowly, Ben set it back down on the counter again.

Looking at the bottle, Ben sneered at it. For years he'd been using this bottle of whiskey as a crutch. He wasn't going to find Ali in this bottle of whiskey. He wasn't going to find his Lizzie or his Jen in there, either. And he certainly wasn't going to find happiness in there. Happiness had been found with Jo. He'd found happiness spending time with Ali. That damned bottle of whiskey would never make him feel warm or cared about like the people in his life did.

Ben raised the bottle over his head and threw it into the sink. It shattered and sprayed whiskey all over the counters, walls, and floor. A shard of glass flew back at Ben and sliced his cheek. Ben just stood there, his anger spent, watching the amber liquid run down the sink and drip off the counter and onto the floor.

Feeling a trickle of something warm run down his cheek, Ben frowned and stared at his reflection in the window over the sink. Blood oozed out of the long cut. He raised his hand to the wound and touched it. Drawing his hand away, he saw blood on his fingertips. Ben grabbed a dishtowel that was hanging over the cupboard door, wet it with cold water, and placed it over the cut on his face, pressing hard. No cut, however deep, could hurt as much as the words he'd thrown at Ali today.

Ben walked through the cabin back to his chair and sat down heavily. He sat there waiting. Waiting for the storm to pass, waiting for daylight, waiting for the pain in his heart to subside.

* * *

The first rays of sunlight fell across Ben as he sat in the chair. His eyes flew open. Despite his fear for Ali, he'd somehow fallen asleep and the sun was already coming up.

Ben stood and stared out the window. The storm had passed, leaving behind huge puddles of water that had turned the gravel road into mud. Looking at the sky, he estimated it to be around five-thirty a.m. Fishing time. Right now, he and Ali should be fishing on the lake, but instead, she was gone.

"Where could she be?" he asked aloud. "Where could she have waited out the storm?" Ben walked toward the bathroom. He'd throw cold water on his face to wake up, and then head out looking for Ali.

Ben passed the desk with the photo of Lizzie sitting on it. He stopped and lifted the photo, gazing at it tenderly. He wished his Lizzie could have met her granddaughter. She would have loved Ali immediately. She'd have never held back her love like Ben had. Ben thought about Ali's kind act of picking flowers and placing them in the lake as a remembrance of a grandmother she'd never met. Ali had even taken the time to find out that Lizzie loved daisies and had walked the woods to pick them herself.

Ben's eyes suddenly snapped to life. Daisies. Ali had picked the daisies on the trail to the old dairy farm. She knew that trail. She knew the barn was there. Suddenly, he realized where Ali was. It was the only place she could have gotten out of the rain. It was the only place that made sense.

Ben ran to his bedroom, pulled on his boots and flannel jacket, picked up his shotgun, and headed out the door.

Jumping into his truck, Ben took off down the gravel road avoiding the muddiest parts in fear of getting stuck. Once he made it to the trail, he turned the truck onto it. When he and Chase checked the bear bait stations, they always drove down this trail. But today, it was difficult with the trail so slick and muddy.

Ben frowned at the thought of the bait stations. They had two in the woods near the dairy farm. That meant that all types of wild animals were in that vicinity. Hadn't they just seen snapshots of a cougar and a huge male bear from the trail cams by the bait stations? He hoped that Ali hadn't run into any of the animals if she'd gone to the barn.

Farther down the road, Ben had to stop the truck. The trail was just too muddy and he didn't want the truck to sink in it. He pulled over on the tall grass as far as he dared so it wasn't sitting directly in the mud, grabbed his gun off the seat, and headed out on foot. Walking was tough. His boots slipped in the mud, and twice he almost landed on his face. But he trudged on, hoping he'd find Ali safe and sound at his destination.

Up ahead, Ben finally saw the barn and his footsteps grew quicker. His eyes were fixed on the barn as he neared it. He hoped that if Ali did come here, she hadn't already left once the sun came up.

A low, deep growl suddenly drew Ben's eyes to the edge of the woods. Ben stopped, his hand tight on the stock of his shotgun. He looked over toward the woods and there, not more than twenty feet ahead of him, stood a large, black bear. As their eyes met, the bear stood up on its hind legs and bellowed.

Startled, Ben took a step back and nearly slipped in the mud. He positioned his shotgun in front of him. If he shot this bear in self-defense, he damned well didn't want to just hurt it. He'd kill it, or else it would kill him.

The bear bellowed again and took a step in Ben's direction. Then another step. Ben lifted his shotgun, cocked it, and trained it on the bear. He positioned his finger on the trigger. One more step toward him, and he'd shoot it.

"Grandpa. No!"

Ali's voice came loud and clear from up above. Startled, Ben looked up. In that instant, his foot slipped out from under him and he fell over backward into the mud and grass. His shotgun fell down just out of his reach.

The bear took another step toward Ben. Ben's heart raced as he stretched out his arm to try to reach the gun. He'd been near bears many times in his life, but this was the closest. Too close. The bear was closing in, and here he sat, defenseless.

"Over there. Look! Over there."

Ali's voice came from up above again. Ben looked up and there she was, standing in the open door in the loft of the barn. She was pointing down to the ground. Ben looked down, and then he saw them. Two bear cubs came bounding out of the barnyard and ran toward their mother. The mother bear had dropped to all four feet by now and stood there, staring at Ben, waiting for her cubs to come to her.

Ben didn't move a muscle. If he tried to grab his gun, the bear would be on him. He'd never have time to shoot anyway. So he lay there, holding his breath, waiting, watching the bear.

The cubs came running up to where their mother stood then ran past her into the woods. The mother bear threw one more long look at Ben, then turned and ambled into the woods after her cubs.

Ben let out a long sigh of relief, but then he remembered Ali up in the loft and quickly picked up his gun and rose. He looked up to the loft and saw Ali still standing there.

"Don't come down yet," he hollered up to her. "I'll come up. I want to make sure the barn is safe first."

Ali nodded, then disappeared from the large opening.

Ben uncocked the shotgun then headed cautiously into the barn. Daylight streamed into the old barn through broken boards, allowing Ben to see around it easily. He noticed the hay bales and loose hay on the other side of the barn and wondered if the mother bear had used this for her den last winter. He made a mental note to be careful in the future when approaching the barn.

Once Ben felt sure there were no other animals in the lower part of the barn, he headed for the ladder. "I'm coming up," he yelled so Ali could hear him. Above him, he saw the trap door open. He wiped the mud off his boots onto the barn floor so he wouldn't slip, then headed up the ladder. Once he was through the trap door and safely on the floor, he called out. "Ali? Where are you?"

Ali was beside him immediately with tears in her eyes. Ben raised his arms to her and she ran into them. "I'm so sorry I ran off," she said through sobs. "It was so stupid. I didn't know what to do, and then I saw the trail and came here to get out of the rain."

"It's okay," Ben said, holding her close. She was still wet

from the night before. "Here," Ben said as he pulled away. "You're cold." He slipped off his flannel jacket and wrapped it around Ali. "I'm the one who should be apologizing," he told her, looking down into her deep blue eyes. "I should never have attacked Chase like that and accused you of something you didn't do. I'm sorry, Ali." He pulled her close again, fighting back tears of his own. "I'm just so relieved that you're safe."

Ali pulled away. "How did you know I was here?"

Ben shrugged. "I didn't know for sure, but I gave it a try. I'm glad you found a place to get out of the downpour last night. You must have been cold, though, as wet as you are."

Ali shook her head as she smiled through her tears. "I stayed pretty warm. I found an old horse blanket to wrap around me and I sat against those hay bales over there to stay out of the wind. It wasn't too bad, except for the bears downstairs. I heard a rustling sound while I was still down there, so I came up the ladder and closed the trap door. When I heard the mama bear growl, I knew it was the bears. That really scared me."

Ben smiled down at Ali. "You did the right thing, coming up here. I'm so proud of you. You're a true Jenson, you are. You knew exactly what to do."

Ali frowned. "But I almost got you killed by that bear. I shouldn't have yelled at you like that. I was so afraid you were going to shoot her, and then the cubs wouldn't have a mother. I'm sorry I put you in danger."

"Ah, don't you worry about that, it ended up all right. I should have been paying more attention to where I was and my surroundings. I came between the mama bear and her cubs, and she was only trying to protect them." Ben stopped, then looked at Ali seriously. "Like I should have protected you. I should have listened to you, and not jumped to conclusions, then you wouldn't have run away in the first place. Ali, I'm sorry. You were right. I'm afraid to let people into my life. I was afraid to care about you because I thought you'd leave me and break my heart. Like when my Jen left. And my Lizzie. What I didn't understand was that I was the one pushing you away."

"It's okay," Ali told him.

Ben shook his head. "No, it's not okay. Because no matter how much I've tried not to care about you, you've still managed to find your way into my heart and if I lose you now, I'd be devastated. Yesterday you said you wanted to go home, back to California. I hope you didn't mean it. I know I'm not the easiest person to live with, and I can't promise I can change overnight, but I don't want you to leave. I'd really like it if you stayed. You're my Ali now. You're my family. I couldn't bear for you to leave."

Tears sprang to Ali's eyes again. "I'm your Ali?" she asked.

Ben nodded. "Yes. Does it bother you if I call you that? My Ali."

Ali shook her head and smiled. "No, it doesn't bother me. I love how you called my mom and grandmother 'my Jen' and 'my Lizzie.' I'd love to be thought of as 'your Ali.' I've never had anyone who thought of me that way before."

Ben hugged Ali hard. "Then you'll stay? I'll do whatever you want to make it nicer for you here. We can build a room onto the house for you so you don't have to stay in the attic. I'll even put in electricity, if that would make living with me better."

Ali laughed, her eyes sparkling. "You don't have to do anything different. I love my attic room, and I've even gotten used to the generator. All I want is for you to listen to me, and give me a chance to prove that I'm not my mother. I don't plan on doing anything stupid that will ruin my life."

Ben nodded. "I'll do the best I can. It may take a while though, so you'll have to be patient with me. I'm an old man who isn't used to change. But I will change, if it will make life better for us."

"What about you and Jo? Will you finally let her in, too?" Ali asked.

Ben grinned at Ali. "Jo's been patient with me for a long time. It's about time I openly admit to loving her, too. Speaking of Jo, I bet she and Chase are going crazy wondering where we are. It was all I could do to keep Chase from searching for you last night in the storm. We'd better head home."

Ali and Ben went down the ladder and out of the barn into the warm sunshine. The day was beautiful. The heat and humidity had been cleared away, leaving behind a bright blue sky and a delicious cool breeze.

In the bright light, Ali saw the deep cut on her grandfather's cheek. "What happened to you?" she asked.

Ben frowned and raised his hand to his cheek, remembering the cut. He chuckled. "I had a fight with a whiskey bottle, and it lost," he told her.

"Your whiskey bottle?" Ali asked.

"Yep. I realized that I couldn't find anything or anyone I needed in that bottle. So I let it go. It was stupid, actually, staring at it all these years."

Ali wrapped one arm around her grandfather's waist as they walked down the wet trail toward the truck. "Let's go home," she said, truly meaning it.

# Epilogue

## *Ten Years Later*

Ali sat on the porch swing at the back of the lodge gazing out at the lake. It was the middle of August and she wanted to sit and feel the lake's cool breeze on her face after the long, hot day. She smiled as she watched the sun make its way slowly below the cliff. Soon, it would be down, but for now, the sun made the lake sparkle like glitter.

Chase came out of the kitchen and onto the porch. He smiled down at Ali.

Ali started to get up. "I should help Jo with the supper dishes."

"No, you stay there and relax. I helped her and she's almost done," Chase said. He sat on the bench beside her and took her hand. "How are you feeling?"

"Fine. Just tired. I just wanted to relax a moment and watch the sun go down over the lake."

They sat there together, slowly moving the swing back and forth. A boat driven by one of their guests came up to the dock and Chase stood. "Back to work," he said. He kissed Ali lightly on the lips and then headed out of the porch and down to the dock to assist in tying up the boat.

Ali watched Chase with a smile on her lips. She remembered the first day they met when she'd moved here to live with her grandfather. He was handsome then and was even more handsome now that he was older. His blonde hair was still light from being out in the sun all summer, but now he wore it shorter. The teenage girls who came to the lodge still flirted with him, but he didn't even notice. Ali knew he only had eyes for her.

Of course, it hadn't always been easy. They had hit a rough patch the first year he went off to college in Duluth. He'd met so many new people there and at one point thought he'd even fallen in love with another girl. Ali had been trying to adjust to the high school in Auburn at the time, and although it had made her sad that she might lose Chase as a boyfriend, it made her sadder that she might lose him as a friend. But the next summer when he came home, he realized that Ali was the only girl for him and they'd been a couple ever since.

Ali had gone off to college in Duluth the next fall so they could be together and she'd still be close to her grandfather and Jo. After his first year of college, Chase decided to change his major from Environmental Sciences to Business Management, the same major that Ali had decided upon. Chase loved the lodge, and he'd decided he wanted to continue working there and keep it in the family. Ali agreed, because that was what she'd wanted to.

Ali's old life in California had become a distant memory to her. After that first year, she rarely heard from any of her old friends and although it was sad to lose them, she accepted the fact that life moved on and things changed. Her new life fit her fine, and she was just as surprised about it as anyone who once knew her.

After college graduation, Ali and Chase were married in a small but beautiful ceremony beside the lake. It was the same spot where Ben and Jo had finally tied the knot a few years earlier. Ben and Jo now lived up at the cabin and Ali and Chase had the family quarters in the lodge. It made sense, since they were slowly taking over the business, although Jo said she'd work till the day she died and Ali knew Ben would, too. It was just their way.

Kat still lived in town and continued helping her mother run the coffeehouse which she would someday take over. She'd gone to college for two years, but had decided to come home and continue the family business. Everyone was surprised when Kat and Jake began dating and married. Ali was happy for her two friends, though. And every now and then the four of them got together and hung out on the lake like they'd done as teens. Ali thought it was nice having another couple to share memories with.

Ali refocused on the lake and saw her grandfather coming up the dock with fishing rods in his hands. She watched as he placed them in the storage shed, then he walked through the porch door with a smile on his face.

"So, how's that great-grandson of mine doing?" Ben asked, sitting down gently beside Ali.

Ali chuckled as she placed her hand on her growing belly. She was seven months pregnant, and despite the heat of the summer, she felt pretty good. "You know, the baby could be a great-granddaughter," she told Ben.

Ben grinned. "Well, as long as it's healthy, that's all that matters," he said. "Although, if it's a boy, I could teach it everything I know," he teased.

Ali placed her hand on her grandfather's arm. "You can teach it everything you know if it's a girl, too. Just like you taught me."

Ben let out a hearty laugh. "You still out-fish me," he said. "I think I'm the one who needed to learn, not you."

Looking into her grandfather's dark blue eyes, Ali thought back to the day she'd almost left here forever. Her grandfather had promised her he'd try harder, and he had. It didn't mean they didn't get into a scrap or two, but in the end he'd always listen to her and consider her opinion. And once he opened up his heart to Jo, he'd softened. He was rarely the gruff, grouchy man he'd been the day she came to Willow Lake Lodge. He'd mellowed as he grew older, and Ali had grown to love him very much.

The sun had made its way below the cliff, and darkness began to settle on the lake. A loon cried out its sing-song call and flew across the lake and over the lodge.

"He's heading home," Ben said. "Just like clockwork, every night."

Ali nodded. She thought back to the first time a loon had flown across the sky above her and scared her with its cry. She thought about the time she and her grandfather had saved the loon tangled in the fishing line. Now, she looked forward to summer each year when she'd hear the loons sing as they flew to and from the lake. She loved that sound. To her, it was the sound of home.

When Ali was young, she'd dreamt about a place she and her mother could call home with family all around. But as the years passed, Ali had decided that the idea of home and family was just a dream. Now she knew different.

As the sun settled down for the night, Ali laid her head on her grandfather's shoulder and he wrapped his arm around her. Home. It felt so good to be home.

###

# About the Author

Deanna Lynn Sletten writes women's fiction and romance novels that dig deeply into the lives of the characters, giving the reader an in-depth look into their hearts and souls. She has also written one middle-grade novel that takes you on the adventure of a lifetime.

Deanna's romance novel, **Memories,** was a semifinalist in The Kindle Book Review's Best Indie Books of 2012. Her novel, **Sara's Promise,** was a semifinalist in The Kindle Book Review's Best Indie Books of 2013 and a finalist in the 2013 National Indie Excellence Book Awards.

Deanna is married and has two grown children. When not writing, she enjoys walking the wooded trails around her northern Minnesota home with her beautiful Australian Shepherd or relaxing in the boat on the lake in the summer.

Deanna loves hearing from her readers. Connect with her at:

Deanna's Blog: www.deannalynnsletten.com
Deanna's Website: www.deannalsletten.com
Twitter: @DeannaLSletten
Facebook: http://www.facebook.com/DeannaLynnSletten
Goodreads: http://www.goodreads.com/dsletten

Please enjoy the following excerpt from
my upcoming novel coming Summer 2014

# Destination Wedding

# Chapter One

Claire Martin discreetly glanced at her watch with one eye as she watched her customer with the other turn this way and that in front of the three-way mirror. Claire had to be out of the shop in five minutes or else she'd be late meeting with her daughter, and she didn't want to be late. Today was important.

Claire smiled and nodded at the woman in front of her, agreeing that the long-waisted sweater did make her look thinner and the dark, skinny jeans were perfect with it. Claire didn't want to be rude. This lady was a regular customer at Claire's clothing store, the Belle Boutique, and regular customers were important for business. But she did wish the woman would hurry up and pick an outfit.

Absently, Claire pushed a stray strand of her sandy blonde hair behind her ear then began twirling the charm bracelet on her wrist round and round. She stole a glance at herself in the floor-to-ceiling mirror beside her to check her appearance. Her hair was still neatly in place, her makeup still fresh looking. She plucked a strand of string that had somehow come to rest on her sleeve. Perfect.

Finally, the customer decided that this was the perfect outfit and Claire politely excused herself and said that Ariana would ring up her purchases.

Rushing to the back room, Claire ran into her office, slipped off her pumps, and pulled on a pair of knee-high, leather boots over her leggings. Today, she was dressed warmly, despite the fact that it should already be spring outside. Unfortunately, spring in Minnesota could come as early as March or as late as May, and this year it chose the latter. To be wearing a sweater dress and leggings in April was ridiculous, but not when the temperature was in the forties outside with snow still on the ground. Grabbing her red, wool coat off the back of her office chair, Claire walked swiftly through the store and up to the front counter where her Assistant Manager, Ariana Flores, stood behind the register.

"Did she buy the sweater and jeans?" Claire asked, noting that the customer was no longer in the store.

"Yes. And the dress and brown trousers, too. I rounded it all up nicely with a set of bangle bracelets and earrings," Ariana said.

Claire smiled at Ariana as she slipped on her coat. Ariana had been working for her for almost five years and Claire didn't know what she'd do without her. Ariana was in her mid-forties, just as Claire was, but where Claire was tall with light skin and blonde hair, Ariana was the exact opposite. Ariana's Hispanic heritage shined through with a golden-brown complexion, big, brown eyes, and straight black hair that she usually kept up in a twist. She was shorter than Claire, which she made up for by wearing very high heels. And Ariana always dressed with a vibrant style, showing off the store's clothes in the most flattering way. Most of all, though, Ariana was loyal, and a good friend who sometimes teased the very serious Claire mercilessly when she felt like it.

"Wonderful," Claire said. "I should hand all my customers over to you so you can add accessories to their purchases."

Ariana shrugged. "It's what we do. By the way, Steven-not-Steve called again to remind you that you are having dinner with him tonight."

Claire held back a smile. Steven Sievers, the man she was dating, did not like being called Steve, and had bluntly reminded Ariana of that the one time she'd dared to call him Steve. Ever since then, Ariana referred to him as Steven-not-Steve.

"Why in the world does he think I'll forget? I've never forgotten before."

Ariana waggled her eyebrows. "Maybe he doesn't want you to forget because he's hoping for a little nookie tonight."

Claire rolled her eyes. "You've been reading too many of those Fifty Shades type books. They're tarnishing your good sense."

Ariana laughed. "You'd better go or your daughter will be angry with you."

Claire waved goodbye and hurried out the door into the dreary, gray day. She picked her way across the parking lot that separated the strip mall her boutique was in from another long strip of shops. Claire's boutique was just one of many in the Ann Arbor Shopping Center in the town of Maple Grove. Everything from clothing boutiques, jewelry stores, and shoe stores to pet supplies and craft stores filled the strategically arranged buildings with restaurants and hotels filling in the gaps. It was a busy place to say the least, and the perfect spot for Claire's business.

The parking lot was splattered with muddy, mushy snow that was melting away but leaving dirty puddles in its wake. Claire stopped at the busy intersection that separated one shopping area from another and waited for the traffic signal to change so she could cross. She pulled her coat tightly around her against the chilly breeze. One thing was for certain, she was looking forward to leaving town for a week and getting away from this cold weather.

After crossing the intersection, Claire walked down past another strip of shops until she came upon her destination. Stepping inside Marissa's Bridal Shop, Claire almost ran right into her daughter, Amanda, and her daughter's best friend,

Kaylie Thompson.

"Am I late, Mandy?" Claire asked, out of breath from her trek across the shopping compound.

Mandy shook her head, her chestnut brown bob swishing back and forth from the movement. "No, we just got here, too," she told her mother.

Claire gave Mandy a quick hug and also gave one to Kaylie. The girls had been best friends since middle school, and Claire felt like a second mother to Kaylie. The two girls were the exact opposites in size and looks. While Mandy was tall and lean with chestnut brown hair cut into a sensible bob and beautiful dark blue eyes, Kaylie was shorter and very petite with long, straight blonde hair and light blue eyes. But their personalities had always meshed well and they had been the best of friends for so long that they might as well have been sisters.

Claire looked around the bridal boutique with raised brows. "Is it just us or will Janice be joining us?" she asked Mandy. Janice Fisher was Mandy's soon-to-be mother-in-law.

"Janice said she'd rather be pleasantly surprised on the day of the wedding," Mandy said, with a sarcastic emphasis on the word *pleasantly*. She shrugged. "So yes. It's just us."

Claire nodded, but what she really wanted to do was say something scathing about Janice. She held her tongue instead. While Mandy might have to occasionally put up with her in-laws for family events, she wasn't marrying them. Mandy was marrying Craig, and he was a lovely young man. Trying to sound generous, Claire smiled. "Well, I suppose it isn't as much fun being the mother of the groom instead of the bride. She probably feels left out no matter how many things we invite her to. Don't give it much thought."

Mandy nodded. Just then Marissa, the owner of the shop, came swooping down upon them in a whirl of energy. She gave hugs all around and then led the small group to the mirrored dressing rooms so Mandy and Kaylie could try on their dresses.

Kaylie went first so they could save the most anticipated dress for last. The strapless, aquamarine, short satin dress she'd chosen fit her to a tee and was the perfect color for a beach wedding. After the three women exclaimed admiration for the dress, it was Mandy's turn to try on her wedding gown. Marissa went in the room with Mandy to help her get into the dress while Claire and Kaylie waited out in the mirrored display area.

Finally, the short, plump bridal shop owner came out through the curtain with a grin on her face and her hands clasped tightly in front of her as if in silent applause. "Here she is," Marissa announced. "The future Mrs. Craig Fisher."

Mandy swept through the curtain in a vision of satin, sequins, and lace amidst gasps from Claire and Kaylie. She glided over to the pedestal in front of the three-way mirror and stepped up on it, then turned to face her mother with a small smile on her face.

Claire stood with her hands over her mouth, taken aback at the sight of the lovely princess standing before her. She had seen the dress on Mandy countless times before, before alterations and without the veil and shoes. But today, with the entire ensemble on, her Mandy, her little girl now grown up, was a beautiful sight to behold.

"Well, Mom? What do you think?" Mandy asked.

"It's absolutely breathtaking," Claire said with awe. "It's just… perfect." And it was. Mandy had chosen a simple satin gown that suit her no-nonsense personality. It had thin shoulder straps and a fitted bust and waist that fell to a full skirt that circled out into a small train in the back. Just the slightest design in beads and rhinestones decorated the bust line, back, and hem of the white satin. The veil hung over her bare shoulders and was also trimmed in a delicate application of beads. It was a sophisticated, yet simple gown and was perfect for a wedding on a sandy beach, Mandy's dream wedding. Looking at her typically serious daughter dressed like an angel in white, Claire suddenly wondered where the years had gone. Twenty-four years. Years of smiles, laughter, and tears. Years of baby dolls, trikes, kissing booboos, and starting Kindergarten. Those years had morphed into prom dresses, shaggy boyfriends, and college dorm rooms. Into a first apartment, a first job, and then engagement. And now, after everything, marriage. Time had passed too quickly.

"It's gorgeous!" Kaylie exclaimed after she finally found her voice. "You look like a movie star."

Mandy smiled at Kaylie, and then her mother. "This is it," she said. "In three days we'll be off to the Caribbean and within the week, I'll be married. It's amazing, isn't it?"

Claire nodded, afraid to speak in case she chocked on the tears she was holding back.

"I can't wait until Dad sees my dress. Won't he be surprised?" Mandy asked.

All the delightful memories that had been embracing Claire that very moment dropped to the floor at the mention of Mandy's father. Claire had been actively trying to forget that one detail—Jim, and his new, younger wife, would be at the wedding, too.

* * *

The wedding gown was carefully bagged as was Kaylie's dress and all the accessories. Claire paid the balance along with buying all the extras like a box to store the dress in after the wedding. The three women waved goodbye to Marissa and headed back out into the gloomy day in the fading, late afternoon light.

Kaylie hugged Claire and Mandy goodbye and ran off to her little sports car, carefully avoiding the larger of the muddy puddles in the parking lot. Claire helped Mandy to her car where they gently hung the bagged gown on the hook in the back seat and laid out all the other purchases.

"So, have you heard from your father lately?" Claire asked, trying to sound indifferent but failing miserably. *Please say he isn't coming and bringing that annoying wife of his. Please, please, please.*

Mandy stared a moment at her mother before answering. "I just talked to him this morning. And yes, he's still planning on coming, Mom. Dad wouldn't miss my wedding day." Mandy threw her mother a sly grin. "Remember. I can read your mind."

Claire had the good grace to look contrite. Of course Jim wouldn't miss his daughter's wedding, she knew that better than anyone. But it didn't stop Claire from wishing she didn't have to spend an entire week on an island with her ex-husband and the woman he'd left her for.

Mandy leaned forward and pulled Claire into a hug. "I know this isn't going to be easy, Mom, but I couldn't get married without both of you there. Please, for my sake, try to make it work?"

Claire hugged her daughter tightly before slowly pulling away. "Of course I'll make it work. I am always polite to him and that woman. I didn't say one mean thing to her or him at the engagement party, remember?" *Of course, I wanted to accidentally spill red wine all over her skimpy, tight yellow dress, but I refrained.*

Mandy rewarded Claire with one of her sly grins, the kind that reminded Claire so much of her ex-husband. Mandy had Jim's thick, wavy, chestnut brown hair and his deep blue eyes, a lethal combination that attracted people easily. But where Mandy's father had an outgoing, easy nature about him, always ready with a rakish grin, Mandy was more serious and reserved, like her mother. Yet, Claire couldn't help but always be reminded of Jim every time she looked at her daughter.

"Mom, that *woman* has a name. It's Diane. And I know you're trying. It's just for a week. I promise you will barely even see them the entire time."

Claire nodded, realizing that this was probably true. After all, even though it was a small island, there were plenty of places she could be that he wasn't. And miles of beach. She looked forward to walking a lot on the warm beaches and enjoying the sun and ocean breezes.

"It's too bad Steven isn't coming with you," Mandy said, interrupting Claire's thoughts. "You're going to be the only person there who isn't part of a couple."

Claire bit her lip. Yes, it would have been nice to have had someone along to share the romantic trip with, but she wasn't going to let that ruin her good time. There were plenty of other people she loved coming along, like her brother and sister-in-law, Kaylie, the best man's wife Angela, and of course, Mandy. Claire would have plenty of fun enjoying spending time with the entire wedding party despite Jim being there.

"Earth to mom," Mandy said, waving her hand in front of Claire's face.

Claire snapped out of her stupor. "Sorry. I was just thinking how much fun we'll all have on the island, even though Steven won't be along." She looked at her watch. "Speaking of which, I'd better get going or I'll be late. I'm meeting Steven for dinner tonight and I have to go back to the shop first then home to change."

Mandy drove Claire over to the boutique and they hugged goodbye. The next time they'd see each other would be at the airport on Monday. They both had plenty to do before taking off for an entire week.

Printed in Great Britain
by Amazon

76430348R00149